I0572749

A VANTAGE OF DARKNESS

Dreams From the End of All Things

NATHANIEL SHRAKE

Print ISBN: 979-8-9989970-0-6 — Ebook ISBN: 979-8-9989970-1-3

All rights reserved.

© 2025 by Nathaniel Shrake and Menagerie Publishing House.

Contact Nathaniel at ShrakeWrites@gmail.com or visit ShrakeWrites.com.

No portion of this book may be reproduced in any form without written permission from the publisher or author, except as permitted by U.S. copyright law.

For Mary.

From the moment I saw you...

"Do not be afraid; our fate
cannot be taken from us; it is a gift."
—— Dante Alighieri, *Inferno*

1

The Huntress in the Snow

Melody stood and, with apathy in her heart, watched Sam die pitifully in the dirt. Not that her name was Melody. Not that she had a heart. Not anymore.

When Sam at last stopped his convulsing, she calmly rested the shotgun against the interior wall of the barn and walked out into the sheets of snow still falling in the darkness of the night. She returned minutes later with a shovel and a bottle of wine that she'd collected from the cellar. As she was in the process of uncorking the bottle, she stood over the body that lay face down and crumpled in the flickering light of the lantern that rested upon the earth nearby.

Thooom, sounded the cork.

"You did this to yourself, Sammy," she muttered, before pulling heavily from the cabernet. "I'd say I'm sorry, but I'm not so sure that I am."

She grabbed the shovel and began to dig. She started on the left side, nearest to the door. She dug along the perimeter of what looked to be the remnants of old horse stalls, an illusion of which she was quite proud. Within an hour, the first body was exhumed. It was José, her most recent addition to the collection before Sam.

José had been a much more difficult kill than Sam. He was a reserved man. Worked as the Emerald Acre caretaker to escape a mile-long rap sheet that he'd acquired in Mexico. As she dug, she thought back to the rainy day, long ago, when she had walked onto the property dressed as a nun peddling bibles. José didn't answer the door, despite her multiple attempts at ringing and vehemently knocking, so she was forced to mimic the sound of a dying cat in the barn the following day. To her relief, he eventually came to investigate, and she left him lying within.

Over the many years that she'd begun collecting on the property, she had come to enjoy the hunt, although she was glad that it was finally coming to an end. It was a dirty business, wrought with careful deliberations. But more than anything, she despised spending so much time on and around the property. It conjured memories that were, at best, uncomfortable to recall.

It seemed like just yesterday when the gaudy house on Emerald Acres was built. She had known several better iterations of the building that had stood in the clearing in the woods, and she longed for the days of the humble farmhouse that had once stood in its place. Those were different times, in more ways than one.

It had only been a month since José's body had been placed in the ground, and it was in a bad state. Large swaths of the corpse's skin had ripped off in the process of pulling it from the dirt, while the skin that remained was a shifting palette of dark green, purple, and pale yellow. Black viscous liquid trailed behind the body while the scene at large reeked of rotting eggs, rancid meat, and shit all mixed together and set on fire.

But Mae—which is what she still considered herself to be named, even after all these years—hardly batted an eye and the wine tasted just as delicate when she took a swig. She'd seen worse, she'd done worse, and today was a happy day. She had at last, after 78 years of collecting, acquired the final piece of her collection. She looked back toward Sam's crumpled body and smiled.

Throughout the rest of night, she dug and pulled corpses from the earth. By the time the sun had begun to shine through the slits of the wooden walls of the barn, nine bodies had been pulled from the earth and thrown haphazardly about. Mounds of dirt and half dug graves littered the area and, not long after she began, she was dragging recently unearthed corpses over ridges and valleys of her own making.

Her hands were blistered and had begun to bleed when she unearthed the final corpse. It was her first contribution to the ritual: Ms. Martha Maxwell. Her remains were reduced to nothing but bones, and Mae was forced to bundle the brittle, crumbling remains in a canvas sack. She was compelled to do the same with others as well. She found that when she dropped the bags onto the dirt, it sounded similar to a bag of heavy sticks being thrown upon the earth.

When she at last concluded her work, she walked through the open door of the barn and lit a cigarette in the warm honey sunrise that glittered on the snow all about her. The sunlight of the virgin day warmed her skin while unkempt strands of her ginger hair fluttered down and littered her gaze. With an airy disposition, she slowly circled the fountain at the center of the driveway as she smoked, crunching into the deep snow with each step. A pair of chickadees dove past, and the sky was an optimistic and unfettered blue.

"Soon, fucker," she whispered into the crisp morning air, raising her gaze to the sky above. "Soon."

She decided that she was due a hearty breakfast, and rummaged messily through the kitchen, an act that felt strangely miraculous. For so many years, she had fluttered about the estate, tending to her dark business, but only rarely did she step inside the house, and never once had she cooked in the gaudy kitchen. She had always been careful to reduce the impact of her presence upon the estate, fearful of leaving too big of a footprint. But that no longer mattered. Her designs were nearly complete and come tomorrow, it mattered not in the slightest. Melody Shilawea would become only a memory, as she would be long gone by the time anyone noticed anything amiss. Society no longer served her. It was a somewhat playful thing to exist in such plain view, but she was ready to disengage and once again ramble through the shadows of the world rather than cosplaying amongst its rabble.

Society was an exhausting thing, and her loathing for its participants had grown sharp edges over the long years. It was but a play in which she was forced to act. How she longed to be in the audience, or better yet, on the sidewalk outside the playhouse, walking carelessly by.

But for now, for the first time without fear of repercussion, she danced through the kitchen making herself a plate of poached eggs, sausage, and toast, while reminiscing upon the long and narrow path that had led her to the breakfast that she now sat down to enjoy.

For years, with help from her "property managers," she would wait to hear word of the new caretakers of the property, and from there she would pounce if the circumstance and person were right. It was easier to kill on the property, and as the bodies had to eventually end up there, it only made sense to commit the acts on the grounds. It was best to not transport dead bodies when one didn't have to. Transporting corpses created evidence and opportunities for long-nosed police officers to stick their smellers where they didn't belong.

Furthermore, Emerald Acres, as it had come to be called in recent years, was a secluded place deep in the ponderosa pine forest of northern Arizona. It was a thirty-minute drive from Flagstaff, requiring multiple obscure turn-offs from the main, secondary, and even the tertiary forest service roads of Coconino County.

Mae had purchased the property years before, with her designs in mind, and through clever and subtle hauntings committed by her hand, she had been able to keep even remotely nearby neighbors to a minimum.

But even though she owned the property, that didn't mean that her name was on the lease. Officially, the property was owned by a wealthy New England victim of affluenza, whom she pictured in her mind as being too uninspired with their wealth to do anything but purchase distant properties that they never visited. That was the story, at least.

But to Mae, it was her private hunting grounds to serve her esoteric and dark designs.

When she got word of a potential match for her collection, she'd slither close and, by hook or by crook, befriend the victim to-be, earn their trust, and when the time was right... well... They'd have a rendezvous in the barn. She took her time. There was no rush, after all. The years came to feel like days, and the bodies she inhabited changed without much ceremony. There were decades that passed without appropriate suitors on the property, and then there were months with multiple, as was the case with José and then Sam.

What mattered most was patience. She waited for the right opportunities, never killing those that might be missed too dearly. Not in order to respect the sensibilities of their families, but rather to reduce any suspicion from those that might spoil her designs. No family men nor anyone too well-known in town. Only the less dead, and loners like Sam.

Once the right victim was chosen and circumstances were ideal, she went about her business in a variety of ways. There were some poisonings. Some were stabbed. With one, she got lucky, as he hung himself from the barn's old rafters without her lifting a finger. One went rogue and thought he'd paint over the original blue paint of the barn with a tacky forest green. Mae confronted him mid-renovation, bled him dry, and painted the barn red with a good amount of his blood just to spite him.

Despite choosing only drifters and the lonely, many of her victims still had friends and acquaintances. Folks would inevitably come to inquire about the missing. Too many disappearing people, even over the span of half a century, was bound to raise the curiosities of those intelligent enough to look for them. So, when it became necessary, she dug up corpses from distant cemeteries and coated them in illusionary magic to change their appearance to appear like the departed. She'd then leave them in carefully arranged scenes of suicide or accidents to justify the departed's abrupt departure.

The process was a nasty one and required hard-to-acquire materials, particularly mandrake and the unsoiled blood of innocents. The latter was what had gotten her into trouble one day outside of Pinesdale years back. When the body she temporarily inhabited was killed, as it was that day—shot up by a police lieutenant appalled by what he had found in her cauldron—her soul simply drift away and latched itself onto another suitable body nearby. Eventually, over the many years, such a thing happened enough times that she gained a semblance of control over the process and could, more or less, select who she wanted to inhabit.

And on that cloudy day outside of Pinesdale, as the police looked on in horror at her bloody acts, Melody Shilawea just so happened to be in the wrong place at the wrong time.

When she finished her breakfast, she looked about the room and noticed a white sheet cast over the diorama of the estate resting on a floating shelf against the back wall. At its sight, Mae was immediately nauseated at Sam's vague half-attempt to distance himself from his fears, and felt compelled to remove it.

She crossed the kitchen and removed the sheet with a flourish to find the hyper detailed diorama of the meadow and the lavish home within it—a gift from the home's developer. Masau'u's kachina doll still stood in the meadow of the display, under its glass dome. She had placed the doll there herself, of course, but after considering the figure with an empty gaze, she decidedly walked to the kitchen and soon returned with a meat hammer in hand. Shards of glass exploded across the floor as the diorama's glass cover met the hammer's face, but Mae didn't so much as flinch. Her gaze remained upon the figure now exposed to the air of the room. She picked up the doll and raised its face to hers. It seemed to have fire in its eyes.

She thought of Vermont for the first time in many years.

She only had half memories of the place. Memories of running through a hedge maze with her sister; her mother singing while doing the dishes; the family huddled about the living room watching the heavy rain fall outside. Then there was the fire and her father sobbing as he watched their home burn.

Her sister Susy was inconsolable, as she had left her stuffed bunny "Maxell" inside.

They were some of her earliest memories, and the burning of her childhood home had triggered a consciousness in her young mind that comes to all children one day. From then on, her memories were more concrete and her relationship with the world more deliberate. It seemed, from Mae's vantage, unfair that all could not exist as unaware as young children were, still playing in the nothing-ness from which we all emerge and to which we eventually return.

But not for her. She was cursed; beset to roam the Earth until its dying days. She wondered, at times, on the coldest of nights, what might happen then. Would she finally be set free, as the sun expanded into a red giant and engulfed everything? Could she then rest and reunite with the universe from which she'd been sculpted? Or would her spirit remain tied to her ego, forever floating through the emptiness of space, until even the stars blinked out, one by one, over the span of a thousand billion lonely years?

The thought terrified her, and quieted the rare trepidations that arose in response to her evil acts. To escape such a fate, she would do terrible things. To recuse one's soul from an eternity of nothing but an impossibly distant view of forever... one was compelled to do terrible acts that had long ago led her to abandon the heavy chains of compassion. Her existence, her experiences, her future... It all made for a universal perspective so far removed from that of the average person that she felt no remorse for the lives that she erased.

She was the huntress stalking the deer, but it wasn't always that way.

2

For the Time Being

Shortly after the fire, the Barretts packed up what remained of their belongings and headed out West. As they waited for the train to arrive at the station, Mae clung to her bag as if her life depended on it, as her mother had assured her that it did. It had pink tulips on its face and had a metallic turquoise handle.

The year was 1895, and over the course of three nights and four days, the Barretts rode the rails westward. Mae felt like they were chasing sunsets and began to wonder if a train could go so fast as to keep the sunset burning forever on the western horizon.

Her mother, Edith, slept often throughout the journey, while her father, John, was dejected and somnolent. Both John's father and grandfather had lived in the house that had burnt down. It was an accident, of course, but regardless, it weighed heavily upon his shoulders. He should have checked the density of the hay he had purchased, and he shouldn't have placed it so close to the house. Turns out hay bales spontaneously combust on humid and warm days, when packed too tightly.

Mae would hear her father muttering while staring out the windows of the train. "Who knew," he'd say softly under his breath when he thought no one was listening.

Mae took the move in stride, more or less. She was still young enough to see it as a great adventure, as her connections to the home they had left behind were only abstract; her memories of it still soft and ambiguous. She passed the days on the train mostly by playing with her sister, Susy, and reading paperback novels about cowboys and Indians, pulp-fiction mysteries, and the occasional issue of *St. Nicholas Magazine*.

One day, Susy, who had taken to long walks throughout the various passenger cabins of the train, approached Mae, whose attention was set upon the pages of *A Child's Garden of Verses*. Susy leaned in toward her sister's ear and whispered, "I met a wizard down the aisle! He said he can tell me the future! Come on!" She grabbed Mae's arm and led her away, leading the latter to drop the book onto the floor, where it slid under a seat, never to be found.

Mae followed her sister down the long aisle of the cabin with only slight hesitance. She would have preferred to stick to her book of poems and not approach strange men on the train, but Susy was an impressive presence, and Mae had yet to develop the muscles of identity that exercised self-advocacy.

They strode through three separate train cars before at last arriving at the door that Susy claimed contained the wizard that she had met. Without contemplation or anything resembling a preamble, Susy leaned forward and knocked upon the door with her right hand while holding Mae's with her left. A proper old man wearing a three-piece suit and a top hat answered the door with grace. He waved his free right hand in a superfluous circle before then bowing low before the girls. May thought he looked as if he stood at the mahogany entrance of a manor.

"Hellloooo," he bellowed in sing-songy Welsh.

"We're here to have our futures told!" giggled Susy.

"Well, then you've come to the right place, young ladies." He stepped into the hallway and knelt to match the level of the young Barrett sisters. "You must be young Mae," he said, addressing Mae intently. He looked piercingly into her eyes, squinting his old, wrinkled eyes in tremendous concentration. He then abruptly shuttered his eyelids and turned his attention inward. A moment passed before the old man suddenly flung his eyes open and gasped, before falling back onto his bottom. He crawled backwards in a rapid scurry, stood, and retreated into his room, slamming the door loudly behind him.

The girls knocked upon the door once again but the man did not answer, and after a few frustrated and confused moments, the girls relented and walked back towards their cabin.

As the years went by, Mae didn't contribute much to the experience. She was struck by the sudden fear in the man's eyes, but over time, the memory faded simply into an odd encounter with a stranger. And that was all.

On a sunny day in August, the Barrett family finally departed the train in Flagstaff, Arizona, and hired a buggy to take them to the property that the girls' father had purchased for them. John had hired some men to begin building the cabin ahead of their arrival, and it was expected that their modest home would be built and ready for them by the day that they arrived.

The buggy ride was long and tremendously bumpy, so much so that shortly into the ride Mae abandoned any effort to read her dime novels. She instead turned her attention to the deep and dark forest that soon enveloped them. It was a gloomy day, and what dim light that did manage to penetrate the stratus clouds above was thoroughly choked out by the canopy of trees that rose thickly from the forest floor that ebbed and swayed all about her. Mae was particularly struck by the jagged gulleys and canyons that littered the landscape, compared to the slow, rolling hills that were common back in Vermont.

Mae's paperback novels spoke at length about Indians that would carve the scalps from unsuspecting settlers, and she diligently scanned the woods for packs of Indians that might be looking for any opportunity to haul her away and scrape the skin from her skull.

When the buggy at last bumped along the path onto the clearing, the Barretts found that their new home was missing a roof, while the construction crew John had hired lounged drunkenly in a makeshift camp nearby.

As the buggy driver unloaded their bags onto the dirt, the girls and their mother milled about the practically empty meadow. To Mae's great relief, the meadow was even more gorgeous than she had imagined it to be. She even thought she saw a deer gazing from the tree line, a sight that made both her and her sister giddy. Furthermore, to the enchantment of the girls, the clearing contained a modest pond, around which a gaggle of geese lazed.

Their father blew his top and angrily confronted the laborers. Mae recalled him screaming about the agreed-upon deadline and the costs of labor, and even heard the word "larceny" being thrown about.

But Mae and Susy were too enraptured by their new surroundings to care. The tall tree trunks of the forest surrounding the meadow captured the girls' imaginations absolutely. It was a stark contrast from the maple, birch, and oak trees that they were accustomed to, back east.

Thankfully, the weather was fair, and John convinced the laborers to give up their tent for Edith and the kids to inhabit while he assisted the crew in finishing the cabin. It took them two additional days to complete the task, days that Mae and Susy spent becoming further acquainted with the land. They circled the meadow hundreds of times, finding favorite logs and boulders to rest upon. They came to enjoy sitting by the pond for hours, skipping rocks that they'd collected from the surrounding forest.

On the third day, the cabin was at last complete, and the Barretts were finally alone in the clearing in the woods.

Not long after getting settled in, John erected a large corral in the meadow in which to raise cattle, and a separate, smaller corral for sheep. Over the coming months, he made frequent trips into town and quickly made enough money to build a barn for the animals to shelter in during the coming winter months. From time to time, butchers, traders, and even the army would arrive to lead the livestock away. Mae despised the visits, as she knew where the animals were being led and had become attached to the sheep in particular. She'd sit and watch them mill about their pens, delighting as they took treats from her hand in slimy slurps.

One day, the butcher came and led away nearly half their head, including a sheep that Mae had come to know well. She had seen the creature birthed and, as much as a ten-year-old could, had helped raise it over the course of many months. She had named the sheep Betsy and spent many hours watching her mill about the corrals. Betsy had a peculiar gait that made Mae laugh, and the animal was always first in line to receive a daily treat from her palm. Susy teased her relentlessly about her relationship with the animal, saying that her attachment showed how young and naive she was, despite Susy being only a year older than her sister. But on the day that Betsy and many of her kin were led away by the butcher, all Mae could muster was a dejected walk into the woods to conceal the steady stream of tears that she couldn't seem to dam.

When Mae was eleven, her brother, William, was born on the fifth of June 1900. Mae recalled her mother calling the boy a "century man." "It's a helpful thing," she had said, smiling. "You'll never have to guess how old your brother is. You'll always know it by knowing the year!"

John was over the moon at William's birth, as he'd finally have a boy to help him with various tasks about the property. In those early days, the good days, Mae would often hear her pa whistling while chopping wood out back, a sure sign that he was in a good mood. Not that their father was often in ill spirits to begin with. He had quit the bottle years before, and was a fair to better husband to Edith and father to his children.

The girls were delighted with the happy child. In the afternoons of the summertime when the storms would roll through with bustling winds and swells of rain and thunder, the kids would all huddle inside the cabin and take turns mimicking the sounds that erupted from the sky. Even as a toddler, William was unbothered by the thunder and was only curious of the sounds. In fact, Mae couldn't recall a single instance of young William crying.

"He just don't have no tears, I guess," his mother would say.

On one of those wet summer afternoons, shortly after a storm had passed through leaving the meadow smelling of clean moist earth before the smell of manure returned, a man emerged from the road behind the trees and approached the homestead with a patient gait. It was evident right away that he wasn't a trader in both the way he dressed and the way their father curtly buttoned his shirt, tucked his revolver into the back of his waistband, and strode outside to meet the man.

The man wore a long purple cloak, but most noticeably, his head was adorned with a crown of long antlers. The sight, naturally, catalyzed both Mae and Susy's curiosities.

The girls couldn't hear the conversation, but after a few minutes of their father shaking his head and pointing in the direction from which the man had come, the antler adorned figure finally turned and walked away with a solemn demeanor. John stood and watched him go, not relinquishing his ground until the man was well enveloped by the trees.

At first, John didn't share much about the encounter when asked, but after a few days he let on that the man was an Indian that had come to "spread nonsense," and that was all he would say about it.

Mae was startled by the admission that the man was an Indian. Even though the man had been dressed funny and had a somewhat darker hue to his skin, the penny novels that she read led her to envision Indians as hulking monsters with bones draped around their necks, eager to suck the marrow from the bones of unaccompanied white children. Even the antler crown hadn't seemed to say such things about him, although the manner in which her father addressed him certainly did.

A week later, Mae was taking her daily stroll along the tree line when she heard a crack echo from deep in the woods. She gazed deep into the trees but saw no indication of deer or anything else that might have produced the sound.

Her latest fear was bears, as she had recently replaced her fear of Indians with the beasts. She and her father had come across the carcass of a dead black bear a few days back. When they examined it, she was horrified at the sheer size of the beast's claws and teeth. Her father assured her that black bears were mostly herbivores and would be much more afraid of her than she would be of it, but that did little to prevent bears from haunting her nightmares and peripheral vision.

But as she gazed into the woods, no bears appeared. She might have gone tramping into the trees to investigate further, but she was alone, as Susy was back in the cabin, sick with a bitter cough. Mae had more sense than to go off into the woods alone. She stepped forward to continue circumnavigating the meadow when she heard another sharp crack and again turned to investigate. Mae saw little William stumbling along the top of a tall, felled tree lying some fifty feet into the woods.

Without a thought, Mae darted into the trees, calling after her brother.

William wobbled across the log like a toddler acrobat, but when Mae got within a dozen feet of him, he lost his balance and fell to the forest floor on its opposite side. Mae yelped in despair and sprinted around the log to retrieve her brother. But, to her dismay, she found only pine needles and moss-covered rocks upon the forest floor.

"Don't be afraid," a voice said calmly from behind her.

Mae spun around to face the voice, finding it to belong to the man that had approached the farm the week before. He wore the same garb as when he approached the house then: a long purple robe beneath a crown of antlers. Mae shook in an endorphin concoction that manifested itself in a light quiver upon her fingers and lips.

For his part, the man's face was old, sunburnt, and wrinkled.

"I want to talk about Betsy," he said.

It had been years since she'd heard the name, but the brash appearance of the man dulled its impact. "What do you want?" she asked. She clenched her hands into fists and prepared herself to fight, if it came to that. She'd fought Susy many times and knew that the first blow was the most important. She steeled herself for the worst. but was only met by a kind smile and open palms.

"Relax, child. I only want to talk with you… about Betsy," he said again.

Hearing the name of the sheep for a second time jostled an unexpected tear from her eye. It was the way he said it, as if he was just as burdened by the memory as she was. She again felt the heaviness of the loss of the animal. She recalled begging her father for weeks not to sell her, to instead let her keep the animal. But her father could not be swayed and refused.

"We're not running a sheep orphanage," he had said.

"It wasn't fair," the man said. "Not to you. Not to Betsy. Not to the land that fed her." He spoke with a steady voice that seemed to carry softly on the wind. The sun had been shining brightly through the trees, but as he stepped forward and approached the log, clouds spontaneously arrived overhead to obscure the sun's rays while a cool breeze blew about them. A chorus of falling pine needles clamored as he sat and gestured for Mae to sit next to him on the log.

Mae contemplated her response to his invitation, still standing fearfully nearby with clenched fists. She considered running back toward the clearing. It wasn't far. But she couldn't shake one thing. How did the old man know about Betsy?

"I know many things," he said, as if reading her thoughts. "I know your name's Mae. Mae Barrett. I know you like reading stories about this land. I even know about Maxwell."

The last word utterly shocked Mae and left her staring blankly into the dirt. How in the world could he have known that?

"I also see things in you, Mae. Things that even you are yet to see. Strength, like these trees." He patted the felled trunk upon which he sat. "They rise from the soil, bend in the wind, give shade when they can, and die when it is time to do so."

"What do you want?" she repeated, tears swelling in her eyes, suddenly overwhelmed.

"I need your help," he said without missing a beat. "I tried to reason with your father. I tried all that I could. But he was raised in a stubborn way; in the way of the white man that has bled this land dry. No patience. No collaboration. Just take, and let might parade as right for as long as their guns make noise."

He stood to his feet and walked to the trunk of a nearby ponderosa that rose high into the sky. He held a palm to its bark. "But you. I see compassion in you. I see an open mind. I see durability, like the trees. I see ferocity, like the wind. You have abilities that you cannot yet understand, but I see it in you, as clear as day. Mae, I want to give you something that might help you save the next Betsy you meet. I want to give you something that few have even dreamt of... Perspective."

Mae stood silent and shaking. She remained unsure of what exactly the old man was saying to her, but she sensed gravity in his words and an absolute sincerity in the way he spoke.

He continued, "But perspective comes only with time, and thus time is what I intend to give to you, so that you might see the things that I see, and eventually, bring your kind to see it as well."

"What do you mean, 'give me time'?" she whispered, her voice quivering. She thought she saw lightning flash in his eyes.

"Just that," he replied. "Time to see what it means to live in harmony with this world. Time to see how what we take from it is taken from our very hands. Time to see how Betsy is a soul that deserves respect, or else the meat that we make of her will come to rot in our mouths. In every circumstance, time shows us the folly of our ways. I intend to give you this blessing, young Mae, and all that I ask is that you listen to what it tells you."

He took a step toward her. Mae made to bolt, to sprint back to the meadow, but found that her legs were lassoed by vines. She tried to scream, but her mouth was covered in leaves.

The man rested his palm upon her forehead and leaned in close to whisper in her ear.

"Don't be afraid..."

3

Entropy's Terms

The gas pump's price gauge cascaded upward as Sam stared emptily into the dials. The number furthest to the left was hesitant in contrast with the rest. It hovered at three, while the number immediately to its right crawled readily upward. Shortly after reaching nine, the latter transformed into a zero, reborn, and resumed an upward ascent just as the far-left dial, at last, transcended into a four. The third digit, separated by a decimal point, flew upward in a flurry while the furthest right number was nothing but a blur.

Sam gazed into the gauge, transfixed, until the sound of metal snapping the valve shut awoke him from his daydream.

He replaced the pump and reentered the cab of the pickup. It had been a long drive, and he was eager for it to be over. Night driving was something that generally agreed with him, but his thoughts roamed wild and untethered for much of the journey and his mind was heavy from the hypnosis of the highway. He raised his view to the rear-view mirror and met a pair of tired blue eyes looking back at him.

"One more," he said to no one. His voice cracked, and he realized that hadn't spoken a single word throughout his hours on the road.

He turned the key in the ignition, ready to cover the final stretch of the interstate, but instead of the engine roaring to life, it produced a series of quick clicks. The dashboard lights flashed angrily, and he immediately recognized his folly. He had known that his alternator was approaching old age as he had been aware of the voltage gauge warning him of the fact for months. It was something that he had managed to stuff into the hidden drawers of his mind to ignore, and as a result, was now confronted with entropy on its terms, instead of his own.

He exited the cab and opened the suicide door to find the jumper cables within. He turned over blankets, a bag of laundry, and a few books that he had forgotten were there. But he found no cables, and only then remembered loaning them to his friend Max not a week before.

Ain't that how it goes, he thought.

He looked about, examining the isolated gas station in which he now found himself stranded. The remaining three pumps were vacant, but an old, rusted Buick was parked in one of the four spots near the convenience store's entrance. The building's exterior was unremarkable. A two-door ice machine with its handles chained together stood beside an unplugged and seemingly forgotten Redbox to the right of the entrance. Around the building's right corner was an exterior door to a restroom, its overhead bulb flickering intermittently.

Sam figured that he could purchase some jumper cables in the store and try his luck convincing the owner of the parked Buick to help him out with a jump. If nothing else, he ought to buy some cables while he was thinking of it. Otherwise, they too might get subconsciously pushed into the dusty drawers of his mind. It was a common occurrence as of late.

Some twenty minutes before, while still on the highway, his mind had been busy flipping through a myriad of different things, rendering the yellow light of the low fuel gauge all but invisible. He was travelling through a day that he had dreamt about for years. Five, to be exact. When he finally lowered his gaze and acknowledged the threat of an empty fuel tank, panic flooded him. Visions of being helplessly stranded on the side of the highway fluttered past his mind's eye, but just as despair began clawing into his psyche, a highway sign approached from out of the darkness, promising gasoline and a restroom at the next exit. He took it, and followed an uncomfortably long and isolated road toward a gas station surrounded by nothing but darkness in all directions.

Sam chuckled to himself. It was as if he was destined to be stranded, one way or another. At least now he had the luxury of a gas station to accompany his acute immobility.

A two-tone bell rang out as Sam pushed into the store, its bright LED lighting pressing heavily upon him. The register counter was uninhabited; however, a door behind the counter opened into a dark room. Sam assumed the employee to be somewhere within it. He proceeded to mill about the aisles looking for cables, which he found in the back corner among the other automobile accessories.

When he returned to the register, a blank-faced woman looked back at him with tired eyes. They reminded him of the pair he had seen in the rear-view mirror of the cab, although hers were a dull green. Her arms rested heavily upon the counter leading Sam to conclude that he must have woken her. Strands of her disheveled black hair fell loosely about her eyes and her left cheek was decorated with three red-lined dents; the sure sign of a quality nap. She mustered an honest smile. Her name tag read *Lilith*.

"Is that all?" she asked, her voice deeper than her thin frame suggested.

"Well," Sam began, "I could actually use a jump." He gestured toward the door. "If that's your car outside, I'd appreciate it."

Lilith grimaced. For a moment Sam thought she might not respond at all, until at last she shook her head sharply. "I'm afraid I can't leave the store, sir. We've got a phone," she said, gesturing toward a wall-mounted payphone beside an ATM.

Sam was surprised and a bit offended by the remark. He wasn't exactly asking for a personal loan. But before voicing his displeasure, he decided that the woman was likely acting in self-preservation, and he didn't intend to give her grief for that.

He sighed and held up his cell phone, indicating that he would not be requiring the payphone.

"Just the cables, then," she said, lowering her gaze and scanning the barcode.

Sam stepped outside, jumper cables in hand, and tucked his chin tightly to his chest as a cold December wind began to blow from the west. It was an unexpectedly frigid night for the outskirts of Phoenix, he thought as he dialed AAA. After a brief dial tone, a robotic voice greeted him and prompted him to press one, three, and four before he was placed on hold. As he listened to the call on speaker, Sam walked to the edge of the concrete and stood with his toes dangling over the dirt that surrounded it.

A loop of hold music repeated as he stared into the darkness, hoping to see headlights approaching from the direction of the highway. The music was a strangely familiar melody, but in an 8-bit execution that reminded him of Lavender Town in *Pokémon Red*. As it looped on and on, the name of the melody was on the tip of his tongue. It began to weigh heavily on him until... there it was! He was listening to an 8-bit rendition of the beginning melody of Brahms' Symphony No. 3. He only knew it because it had been a favorite of his piano teacher, and he was compelled to perform it routinely throughout his lessons. Sam thought it an odd selection for roadside-assistance hold music, but it brought fond recollections, and he suddenly felt overwhelmingly glad to be so close to his home in the desert.

A human eventually answered and promised an ETA of approximately two hours for a service truck to arrive. Sam balked when he realized how late he was going to be, but he recognized that he hadn't any better options for the time being. He could always call and cancel if a friendly traveler arrived and helped him with a jump.

As he stared into the darkness of the desert, Sam kicked himself for not fixing the alternator earlier. He kicked himself for not getting gas in a better location. But most of all, he kicked himself for being so thoroughly thoughtless lately. It had been a wild month, and he intended to give himself grace for that, but it was something he resolved to be better about in the future.

It felt like he had been existing in a cloud since being stateside again. "You just need time to adjust to things," his father had said. "It'll get easier," "be patient," and all the other lines with similarly well-intentioned yet meaningless impact seemed to blend together like the fog of his recent days.

No headlights appeared on the horizon and the breeze became persistent, prompting Sam to retreat to the relative warmth of the truck cab to wait. He leaned the seat back and tried his best to find a comfortable position. There might be a silver lining in this whole ordeal, after all, if he could find a little rest before arriving at Sawyer's that evening. It was going to be a wild night, and a little sleep would go a long way. He closed his eyes and thought back upon the long day he'd already had.

That morning, Sam had walked into a building for the last time. It was a raised trailer-turned office that stood atop strained cinderblocks that betrayed the building's age. The overnight rain had perfumed the black sage that accompanied the grated stairs that led him to the door, and a bell rang out as he stepped inside.

He approached a desk and handed a disinterested clerk a piece of paper before being prompted to sit in a nearby plastic chair produced by the lowest bidder. He obliged, and after several minutes of staring into ceiling tiles and nostalgic carpet patterns, was at last called to a separate counter to verify his date of birth, enlistment, his mother's maiden name, the signature of his commanding officer, and a good address should it be required that he be contacted again in the future.

"For reasons," said the clerk when pressed on the latter.

He sat back down and waited once more. After a few minutes, the bell nailed atop the door's entrance rang once again as a young man walked in, this one half drunk, unshaven, and ragged in seven other ways. His belt missed a loop, and he smiled queerly when he saw Sam sitting in the lobby. Sam returned the smile gently and extended a hand to Private Shaefer as he approached.

"Well, well, well," Shaefer swayed slightly before correcting himself. "Sergeant Yellowstone. May he find greener pastures."

"Doesn't seem real, to be honest with ya, Shaef."

"Eh," he burped, "This is as realllll as it comes, buddy." His voice began to rise. "That chair over there," he pointed to a chair among chairs, "it's my favorite real chair. That desk over there..."

"SHUT THE FUCK UP, PRIVATE SHAEFER!" roared a voice from behind a door. "IT'S TOO GODDAMN EARLY FOR YOU, MOTHERFUCKER. SIT THE FUCK DOWN AND SHUT THE FUCK UP."

Private Shaefer silently mocked the voice with a contorted face before ultimately obliging.

"That's real," Shaefer gestured toward the voice. "but it's not my favorite anything."

"I'm sorry things went this way for ya, Schaef," Sam said quietly.

"Eh," he grunted. "If I can be honest with ya, buddy, and I guess I can now as I don't expect I'll see ya again, I never really wanted to be here. My dad wanted me to." He smiled and tilted his chin towards the blinding lights above him. "I don't know. Maybe my pride wanted me to be here. Either way, it just took me too long to realize it."

Sam had genuine sympathy for the platoon's mascot of "don't" sitting before him. "Things have a way of working out," said Sam.

Private Schaefer chuckled. "So I've been told." He closed his eyes and drifted off to a version of sleep known only to alcoholics and the parents of newborns.

As Sam concluded his waiting in silence, he heard Schaefer humming a tune softly to himself. It wasn't until later that day that he identified the tune: *They're Hanging Me Tonight* by Marty Robbins.

The door to the room from whence the screaming had erupted minutes before ripped open and a caricature of a Marine stepped out into the doorway.

"YELLOWSTONE!" he bellowed.

Sam stood and approached casually. "Yes, First Sergeant."

"I've never seen you before. Why is that?"

"Common sense, sir."

"Good answer. What the fuck do you intend to do with your life without the Marine Corps, Sergeant?" He glared paternally down at Sam. It was a look that Sam had come to know well throughout his tenure in the Corps. Stern, unwavering, and self-assured. In a way, the man's demeaner and resulting gaze embodied what the Marine Corps represented as a whole: getting the job done and not worrying about your feelings. The ends always justified the means, and albeit necessary for his country's aspirations, Sam was eager to no longer be a means to a wider end.

Sam hadn't a clue of what to say in response to the man's question. What *did* he intend to do with his time once his purpose was no longer dictated to him? He was pondering what an honest answer might be when he was interrupted by the sound of his own voice rambling on about university, contributing to society, and utilizing the tools the military had given him to better himself and those around him.

The caricature before him, oblivious to the lack of sincerity in Sam's voice, felt genuinely touched by his words. That evening, he went home and shared with his wife what Sam had said. She was equally inspired, and they both slept well that night.

4

Lasciate ogne speranza, voi ch'entrate

Sam awoke with a jump. He looked about the cab, at first utterly confused, then quickly regained awareness of the situation. He pulled out his phone which read 10:15. It had already been two and a half hours since he'd called AAA. Did he miss them? Surely they would have noticed him asleep in the car and woken him, right?

More troubling, was the *1%* displayed in the top-right corner of his phone screen. He scrambled out of the cab, and with his phone charger in hand, walked toward the convenience store, searching for an outlet. He saw no new vehicles in the lot and the scene appeared to be unchanged except for a noticeably colder breeze pushing against him from the west. As he circumnavigated the building counterclockwise he passed the flickering bulb of the bathroom. He had to pee, but decided that he would rather test the blackness of the desert than whatever awaited him behind the ominous-looking door.

He continued around the building and found an outlet on the back wall facing nothing but desert. He plugged in, rested the phone on the concrete floor, and walked into the night to relieve himself.

He walked far enough into the desert to be enveloped by sufficient darkness. He didn't wish to be seen by Lilith should she break her oath of not leaving the store and find him peeing but a stone's throw from the restroom promised to him by the highway sign.

As he relieved himself, he looked up and felt immediately swallowed by the stars above him. When he had free time back in the barracks, he often enjoyed learning about space and the mind-melting distances that it encompassed.

Something in the way it humbled him and made his troubles seem small and insignificant had made it a favorite pastime.

He looked up into the dazzling sky and recalled some statistics that he enjoyed pulling out whenever appropriate. Specifically, he enjoyed sharing, with those that would listen, the journey of a particle of light travelling through space, to demonstrate its vast emptiness. He'd ask the listener to picture themselves flying through space at 670 million miles an hour, which was the speed of light, the speed limit of the universe. It would take the listener nearly five years just to reach our nearest star, Proxima Centauri. It would then take an additional 100,000 years to cross the Milky Way, and an additional two and a half million years to reach the closest galaxy, Andromeda. He'd finish by reminding the audience, if they remained present, that Andromeda was only one of an estimated two trillion galaxies in the observable universe. His story was oft to elicit eye rolls, but the perspective gave him a warm sensation of humility and wonder that he thoroughly enjoyed sharing with others.

A gentle ease overcame him as he gazed upward. *Eternity, there and here*, he thought. *All would be well.*

But just as he felt utterly content, something wholly unwelcome and unexpected rose from within him. Loud tinnitus started to ring in his ears. He winced from the abruptness of the white noise and simultaneously endured a vague suspicion of being watched. Still peeing, he turned to look back toward the building but saw no voyeurs. He returned his gaze to the desert but saw nothing but darkness. He pressured his bladder, finished his business, zipped up, and walked briskly back towards the building. The white noise persisted, rising slowly until it crescendoed and maintained a pinnacle pitch. It wasn't a wholly unfamiliar experience, given the many rifle shots he'd fired without ear protection, but its persistence unnerved him.

He returned to the light of the overhead LEDs that lined the building's rear exterior, turned back, and still saw nothing, although the strange feeling of anxiety persisted. A heaviness within the darkness pressed upon him, and he had an overwhelming urge to get away from it in an utterly primal manner. An urge to run. Flee. Get or get got. He hadn't felt that sort of fear in some time. Not stateside, at least. His trigger finger twitched. He considered bolting, but just as he was about to, his phone buzzed on the concrete below him. He reached down and picked it up. A call from an unknown number begged to be answered.

"Hello?" he asked, still eyeing the darkness as his ears stopped ringing with a peculiar swiftness.

"YEAH!" the caller replied. "This is Mike with AAA. I'm at the station. Where are you?"

Sam walked to the front of the store and found a tow truck idling in the lot. Its diesel engine gurgled loudly, prompting Sam to be surprised that he didn't hear its approach.

Within 15 minutes they jumped the battery and ensured that his truck had enough charge to get him into town. Sam wanted to tip the man for his help but realized that he was cashless, and didn't intend to wake Lilith again. He promised to leave the man a good review, to which he grunted with disinterest. "Nobody reads those," he said, climbing back into the tow truck and driving away.

Sam wasted no time in getting back onto the desolate highway. Before long, it grew from two lanes into three, then four, until the looming lights of the freeway came to decorate the cab's interior in a fluorescent orange. He took Interstate 17 north, and as the bridged exit rose high and bent over the various freeways crisscrossing underneath it, he caught a glimpse of the glittering Phoenix skyline to the east as Brahms' Symphony No. 3 played on the speakers. A specific melody from it had been stuck in his head since hearing it on repeat earlier, and he felt compelled to hear it once again. He recalled his mother saying once that the only way to get a song out of your head was to play it in its entirety.

And so he did, and it worked.

Even at the late hour, the traffic was considerable. It was better than what he had become accustomed to in southern California, but the Phoenix traffic seemed to increase each time he returned. He passed beside the flashing roller-coaster lights of an amusement park on his left and under the arched pedestrian bridges that were common along this particular stretch of freeway. He appreciated, as best he could while maintaining safe control of his vehicle, the geckos and lizards painted onto the walls along the sides of the freeway, each erected to keep its sounds out of the neighborhoods that flanked the artery of the city.

Eventually, however, the freeway began to revert back into an isolated highway as he drove north and out of the city proper. The looming orange lights that had lit the freeway disappeared, and once again he was surrounded by darkness while a redness painted the skyline just above the horizon in his rearview mirror.

He took an unassuming exit and drove east for a handful of miles into the desert.

After a considerable distance had been placed between him and the highway, the sound of thumping bass in the distance was the first sign that he was getting close. Cool air poured through the rolled-down windows of the pickup as it hummed along the lonely desert road. Blackness in all directions was Sam's primary company as the faded yellow lines of the road dove down under the hood and away forever.

When the street sign for Tequila Lane came into view, Sam turned right and exchanged pavement for dirt. As he drove, the far-away heavy bass began to mix with the intermittent high-pitched melodies of electronic music, prompting Sam to turn off his own radio and listen. His gaze lifted upward as a firework shot high into the sky, up and away from the horizon. The slick hood of the truck mimicked the ascent of the rocket like lake water interpreting the moon. There was a flash before a bang, and the dirt road illuminated in hazy greenish-white luminescence and the sky flowered.

Sparky must be with them. Drunk, too, he thought.

As the glittering remnants of the fireworks descended and atrophied into dark sky once again, Sam encountered a renewed excitement of the proximity of his destination. He looked to the left and saw the black silhouette of a familiar set of hills making an inky contrast against the sky.

He passed a homemade road sign that read: *Landmines ahead.* Two hundred yards beyond that, he passed another, this one stating *USAF PROVING GROUNDS – TURN BACK.* Two hundred yards further, he passed a final sign, this one Latin, stating something Sam had never thought to look up. It read: *Lasciate ogne speranza, voi ch'entrate*. He was getting close now.

The memories associated with the house at the end of Tequila Lane held court in a fond place within Sam's mind. He knew the memories were surely growing like big fish, but that was half the charm.

Sam had initially been introduced to Lane Sawyer by friends who had since gone their own ways in life, leaving Sam with an eccentric, curious, lavishly affluent, half-friend that had, for one reason or another, taken a liking to Sam in the brief interactions they'd had since.

They'd shared drunken dialectics in the few parties that Sam had been able to attend while on leave, and the memories remained as emotional bright spots after nights of heavy drinking. Their associations came to amount to nothing truly substantial, nothing especially profound, but apparently they were enough for Sawyer to remember Sam fondly.

Regardless, for one reason or another, Sawyer had reached out to Sam the moment he heard that he would be driving back into town, and had asked that he attend a party that Sawyer was throwing that evening. Sam had only a half plan for his return to civilian life and figured that swinging by Sawyer's would be a good story, if nothing else. Visits to the house at the end of Tequila Lane always were.

The truck rose above a bluff to reveal the infamous house at the end of Tequila Lane, which flooded the Sonoran Desert in fluorescent light. A disco ball's dancing colors bled from one window while solid red floodlights poured from another.

To the right of the home, an open courtyard bleeding into the unmitigated desert was overrun with a crowd of drunken, writhing miscreants.

Sam brought his attention back to the road, as Tequila Lane had quickly become flanked on each of its sides by parked cars. The headlights revealed a man up ahead, raising his arms high into the air, imploring the vehicle to stop.

As Sam slowed, the man approached the driver's-side window with a sashaying gusto that suggested a Latin dance number playing in the headphones that he removed upon approaching the vehicle.

"Valet!" he yelled, sweating and panting profusely. He had a thinly curled mustache and wore neon green running shorts below a vest bearing two large printed words across the chest. *Boom Shakalaka*, it said. There was nothing underneath the vest, of course.

"Valet!" he repeated, gesturing for Sam to exit the vehicle.

Still shedding the crustaceaned bark of highway hypnosis that he'd acquired over the past 400 miles, Sam had forgotten his social cues and simply stared at the valet, trying in vain to interpret the mannerisms of the eccentric man before him.

"SIR!" the valet exclaimed.

Sam snapped to attention. "Oh, um, I'm Sam. Sawyer told me to..."

"OH SHIT," the valet proclaimed abruptly. "I'm sorry, sir. I was starting to think that you weren't going to show. Go on ahead, your spot is waiting for ya. Just park in the driveway."

The valet then stepped back clumsily, collected himself, and made an obvious point of standing as tall as he could before rendering a sharp salute. Sam stared in awe before pulling forward slowly, unable to think of a single thing to say.

As he drove away, the valet, whose name was Fletch, congratulated himself on executing a salute he deemed quite excellent indeed. Sawyer had paid him twenty dollars an hour to watch *Full Metal Jacket*, *A Few Good Men*, *Flags of Our Fathers*, and *Patton*—twice—in the name of studying a proper salute to give Sam when he arrived at the party.

"Semper Fidelis, Marine," the valet whispered to himself as he stared at the taillights pulling away. A single tear fell from his cheek.

As Sam approached the driveway, he found taped to the garage door a vinyl banner of a photoshopped Sam Yellowstone, adorned in a uniform displaying every medal that was possible to be earned in the United States armed services. In the background of the banner was a fighter jet, a bikini-clad bombshell holding a M249 machine gun, a hamburger floating on a cloud, and a great white shark, all before an American flag waving in the wind.

Sam pulled down the banner, folded it into neat squares, and placed it into the back of the truck's cab. Just as another firework ascended from behind the building and into the sky above him, Sam walked around the back of the house and joined the party swirling about the courtyard.

The fish were as big as Sam had recalled them to be. In fact, they seemed to have been eating quite well over the years and had grown substantially since he'd last seen them swimming.

The police never came, or rather, they were there the whole time. Sheriff Sparky O'Hare was wearing flamingo sunglasses as he orchestrated the firework operation near the gazebo.

The party was themed as an "Every Holiday Party," as banners proudly proclaimed throughout the property. The first thing Sam noticed as he walked around back was a piñata strung to the arm of a saguaro. As he rounded the corner and began milling through the crowd, a man in a sombrero swung a Louisville slugger into the piñata, breaking it open and sending tequila shooters flying across the pool deck.

A woman wearing a flapper dress while carrying a jack-o' lantern approached Sam and encouraged him to write his name on a piece of paper and place it into the pumpkin. Sam proceeded to do so, on blind faith of the eccentricities of the evening, just before the woman carried the orange ball of names to a raised table where Lane Sawyer waited to receive it. The ceremony included a small marching band, which provided a drumroll as Sawyer rummaged his arm blindly into the pumpkin, squeezing his eyes shut, feigning an intense effort to the crazed encouragement of the crowd. A lesser man would have taken off his tuxedo jacket before doing this, but not Lane Sawyer. Chaos was part of his charm, or at least his curious allure.

Sawyer was a tall, well-built man, likely in his forties or early fifties. Without fail, he was the best dressed person in any room. Girls giggled when he walked by, and he made a point of mingling with every single person that came to his soirees.

Sawyer drew from the jack-o'-lantern the name of Greg Filson, who was already passed out drunk in an armchair on the patio. That didn't stop the party from presenting Greg with a hundred-candle birthday cake and singing him "Happy birthday." He required assistance to have the candles blown out, but when the crowd chanted "Speech, speech, speech," Greg briefly came to, and managed to mumble, to the delight of the crowd, "Where are my shoes?"

Inside, a Christmas tree glistening with elegant white lights towered above the living room. Below it rested nearly one hundred carefully wrapped presents, each with the name of a partygoer taped to its tag. In the kitchen, a Thanksgiving spread complete with three turkeys, homemade cranberry jam, mashed potatoes, Hawaiian rolls, garlic herb stuffing, and a row of pizzas recently delivered by Jumbo's Happy Pizzeria was intermittently picked at by the attendees. The man who had delivered the pizzas was offered three hundred dollars to quit his job on the spot and join the party, to which he happily agreed.

Sam had missed the New Year's Eve event while in the restroom, but a detailed account was provided by Sawyer when the two finally caught up. According to Sawyer, the party had shouted a countdown as a 12-foot-tall digital clock on wheels tracked the final seconds until midnight, while Fletch, dressed in his valet uniform, stood atop the roof, carefully lowering a disco ball tied to the end of a fishing pole. The ball dipped into the steaming hot-tub water at the precise stroke of midnight.

The only true snafu came when it was time to celebrate Veteran's Day. A triumph had been arranged, in the style of the ancient Roman republic. Sawyer's plan was to have Sam paraded around the property in a horse-drawn carriage, while Miss Arizona sat beside him whispering sweet nothings into his ear. Upon hearing this, Sam vehemently refused and threatened to leave if Sawyer insisted upon it. Ultimately, Sawyer relented and, in an impressive show of improvisation, turned the spectacle into an interpretation of the Macy's Day Parade, "with less fuckin' capitalism," he remarked to the crowd.

Nobody knew exactly where it came from, but somehow an inflatable arm-flailing tube man was produced and placed in the seat next to Miss Arizona, where Sam was originally intended to sit.

After this point, things blurred quite agreeably for Sam, especially near the end of the night. He bumped into friends, old, new, fake, and some he suspected, in his stupor, might become good friends down the road. He smiled and shook hands with people whose names he should have known. He laughed politely and tried to listen more than he spoke. He told favorite stories, smiled often, and even spilled a drink into the pool at one point, after losing his balance in a loose bout of laughter.

He knew his limits with drinking. It was something that had come after years of not being acquainted with them.

And so, the night, and eventually the early morning, went. At some point, sooner than seemed fair, he found himself walking east into the desert, in the direction of a rising sun still hiding behind the hills. Not long ago, he recalled, these hills had been black against an inky purple sky. Now they were a proud soft blue before a rapidly blooming amber, indigo, and rose sunrise.

He'd thought of these hills often over the past few years. In his mind's eye, they were smaller than they appeared now. As he took in the scene, complete with intermittent quail songs, a cool December breeze kissing his skin, and the smell of creosote in his nose, he tried to find the words to match how it all made him feel. He searched for some time, but eventually relented and embraced passivity, happy to be an observer unbound by the responsibility of tying words to his experience.

As he found a boulder worthy of a sit, and did just that, a lavender voice called out to him from behind.

"Sure is something, ain't it?" said the voice.

Sam turned to see Lane Sawyer approaching from the direction of the house, his stride typically confident. He had finally removed his tuxedo jacket to reveal a pearl white undershirt with the sleeves rolled a third of the way up his arms. The top three buttons were undone, and a carpet of chest hair peeked out from underneath. Sam thought him dressed as if he were about to sell him a cologne that neither of them could pronounce.

"I've thought of this place quite a bit while I was away," Sam remarked as he turned back to the hills. "Do they have a name?"

"Well," Sawyer replied in a patient iteration of the word, "I suppose on a map somewhere, in a place deemed important by someone, they've got an official name. I call them something all my own."

"And what's that?" asked Sam.

"I'd have to show you," replied Sawyer without missing a beat.

"You can't just tell me?" Sam chuckled.

"No," Sawyer replied in a suddenly curt manner. Sam was expecting a playful response but was provided with a thoroughly direct demeaner in the man's response. "I mean, I could. But that wouldn't mean much, would it? Words are just symbols. Maps. And the map is rarely, if ever, the same as the territory." He paused to measure Sam's expression with a thoughtful attention. "What do you say I show you what the words represent? Then we can talk symbols."

Sam took a moment to unravel Sawyer's riddles. "You mean... go up into the hills?"

Sawyer shot finger guns at Sam while simultaneously flashing a grin.

Sam thought the offer of ascending into the hills a joke at first, considering he'd never seen Sawyer in anything but a suit or some variation of formal attire. He also hadn't slept in over 24 hours, and both men had been up all night drinking. If Sam chose to look for even a sliver of an excuse to say no, to instead go inside and sleep comfortably... well, he'd have found a library of excuses to choose from.

But Sam detected no jest in Sawyer's expression, and a tingle of excitement traversed his spine, beginning in the lumbar and rising from there. This was the first morning of his post-Marine Corps life, and Sawyer's aura was undeniable. He looked at Sam as if neither of them had a thing to lose. In his gaze, a sly grin and wink that could have easily been missed by a casual observer, Sawyer seemed to proclaim ancient axioms that scoffed at the idea of sleeping through an adventure worth having.

"Let's go," Sam heard himself say confidently as he rose from his seat.

Sawyer laughed abruptly, his eyebrows rising to accentuate the fact. He was obviously surprised and impressed with Sam's response. He paused for a long moment, turned to look back at the house, and then back at Sam.

"You're crazy in all the right ways, kid," he said.

A wave of embarrassment flowed over Sam as he realized suddenly that Sawyer hadn't intended to go immediately. Sam had always been a bit brash when he was inspired.

"Come back Tuesday, an hour before dawn," said Sawyer. "Today, I'm seeing a man about a horse."

5

Slivers

Mae heard the tires of a heavy vehicle crunching the snow as it approached the front of the house. She walked outside and found Lane Sawyer approaching the circular drive in his lifted Wrangler, cherry red with a cloth top.

"Cloth-top convertible, huh?" she called as he disembarked. "You realize it's January, right?"

"Down in the valley it's still Phoenix," he said. "You didn't exactly give me time to make arrangements." He looked tired and a thick five o'clock shadow was prevalent on his jawline. He spoke as if he hadn't the patience for social nuance, nor much respect for his host. "Drove through the night to be here, ya know."

"Don't forget who's in charge here, Sawyer," Mae replied sharply. "I'd hate to let a certain somebody know about a certain something."

Sawyer didn't respond but merely cocked his head to the side as he walked past her and into the house. He dropped his bag on the kitchen table with a thump before turning to face her. "Should we go dig up our friends?" he asked.

"They're already awake. Just need to get them into position. You brought the text?"

Sawyer's mouth opened abruptly in astonishment. "You dug up ten bodies? All on your own?"

"What can I say? I hit a stride. Felt like strolling down memory lane," she said.

"Whatever," he replied, shaking his head without nuance. "I've got the text. I've got the blankets. Let's get this over with."

The two walked toward the barn in the bright sunshine of what was undeniably a beautiful day. The bright white snow beneath their feet glistened in striking contrast to the acts they were about preparing to conduct.

"What happens after this, Mae?" Sawyer asked gruffly. "When we're done here... are we done here?"

"We'll see," was all she said in response. In reality, Mae hadn't given half a thought as to what might come of Lane Sawyer after the ritual was complete. It didn't matter to her in the slightest. He had been a useful tool in the pursuit of her collection, but she felt no obligation to the man, and ultimately thought of him as nothing more than a self-indulgent glutton deserving of the blackmail that she weaponized against him.

Once the ritual was complete, he could spontaneously combust for all she cared.

The pair began carrying the bodies from the barn to the house, one by one. They began with Sam, then José, and so forth, in roughly the same order that Mae had removed them from the earth earlier. With each trip, the weight of what they carried grew lighter, until at last they were burdened with only rattling bags of bones, one in each hand, into the house.

Each of the remains were brought into the master bedroom, where Mae had been making preparations since her arrival with Sam the day before. The bed had been dragged through the colossal sliding glass door and lay outside under a thick coating of snow. Its mattress had been thrown outside as well alongside the carpet that had been ripped out and rolled into a crumpled cylinder beside it in the snow.

Upon the concrete floor that remained, Mae had drawn a large pentagram with red chalk. Each of the five lines within the polygon had a small line drawn perpendicularly upon it, exactly halfway, resulting in ten six-foot-long stretches of chalked lines in total.

Each line awaited a set of remains to be placed upon them, and one by one, as Mae and Sawyer brought in the remains in their various stages of decay, such was achieved. When it came to the bags of bones, they were carefully emptied into narrow rows upon the chalked lines that awaited them.

Every depiction of evil ever depicted across humanity's long relationship with vice smiled upon the scene. Mae was equally glad for it. Her patience for acceptance and empathy was tired and jaded after her many years of being subjected to humanities self-righteous opinions and perspectives.

Trite was the word that came to mind, more than others.

Mae and Sawyer took a break outside, correcting a pair of upturned patio chairs and then basking in the sun. They drank glasses of strawberry daiquiri mix that Mae had found in the fridge.

"So," Sawyer began, "how'd the spider catch her final fly?"

Mae scoffed. "By holding his hand and whispering sweet nothings into his ear. He was like a dry sponge, that one. Just needed a touch of water, and he expanded into whatever shape I needed him to be."

"And what shape was that?" Sawyer asked, only half interested.

"A leaf in the wind. I didn't lie to him, though. I told him why I was here from the beginning—in a sense, at least."

Sawyer suddenly regained an interest in the conversation. "Why the fuck would you do that?" he asked.

"For fun," she replied sarcastically. "All I did was conjure some illusions of Masau'u on the security cameras. Another day, I drove up and disappeared like a fart in the wind. Just fucked with him a bit. Just enough to get him unnerved and willing to accept the help of a pretty face. Took him to Kyao and got him all riled up. Then I told him I needed his help to come back here and kill that ancient bastard."

"That's very meta of you. And very stupid, too," Sawyer said boldly.

"He wasn't a threat. If I batted my eyes enough, he would have dug up those bodies himself."

For a moment, Mae considered if Sawyer was of any use to her any longer. His growing insolence was agitating her, and she could perform the ritual by herself, after all. But the longevity of her day was beginning to catch up with her, and she decided that after a nap, she would reconsider the matter. "I'm going inside to rest. Wake me when the sun goes down."

Mae walked into the living room and laid down upon the living room couch, quickly descending into a deep slumber. A pleasant darkness overcame her, and she drifted softly through a timeless nothingness that she hoped to experience outside of her dreams, one day soon.

It was a welcome sliver of death—that is, until her dreams played a wicked drama of flickering memories and fears upon the folds of her temporal lobe.

Her perspective fluttered from one thing to the next without pretense or concern for logical transition. She quickly found herself looking down a long, dark cave with a distant light shining from within its craggy depths. She could feel the dampness of the space, and as the light at its end began to flicker out, a bloodcurdling scream echoed through the walls from a larynx vaguely familiar. She then saw a cobblestone well beside the burnt-down remains of a building somewhere in the forest. The concrete foundations lay beneath a chimney still rising into the sky against a backdrop of trees mocking its ascent. A smattering of charred wood lay scattered about the scene, and a dozen head of cattle grazed lazily by. A pair of pale hands suddenly emerged from within the well, grasped the lip of the cobblestone brim. Just as the waterlogged head of a translucent figure breached the wall, her perspective shifted to a desolate path in the forest, the rain pelting its unmaintained surface. She gazed down the wide path flanked by tall ponderosas. From the tree line on the left, a donkey emerged onto the path. Upon the donkey's head was the obviously taxidermied head of a lion, the saw marks on the lion's neck still bleeding down the donkey's legs and its front hooves as it trotted slowly onto the soggy road. Once upon the center of the path, it paused, its lion-head dipping as it looked downward before continuing into the trees on the right side of the road. Mae's view then shifted to an all-encompassing view of space from space with stars surrounding her in every imagined axis of direction as if she were floating weightlessly through the cosmos. All that could be seen was a suffocatingly distant view of the universe; a thousand billion stars staring back at her with a heaviness that snuffed out the very breath of her thoughts, while the galaxies, more distant and numerous than seedlings beneath the hard crust of the earth in winter, glistened in the tears that swelled unexpectantly in her eye's perspective. She waited and pleaded for her perspective to shift, but in the elongated experience of her dream, the stars seemed to threaten, in no uncertain terms, that it would forever press upon the corneas of an unfathomably long, desolate, and impotent existence.

6

Threads in the Frost

Mae awoke to a view of Orion's Belt peeking sheepishly through the canopy above her while the shifting branches of the pines danced to a slight breeze. From somewhere off in the distance she heard her father calling her name.

She sat up slowly, prompting needles to cascade off her shirt and into her lap, where she found a centipede casually crawling along her pant leg. In a mad flurry, she swiped at the insect several times and shot to her feet, shaking from the adrenaline that had been injected into her bloodstream.

The creature scurried away in terror, and Mae briefly considered killing it, but the act of killing had always disagreed with her and she decided against it. She was glad that Susy wasn't there to see her mercy, as it was another topic of ridicule for which her sister routinely berated her.

She peered into the darkness of the woods in the direction of the bellowing voice, and saw a lantern being carried by her father a short distance away.

"Pa!" she called after him.

John turned with a start before quickly bounding over. "Mae! Darling!" he called. Upon his arrival at her side, he rested the lantern upon the felled log beside Mae and gave her a tight squeeze. "We thought we'd surely lost you! Where did you get off to?" he asked frantically.

Mae considered telling her father about what she'd experienced. The visage of William walking along the log. The Indian. The curious things he had shared with her. But for reasons not yet fully known to her, she kept it to herself. "I... I must have tripped and hit my head. The last thing I remember, I was walking on that," she said, pointing to the log on which the lantern was now placed.

John knelt and reached for his daughters' hands, leaning in close with a progressively tense demeanor. As he drew near, his brow furrowed and his lips tensed. He held her hands softly at first, but as he began to speak softly to her, as if telling a secret, his grip grew stronger with each word.

"Mae... do you know why we don't want you going into the woods alone?" Mae nodded her head, but he interrupted her as if she had shaken it. "It's not Indians. It's not bears. No. It's an old witch that wanders these trees, looking for little girls to put in her stew." Tears began to well in her eyes as his grip continued to tighten. "It's true, Mae. The traders told me about her. She lures little girls into the tall trees, snatches them up, and boils them alive in her pot. Do you know why she does it, Mae?" he asked, his voice rising sharply into a crescendo.

Mae thought he might crush the bones of her palms. Tearfully, she shook her head.

"Just for fun," he said with finality. He relinquished his heavy grip and stood tall above her like the trees that surrounded them both. "Let us get back now, to release your poor mother from her worries."

And so, Mae and her father walked hand in hand back toward the farmstead to do just that.

Mae came to regard her interaction with the Indian under the trees as just another odd event that she only occasionally considered, not unlike her interaction with the old "wizard" on the train, years before. The rare occasions when she recalled the interaction were typically late at night when she couldn't sleep. She would lean against the windows of the cabin for hours, gazing into the blackness of the forest. Every once in a long while, she thought she saw black shadows running amongst the trees.

She never gave much credence to what the Indian had said to her. When she recalled the instance, she mostly just remembered the racing of her heart and the impotence of her will to run away. She remembered the man saying that he was going to give her "time", but that made little sense to her, no matter how long she considered it. How could he give her something as intangible as time?

In the end, she came to see the interaction as nothing more than a conversation with an odd bird culminating in her having a panic attack and falling unconscious as a result. It was a theory that satiated her fairly well, until she at last came to acknowledge the reality of the situation years later... above the cave, and in the rain.

***

On his eighteenth birthday, William was drafted into the Army to go off and fight in The Great War. In the months leading up to the U.S. becoming involved in the conflict, Mae recalled her parents huddling around the kitchen table, concernedly reading the newspapers that they had greedily gathered from town. They became convinced by and rallied around Woodrow Wilson's belief that the country could and should stay out of the conflict. They knew that if the U.S. was drawn into the war, their William would likely be among those compelled to fight in it. That was simply the writing on the wall. William, for his part, was unapologetically eager to go off on his great adventure and confront the Huns. Mae recalled him fishing the newspapers from the trash when their parents were done with them, as his youthful perspective resulted in a strikingly different interpretation of world events than his parents'. When the day that his letter of summoning eventually arrived, it wasn't difficult for Mae to see his shaky smile thinly cloaked from his thoroughly despondent parents.

Mae's parents threw a party for William on the day before he shipped off to France. Half of Flagstaff was there, mingling in the meadow outside the cabin. A modest string quartet played behind the house beside an impressive spread of appetizers and drinks. Her mom thought a string quartet was just about the classiest thing someone could have at a party.

William had returned from basic training the day before and proceeded to fill every room he entered with a radiating smile. He seemed, Mae thought, to confer importance upon every person with whom he crossed paths with. And it wasn't just a show, either. Mae knew that for a fact. For the rest of her life, Mae thought William Barrett to be the single most compassionate and genuinely thoughtful person she had ever known.

Mae recalled their father taking Will aside at one point and shaking his hand with a quiet word. Her mother concealed her worry poorly by attending to as many chores as she could possibly summon.

And then he was away.

That August, a pair of uniformed men walked the long aspen-covered pathway onto the property and handed John Barrett a letter.

Mae took it hard. The whole family did, and they processed the loss in their own ways. That's the only way pain can ever truly be felt. Individually.

Most of that period... well... Mae had only abandoned memories of. Half recollections of her mother sleeping for days on end, although, one memory in particular from the weeks following the news of Williams death couldn't be abandoned, as much as she wished that they could. One day, after not rising for nearly a week, Edith stood stoically from her bed, fully disrobed, and walked calmly toward the woods before John could throw a blanket around her shoulders and wrestle her back into the cabin as she screamed and pleaded with the sky.

After some time, which is the only true medicine for such things, Edith got better. Mae even heard her humming on a sunny afternoon while she tended to the dishes. It was something she was known to do often before the war came, looking out the window and into the meadow beyond.

Her father showed little, if any, emotion on the subject. Even on the day he received the letter saying that his only son was missing in action, Mae witnessed only a single tear drop from his eye before he went outside to chop firewood long into the night. And that was it.

Later, Mae decided that all the grief that he was surely holding inside for so many years must have been hellish. She felt remorse for few things more in life than the unrelinquished pain of her father over the loss of his only son.

She didn't blame him, though. She even came to suspect that she had come to do the same thing herself... in her own way.

Years later, Mae couldn't help herself and went to the city archives to conduct research into her brother's fate. She discovered that Willam Barrett had likely been buried alive by earth cast into the air by artillery fire during the Second Battle of the Marne. She regretted her curiosity.

But time went on for all involved, whether they were healed, ready, or not. Susy fell in with a well-to-do son of a trader by the name of Thadeus Tremour. Mae thought very little of Thad, as most called him. He was a surly man raised with an unshakeable confidence that he would one day become a titan of industry, known the world over.

It was unearned confidence, yet he waved his flag high upon the pole of his own estimation.

Regardless, he and Susy fell in love, and the two quickly shuffled off to Los Angeles in the early 20s. Thad promised that he had a flat, and even a secretary job waiting for Susy upon their arrival.

"Our Susy! Working at a law firm! Well, I for one am just tickled!" Edith sang across the dinner table on more than one occasion.

With Susy out of the house, Mae was abruptly confronted with an itch to leave her parents' home as well. She hadn't been too keen on any of the boys that had come to call over the years, but her interests did come to expand beyond the tree line of the homestead. She had become enraptured by some of the latest books that she had stumbled into, and her imagination blossomed with thoughts of how she fancied her own story unfolding.

On the first of each month, she and her father would ride into town. She would step into the library while John addressed his business with the butchers and traders. Mae would often walk out of the building carrying three or four books in her arms, to the bafflement of her father who understood little of the joys of reading for pleasure. He was simply happy that she had a reason to join him on his trips into town. As she grew from a child into a young woman, he became more and more appreciative of the increasingly brief moments that they shared together. He knew all too well that one day such little moments would be but happy memories.

Once, over the course of a single rabid month of reading, Mae read *The Odyssey*, *Crime and Punishment*, *Frankenstein*, *The Picture of Dorian Gray*, *Thus Spoke Zarathustra*, *Pride and Prejudice*, and *Frankenstein* again. Upon the conclusion of her second pass through the Mary Shelley classic, Mae strode outside the cabin to find her parents attending to an unruly sheep and announced boldly that she intended to attend the university that fall to study literature.

Neither of her parents understood her decision, but they were ultimately nothing but supportive. The cattle business had been good to them, and with Susy married off, they had plenty of money to help with the costs of tuition and attendance. Not to mention, with one child passed on and another a state away, they were more than happy to help Mae with an endeavor that ensured her staying close by.

So that September, with much fanfare—her mother couldn't help but throw another party, string quartet and all—Mae began her studies at Northern Arizona University. At first the transition from living in the small cabin in the woods to a bustling dormitory was somewhat overwhelming, but after a short time, Mae settled into a routine and made friends. As the months came to pass and the snow began to fall in the deepening winter, she came to thoroughly enjoy her new life and the varying perspectives and ideas that it afforded her.

One night, however, everything unequivocally changed.

Inferno lay open upon her dorm room desk with the words *CANTO XXIX* proclaimed boldly atop the open page. Handwritten notes were scribbled liberally across the pages, and a cooled coffee sat forgotten beside it. Mae leaned against the open window of the dormitory watching a peculiar sight far below. In the field across the street, a figure paraded through the three-day-old snow dancing and singing with an apparent apathy for any potential audience that might have been listening in. That alone wasn't enough to make the occurrence noteworthy, of course, as rambling drunks were a common sight on campus. No, what made the sight capture Mae's attention was the slow recognition of a certain symmetry in the lines left behind by the figure as they danced. It was almost like they were drawing something in their tracks while spinning, shuffling, and skipping through the deep powder.

The sketch beckoned to her strangely, as if its angle and orientation was constructed to face her open window directly. In her gaze of its angles, it whispered sweet nothings into her mind that were beyond word and without symbolistic meaning. It just was.

It almost looked like a sigil of some kind, like something straight out of *The Book of the Law*.

The man's singing—as the more she listened it, the more it became clear that it was the voice of a man—was muted by the glass of the window, prompting Mae to slide the pane open an inch to listen. It was a throaty rendition of Schubert's *Der Doppelgänger*. That was the final straw. The song's lyrics so soaked in vibrato catalyzed her curiosity into action.

She donned her coat and descended the stairs to investigate what was occurring in the deep white field below.

The man continued to sing into the night in his throaty baritone as she approached. When she got close enough to see his features in the ice-blue glow, she saw that the voice belonged to old black man with a messy white beard dancing in a neat black cloak.

"Der Mond zeigt mir meine eigne Gestalt. ..." He stopped abruptly as his pirouette spun him to face Mae, now standing nearby under a gas lamp post. He finished the last word of the line, albeit in but a hushed monotone. "...Gestalt."

"Would you give me a hand, young one?" he asked in an elegant cockney that compounded Mae's curiosity.

She nodded.

"Do you see that bench over there?" He pointed toward a stone bench resting caddy corner to where she stood.

"Yes," she said with a coy smile.

"I would be much obliged if you, my darling, would walk to it." Before she could take a step, he shouted: "Directly! ...my dear. Directly, and exactly... from where you stand now."

Indeed, she had intended to take the sidewalk around the corner, but now understood that the man wished for her to contribute to his masterpiece and walk through the snowy field and leave a trail behind her.

She obliged.

"Marvelous. You move like the wind," he remarked as she reached the bench and turned calmly to face him once again. "And now you must close your eyes and move in whatever direction takes you. Would you do this for me?" he asked.

Something about the man made her overwhelmingly comfortable. Trusting. Calm. She had long relied upon an ability to sense danger in others, men in particular, but none of her warning bells rang while in the man's presence.

After a moment of silent stillness, she closed her eyes and began to walk into the field, shifting her weight when the impulse took her. She spun, backed up, ran, and shuffled, all while holding her eyelids tightly shut. It felt so obvious and queerly blissful, like she was but a leaf upon the currents of a raging river that she had always known to be flowing from mountains yonder toward valleys below.

Suddenly, an uncanny whisper came from somewhere deep, and yet, nearby. "Open your eyes," it said. She again obliged, and when she did, found that she stood a mere foot away from the man. His grin grew slowly and steadily, and before long, both he and Mae shared in full-bodied laughter.

When their giggles finally subsided, the man gazed at her with a smirk that risked erupting into laughter once again. His lips didn't shape the words, but again she heard the same voice that had whispered for her to open her eyes. This time, she had no doubt as to who's voice it belonged.

"Your gifts remain unopened," the voice said. "Would you like me to open them for you?"

7

The Map and The Territory

Come Tuesday, in the pre-dawn darkness, Sam returned to the house at the end of Tequila Lane with bells on, as his grandmother would have said. He had gotten his alternator fixed the previous day and while attending to other miscellaneous to-do's. It felt wildly unbridled to be living his days so spontaneously after years of enduring the Marine Corps' yoke. He was no longer forced to inform a superior of his every move, and, as a result, life was a already a simpler thing to carry.

He walked around the back of the house, stepping carefully between towering saguaros and jumping cactus. He was a bit tired, as he had only slept a few hours the night before, mostly due to his eagerness to indulge in Sawyer's enigmatic presence once again. He couldn't help but be strangely curious of the man and the odd, yet wise, things he'd say from time to time. "What a character," Sam would say when describing him to those who'd never met him.

He found Sawyer standing on the cobblestone patio, smoking a cigar beside a chiminea burning what smelt like creosote. The air was calm, and the smoke rose from the cigar in a neat line before finding a current of air and becoming unkempt. As Sam approached, Sawyer bellowed into the cold air without turning to face him. "Good morning, Rocket!" His breath, warmed by the cigar, emerged from his mouth in a visible cloud that mixed readily with the smoke of the cigar.

"Rocket?" Sam repeated as he approached. His hands dug deep into his pockets, clinging to the warmth that they found there. He was wearing a tan beanie that he had permanently borrowed from the Marine Corps. It had been around the world with him, and he figured it was a fair parting gift. He had known men that had taken their helmets with them. The Corps could afford to part with a beanie, he reasoned.

"You're a rocket, Sam," said Sawyer, turning to greet him at last. "The only question is, are we talking Columbia or Apollo?"

Sam hadn't a clue what Sawyer meant by this, but decided to indulge him. "I guess I should call you Houston."

Sawyer smirked, implying to Sam's indulgent assessment that he had deemed it an excellent response.

The two collected their effects and marched eastward into the hills of the Sonoran Desert. They followed a scant dirt path that zigged and zagged between boulders and cacti forests. They rested their weary feet at uneven patches of dirt and rock, and occasionally let loose small rockslides that tumbled small distances before finding rest once again.

There is a certain magic one comes to know when hiking before dawn, particularly in the cool months of the year. Sam had come to know this well after many humps through the hills of Camp Pendleton, and other more distant and less hospitable mounds of Earth. The lungs burn with each pull of cold air and the legs begin to protest and threaten to strike—however, after some momentum is given to each, the blood finds inertia and warms as the body coalesces into a comfortable numbness. With enough practice, the brain even abandons its grievances and becomes more similar to the hills than the legs that traverse them.

After an initial surprise at finding Sawyer's pace to be quite quick indeed, Sam found himself slipping into a pleasant cadence, doing his best to match the steps of the man leading the way. Although the pace was brisk, Sam's body had been sculpted by longer and steeper hikes, while carrying many more pounds than he was now. The lack of a rifle slung across his chest was also a pleasant absence. He despised the jostling of the long heavy metal, particularly when it would inevitably bounce against his kneecaps while climbing steep ascents. Now, his hands were free to hold air and nothing else.

The hike soon became a meditation, and time passed unobserved by his conscious mind. Before many more thoughts came to be, Sam looked up and found that they had reached a small plateau overlooking the valley below and to the south. They paused to catch their breath and took in the view, sharing in a silence hard to find in daily life. A soft breeze rustled one branch against another, but that was all that Sam could hear. The moon hung bright and full, and a hawk flew high overhead.

From their vantage point, Sam could see the northern fingers of Phoenix extending into the otherwise unmolested desert in shimmering veins of roads and houses. The sun had begun to brighten the eastern horizon behind them, but streetlights still illuminated the roads and suburbs below.

"I s'pose they'll keep developing north until they hit Black Canyon City," said Sawyer. His voice was jarring in contrast to the silent ascent that Sam had enjoyed much more than he had been expecting. "You see that development down there?" He pointed toward a tightly clumped grouping of homes far removed from the other larger signs of humanity amongst the desert. "That got built just last year. Popped up like a weed after a monsoon."

"Seems like it'd be quite the commute to Phoenix from there," Sam remarked.

"There's something awful interesting about people that are undeterred by a commute like that," replied Sawyer, dropping his pack to the ground. He removed a canteen and pulled from it. Sam assumed it contained water, but he could never be too sure where Lane Sawyer was concerned. "These folks would rather spend two hours in a car each day, before and after working jobs they hate, than live too close to the city, or too far from it. Seems indecisive to me."

"Maybe they just like the desert," said Sam.

"If they liked the desert, they'd leave it be."

"But *you* live in the desert," replied Sam, trying his best to not sound confrontational.

Sawyer smiled and winked. "I *am* the desert."

The two ate their breakfast on the plateau without much further conversation. Sam produced a bag of nuts and poured electrolyte concentrate into his Camelback while Sawyer bit into an apple and continued drinking from his canteen. Both sat on their packs and stared listlessly west.

Before resuming the hike, Sawyer shared that the plan was to ascend to the saddle ridge a few hundred yards east and take the ridgeline south towards the highest summit of the surrounding hills. He said that it shouldn't be too much trouble if they managed to stay out of the cholla fields, and that the views would be worth it.

True to his word, the remainder of the hike passed without incident, and despite a few craggy rocks jostled loose when stepped upon, the two summited the peak just as the sun was threatening to rise above the Mazatzal Mountain range in the east. The two, now on top of the world as they knew it, became withdrawn and quietly appreciated the panorama before them for several minutes.

To Sam's surprise, he could see the slight shimmer of Bartlett Lake, a distant, crooked blue line just below the rapidly brightening eastern sky. As he appreciated the view, the breeze grew strong, making any attempt to walk near the edge of the peak a flirtation with disaster.

Both men dropped their packs and sat, marinating in both the view and the endorphins still racing through their veins. Sam stole a glance at Sawyer and realized that this was only the second time he'd seen him in the light of day, the first being the morning after the all-holiday party a few days before. Most of their encounters were at night and fuzzy from the vignette of alcohol.

But looking at him now, he saw a face much more touched by time than he had previously realized. Lines flanked his mouth, and a few prominent ridges ran east to west across his forehead; both signs of an optimistic and happy life. His well-maintained beard showed more salt than pepper, and the skin beneath his eyes sagged.

As if sensing Sam looking at him, Sawyer spoke without turning from the view.

"So now that you're here, what are these hills called, Rocket?"

Sam chuckled. "I thought *you* were going to tell *me*?"

"Here's the thing." Sawyer paused to pull from his canteen. "I believe that our purpose in life is to create a purpose in life. It's all up to interpretation and there are no wrong answers. But everyone's purpose is their own. And if I were to sit here and tell you that my purpose in life is one thing, I'd hate for it to impact yours, especially if you're still searching for it."

"What does that have to do with the name of these hills, though?" asked Sam, again surprised and impressed at his own confident interjections. Despite his position of non-commissioned authority in the military, he had always been a relatively passive person, something that he had recently resolved to improve.

"The point is," Sawyer continued, "that if I tell you what these hills are to me, I wouldn't want that to impact what they are to you."

Sam contemplated this for a long while, and neither man spoke for some time. The same hawk that had flown above them at the beginning of their hike made a slow arching pass nearby, much closer now. In fact, Sam had never seen a hawk pass so near. He could see the golden rings of its eyes scanning the steep cliffs for mice and rabbits. Sam looked out into the void before him and sensed the vastness of the space pressing upon him. It hit him heavily, like the weight of one's first understanding of sonder; the appreciation that one is but a single perspective swimming in an ocean of a thousand-billion others.

This must be what the ocean would look like without the water, he thought, picturing whales floating through the morning air.

"Orca Cloud Hill," he said aloud.

"Now that sounds like a place I'd like to visit."

"And you?"

"I've always called it Happy Jack's Hill Emporium," said Sawyer with a straight face before slowly growing a wide smile.

Sam took note of the expanding lines across Sawyer's face while subduing an urge to roll his eyes.

"No," Sawyer said finally. "To me, this is Dusty Hill." There was a long pause as Sam recalled Sawyer having a brown labrador named Dusty some years back. He didn't pry.

"So, what's the plan, Rocket?" asked Sawyer happily.

Sam hesitated. He had been following Sawyer's lead throughout the adventure, and was surprised by the question. In general, he had been enjoying not making decisions lately. Years of being responsible for so much had siphoned the initiative right out of him. At least for the time being.

"I guess we can head on down when you're ready," he said. "Get some lunch at that bagel shop in town."

"No," Sawyer said, waving Sam away. "I mean, what's the plan now that you're a free man? You planning on sticking around Phoenix, or what do you have in mind?"

"Not much, if I'm being honest," said Sam. "I'm just jumping from couch to couch for the moment. I'll probably enroll in school next semester. Use that GI bill, ya know? But for now, I'm just enjoying being a leaf in the wind."

"I don't blame you," said Sawyer. "When I got out of the Army, after Vietnam, I bummed around for months."

Sam was thoroughly startled by the statement. In all the times that he'd interacted with Sawyer, trivial as those interactions may have been, Sawyer had never shared that he was a veteran, and his demeanor didn't exactly scream Vietnam vet, either.

Sawyer continued, "I was just beyond everything at the time. It felt good to just... not. I hitchhiked a lot, ending up where I ended up. I'd get up and go when the time felt right." Sam noticed Sawyer fiddling with some dirt between his fingers. "Then I woke up one day and found myself in Cheyenne, Wyoming. Couldn't tell ya how I ended up there or why, but I met a pretty girl and stayed there a while. That was in early seventies, long before I came out here."

"I guess there's a lot I don't know about you, Sawyer."

"I can say the same about you, young Rocket, and yet I think I know enough." Sawyer looked down at the dirt before raising his chin toward the sky, as if he were at the precipice of a decision. "Listen," he continued, "if you're looking for work, I might have something for you... Do you know what I do for a living?"

Sam did not, and had long been curious about the subject, but not quite curious enough to ask outright. He shook his head.

"I own an estate management business. Most of the time, we take care of properties that rich folks have forgotten about, gotten bored of, or only visit from time to time. Anyway, I've got this property up north, just outside of Flagstaff. Real pretty place. The guy who'd been working it just quit on me, and I'm thinking maybe you'd be interested in taking his spot. Free room and board, and I'd pay you more than fair. Whaddya think?"

"To be honest, it sounds a bit too good to be true," said Sam, still cynical from his last contractual agreement.

Sawyer laughed in agreement while nodding his head. "You're not wrong, my friend. You're not wrong. But the thing is, it's harder than you might realize to find reliable help these days, and I prefer to hire veterans when I can. And to be honest, I think you might just enjoy it."

Sam thought long on the idea. He'd always enjoyed his trips up the mountain and, on its face, it appeared to be a rare opportunity to reset and relax for a bit. The silence on the hike up the hill reminded Sam of how valuable time spent alone in nature could be. The hawk made another pass above their heads while he pondered. "Does this place have a name too?" he asked.

"It sure does," replied Sawyer with a grin. "It sure does."

8

Dust Bowl Eyes

The drive north along I-17 towards Flagstaff was a route that Sam had taken many times over the years, and it was one that he was particularly fond of. As the highway rose out of the valley, it began its ascent by first rising into the dramatic New River Mountain range, full of saguaro thickets and jagged cliff faces, a place Sam thought to be unlike any other in the world. When he was young, Sam would descend into the hills to ride dirt bikes and shoot propane tanks with his friends. As he passed the Bumblebee exit, he thought back on all the times that he could have, and likely should have, been killed by the reckless decisions of his adolescence.

Further north was Sunset Point, a plateau that had an excellent view of the Castle Creek Wilderness to the west. The road then continued on through the high hills and bleached grasses that passed the enigmatic attractions of Arcosanti and Montezuma Castle, but Sam had never taken the time to stop and visit either. Instead, the landmark that mattered to him was an eclectic juniper that stood tall in the median around this stretch of highway. It had been ornately decorated in Christmas lights every winter for as long as Sam could remember. The tree was some twenty feet tall and nearly as wide, looking more like a bush than a tree. Regardless, it brought a smile to his face every time he saw it, and this day was no different.

Soon, he approached the 179. Briefly, he considered taking the scenic route through Sedona on his way into Flagstaff, but ultimately decided against it. The weather was gorgeous, a cool late December day, and therefore he knew that the rust-colored mountains and the city's roads would be choking with tourists. Better to pass through on a blistering day in August, he thought.

In the years after high school but before his enlistment, Sam had driven to Flagstaff often to visit friends that were attending NAU. The place represented fond memories of youthful debauchery but with a tinge of regret, as he had wanted to go to the university himself, but he was too high and apathetic throughout the latter years of his high school tenure to earn the grades for it. Money was a problem too.

But Flagstaff remained a town that he was always happy to visit, even in December, as both cold and snow remained novel and exciting phenomena to him. He had never lived in a place where he had to scrape the ice from his windshield, nor had he known the stress of driving on icy roads following a frozen fog. The cold was an exotic beast while Flagstaff, and its surrounding forest, remained a romantic bastion for Sam's imagination.

The drive was a pleasant and uneventful hour and three quarters. When he grew near, he began to spot clumps of snow dappling the countryside, prompting him to smile widely while thrusting his arm out the window to embrace the frigidity of the wind. He had always felt optimistic on the mountain.

As he passed the exits for Kachina Village, he looked up and saw the San Francisco Peaks rising high above the tree line. His destination, "Emerald Acres," as Sawyer had called it, was 30 minutes east of Flagstaff and Sam figured that he might as well stop for a late lunch while he was in town.

He parked on San Francisco St. and meandered about the downtown in no particular hurry. School was still in session and groups of students roamed the sidewalks in packs. Sam walked past the corner of Aspen, where he saw men on a scaffolding hanging a large pinecone high on the corner of the Weatherford Hotel. He made a mental note to return on New Year's Eve, in just a few short weeks, to see the Great Pinecone Drop, if he could.

Maybe I'll stay at the Monte V, he thought.

The Hotel Monte Vista loomed over the corner of San Francisco and Aspen. It was built in the 1920s to accommodate the expanding tourism of the west, and had its chapter in the history of prohibition. To Sam, though, it was a favorite spot to crash when he was in the city and a couch was unavailable. Its historic rooms outfitted with rotary phones and faded antique furniture painted his thoughts in a transatlantic hue. Not to mention that the bar on the ground floor was decent and live music was common on most nights. It reminded Sam of Hotel San Carlos in downtown Phoenix; however, the latter had a pool on the roof, which would be an interesting choice for a city with a climate such as Flagstaff's.

He walked all the way across town to Macy's for lunch, enjoying the cool air and the bustling streets. Shortly after crossing the tracks, he passed a man in a ragged coat playing the harmonica while leaning against a street post. The man faced in the opposite direction, but as Sam passed by, he stopped playing, turned, and gave Sam a piercing gaze that startled him, as the man's right eye was absent from its socket, leaving a hollow, fleshy cave within the skull.

He spoke to Sam in an Irish accent. "Dontcha let her catch you, now," he murmured before cackling wildly. Sam continued on briskly, having learned long ago that it's best to just put one's head down and continue walking in such circumstances.

"Moth to the flame! DANCE AS YE GO, NOW!" the man called out between his gasping laughter.

At Macy's, Sam ordered a Reuben and a pilsner and sat on the patio alone. Quite reasonably, all the other patrons sat in the warm café, but Sam didn't mind. He always felt somewhat offput in crowds. The view from the patio overlooked a street overwhelmed with parked cars. Across the way was a brick wall muraled with a vivid interpretation of cosmic consciousness and a correlating acceptance. At least, that was Sam's interpretation of it by the time he finished his beer. As he did, a shivering waitress approached his table with his sandwich.

She had a gentle face beneath blonde hair pulled messily into a bun. A single unruly strand danced about her face, and Sam experienced secondhand ticklishness due to the way it lightly bounced across her cheeks, which were rosy from the cold.

As she bent over to put his plate on his table, she hesitated, looking at him with alternating curiosity and sheepishness.

"This is silly… but do you by chance know Lane Sawyer?" she asked.

"I... I do," Sam said slowly. He then saw, in his mind's eye, a flash of a memory from his admittedly fallible recollection of the all-holiday party a few days before. He remembered watching the girl who now stood before him, from across the pool in Sawyer's backyard as she laughed awkwardly with her friends. He remembered thinking that her eyes belonged to a portrait portraying dust-bowl sorrows, and yet she laughed and swayed elegantly in the desert's moonlight. They had walked past each other twice, exchanging smiles as they did, but no words were exchanged. She had mingled mainly amongst what appeared to be close friends, making the prospective act of introducing himself impossible without a boldness that Sam did not possess.

But on the patio of Macy's in the gentle light of day, she smiled with relief when he spoke and laughed when he smiled. "I thought I remembered you! You're Sam! You were replaced by an arm-flailing tube man in the parade!"

"Here's hoping they put that on my grave," he chuckled.

"Well, serendipity," she said, pulling out the chair across from him and sitting down. She reached for the upturned glass on the wooden table and flipped it upright before grasping the table's carafe and pouring. She did it with an efficient flourish obviously learned from running and serving tables for a considerable spell. "What brings you up the mountain?" she asked.

"Aren't you cold?" he responded, flatly but not intentionally ignoring her question.

"Of course," she replied matter-of-factly. She wore only a Macy's T-shirt and jeans. "It's Flagstaff. You get cold sometimes." She tucked the renegade strand of hair back behind her ear and Sam was lost to the world. She might have been the prettiest girl he'd ever seen.

She explained that her older sister was a horse trader in Phoenix, selling prized steeds to wannabe cowboys like Sawyer, and that she was often invited down to the valley for his escapades. She was still in school and only rarely made the trip, "however, I'm glad I did this time," she said, looking up to meet Sam's gaze.

Sam was enraptured. Her words seemed to carry away from her in a miraculous current that he wished with all he had to wade into. Her eyes seemed to spell out...

"I...I'm studying timber!" she exclaimed in a quick shift in tone and cracking voice that awoke Sam from his daydream. It was obvious in her suddenly darting eyes that she was embarrassed, as it was now clear to Sam that he was not paying attention to whatever it was she was saying. The girl put down the glass, grimaced, and stood. "I'm... I'm sorry. Please enjoy your sandwich," before quickly shuffled toward the door.

Sam begged her pardon, but her embarrassment hurried her retreat and before he could mutter a cohesive apology, the door closed behind her.

The day was getting late, so he made his way back to the car and headed east on the interstate. He drove on the 40 for a short while, before taking an exit onto a forest service road that led him into a dense thicket of ponderosa pine and Douglas fir. As he turned onto the road and crawled over a cattle gate, he acknowledged a sign that read: *No services. No outlet.*

"Well, that's welcoming," he said aloud, before winding through the labyrinth of swallowing trees that led him into the forest.

Snow had evidently swept through the area sometime in the past few days. There was noticeably more white on the ground here than there had been in town, and the crunch of the compacting snow on the unplowed road suddenly reminded Sam that Sawyer had suggested he buy chains before he arrived at the estate. Sam experienced a twinge of uncertainty. Should he turn back and get the chains now? The sky was already threatening dusk, and finding the property in the dark would be less than ideal.

Ultimately, he reasoned that it likely wouldn't snow heavily again in the next few days, and so he carried on. He would get chains the next chance he got.

Sam considered himself to be quite capable when it came to directions, often taking pride in the fact that it was a tall task to get him lost. "I'm spatially oriented," he would tell others proudly whenever the chance arose. But after 15 minutes of winding through the forest, Sam had to admit that he had no idea which way was north. Low-hanging clouds obscured the setting sun with dull efficiency, and greyness seemed to cover and desaturate all.

Just when Sam began to wonder if he had taken a wrong turn, he at last came upon the promised turn-off, decorated by a large hand-made sign reading

Emerald Acres. Beneath the arched words was an idyllic painting of a homestead before a rising sun. The paint on the sign was chipped and faded, and the stakes supporting the sign were overgrown with underbrush that threatened to cover the sign entirely.

Sam turned onto a path tightly flanked by aspens, their limbs reaching overhead to one another, creating a long archway. At the end of the path, a tall wrought-iron gate blocked the way.

As he approached the gate, Sam could see that the twisting bars of its black metal met along a vertical line of separation that, in its muted ebony hue, seemed to dare approaching visitors to cast its arms yonder and enter between them. What appeared to be Greek lettering was worked into the metallurgy. Beyond the gate, the path turned towards what appeared to be a gorgeous home settled amongst a wide clearing in the woods.

The building flaunted high rising windows and promised to be quite lavish if the feathering along the fascia and dormers, that he caught between the still obscuring trees, were any indication of what awaiting him inside.

Sam pulled the truck up to the keypad that rose out of the ground like a sunflower. As he rolled down the window, he was immediately overcome by the concentrated and mingling scents of evergreen and moss, suggesting the presence of a nearby body of water. He entered the code, 4259#, which prompted the gates to part and open outward, allowing Sam to pull forward and onto the property. The gate closed behind him without a sound.

The building was indeed beautiful. Predominately modern in design, it displayed minimalistic clean lines along its roof and sidings, although just as he had spied through the trees on approach, the builder seemed to take peculiar liberties in ordaining the gables and ridges of the home with surprising flourish. It was a disorienting and rather tacky concoction, Sam decided.

Before the building stood a fountain, dry now, surrounded by a circle gravel driveway. A single-car garage with horizontal wooden panels protruded from the home, while a decrepit barn peeked out from behind the building, pressed up against the resumption of the woods at the edge of the clearing. Its red paint had been flayed by the elements and time itself.

To the left of the home was a small pond. It was mostly frozen over; however, a thin, crooked line traversed it from one side to another, effectively separating the frozen and still liquid surface upon its face. A handful of Canadian geese milled about the frozen beach, while some floated lazily in the water. None seemed perturbed by the vehicle's approach.

Sam parked the truck and took a moment to marvel at the unexpectedly idyllic scene. Behind the pond was an elevated hunting stand positioned in a way to afford a clear line of sight of the grassy meadow extending out from behind the house. In his peripheral vision he thought he noticed a figure standing in the loft of the stand; however, after performing a double take, he found it to be empty. The vertical lines cast by the forest behind the stand were playing tricks on his eyes. The day was growing long, as were its shadows.

Sam grabbed his bag from the cab and walked to the door, punched into the keypad the same code that he had entered to part the ebony gate, and entered the house.

9

Or All Will Be Ash

"Wake up," a voice whispered.

Mae gasped and opened her eyes. She was lying in a pitch-black room. Her mind was still foggy from the thickness of her dreams, and it took a long moment for her to recognize where she was and who had just spoken.

"You told me to wake you when it was dark," said the voice.

Her circumstances at last flooded her awareness. It was Sawyer before her, shifting uncomfortably in the darkness. She rose from her supine position and into a seated one to look out the open window nearby. She found the view to be that of the meadow in the dead of night. She must have slept for 12 hours, at least.

"Any sign of our friend?" she asked.

Sawyer hesitated. "Not exactly. But some friends of his." He paused to hear her response but heard nothing. "They're still here. Come outside. Say hello."

Sawyer led Mae out the back door that led to the patio overlooking the meadow. The sky was clear with the Milky Way and a speckled moon shining above them. The former sent a shiver down Mae's spine when she saw it.

"What's wrong?" asked Sawyer, apparently noticing her suddenly unsettled demeaner.

She swallowed and collected herself, bringing her focus back to the current moment and the coming developments that would require her undivided attention.

"Nightmares. Where are they?" she asked.

Sawyer handed Mae a flashlight and pointed toward the tree line opposite the snowy meadow that shimmered in the moonlight. She slid the switch with her thumb and pointed the impressively bright beam into the trees.

Between the rising trunks of the ponderosa pines stood men cloaked in black robes, their hoods draped loosely over their heads, concealing their faces in blackness. There must have been a dozen of them in just the small patch of trees she illuminated, but when she slid the light along the perimeter she found that the robed men lined the forest's edge in its entirety. She walked to the left, toward the pond, and when she passed the edge of the house, raised the flashlight's beam toward the pathway leading out of the property. More robed men staring back at her.

They were surrounded by a thousand cloaked figures watching them from the forest. They didn't appear to be moving. Only watching. The illumination of the flashlight didn't seem to disturb them, either. Only the sound of a slight breeze rustling the branches of the trees could be heard above a distant owl, hooing at the moon.

"How long have they been here?" she asked.

"I saw the first one about an hour ago. What do you make of it?" Sawyer asked.

Mae turned off the flashlight and tossed it back to Sawyer, who missed the catch. Mae sighed in disappointment as he fumbled for it on the snowy ground. "It just means we need to hurry. Let's get going," she said.

Leading the way, Mae slid open the glass sliding door of the master bedroom and found the pentagram of bodies and remains untouched. Mae walked across the room and approached the dresser, now covered in miscellaneous effects: three red candles, a corked vial of liquified nightshade, a dozen hawks' feathers, a hammer, a single nail, a bundle of hemp string, three cleaned mandrake roots, a dagger, a box of matches, and the *Tome of Instruction*. She reached into her jacket pocket and placed beside it Masau'u's kachina doll and an oak keepsake box.

She considered the *Tome of Instruction* to be her only possession of any true value in this world. It was given to her many years ago by Malaki, and she prized it like a family heirloom. It had become a part of her: wicked, magnificent, and decidedly different than the rest of this world's inhabitants. She was unlike any other human on Earth, and it was unlike any other book.

As she picked it up and began to flip through its oily pages, she was soothed by its presence. She had been hesitant to have Sawyer deliver it to her from the bookstore, but she knew that he was nearly as afraid of it as he was of her. He would treat it with care, she knew, and he did.

She flipped through the pages deliberately and eventually stopped upon a handwritten page with the words *Material Bounding* and *Mortalization* written upon it. The ritual would be a combination of two separate spells within the book. Material Bounding was a spell that conjured and trapped supernatural beings in a temporary cage of ethereal magic, while Mortalization involved the removal of a creature's immortal state of being.

The much simpler of the two spells, Material Bounding, was one that she had successfully trialed in preparation, on a smaller scale. In the test, she required only a single human sacrifice to be laid upon a drawn pentacle, while a totem of the creature to be summoned was placed within a box of oak that was then sealed. To complete the ritual, she burned a mandrake root wrapped in the feathers of a bird of prey and engaged in an hour of silent meditation in utter darkness.

For the practice run, she had managed to sneak inside and seal herself within the mausoleum of a wealthy oil magnate from days long gone. She had brought with her a small bag of supplies and the (compacted) body of a hiker that had lost his way the day before. She followed the directions within the *Tome of Instruction* to its finest of detail and managed to summon the magnate's specter and hold it within the walls of her holding for nearly two minutes. While the specter was conjured, the sacrificial body of the hiker caught flame and burned with a wild blue hue. The specter wailed and cursed Maw in a dozen languages, but within its cage of glittering luminescence, it was completely impotent to do her any harm. Once the sacrificial corpse was burnt in its entirety, the spell lost its potency, and the wraith disappeared as quickly as it had arrived.

If the Material Bounding was the *how* of the ritual to come, the Mortalization, on the other hand, was the *why*. It was, however, much more difficult to achieve any degree of success, even on a much smaller scale, as it required a huge amount of arcane energy that was not easy to attain. So demanding were the energy requirements of the spell that the only conceivable manner that Mae could think of to satisfy its thirst was to trap a creature of colossal power and suck it dry of its energy.

Thus, the necessity of the Material Bounding in the first place: to make the Mortalization of herself even remotely possible.

But what creature was she to suck so horribly dry? She had crossed paths with plenty of suitably vile and powerful entities in her day. Any of which would do just fine. But on a moonless night a dozen years before, as she starred deep into the forest's edge while contemplating the question, she saw something she hadn't seen in years. She almost thought she saw dark figures running amongst the black that hid behind the trees. She knew then and there that only a single entity was worthy of her designs and its repercussions: Masau'u would do just fine.

And if the process left the bastard as but carbon scattered upon the dirt... so be it. It would be two bloody birds smashed upon a single stone.

She replaced the Tome upon the dresser and looked about the room, scanning for anything that might be out of place or forgotten. She would likely have only a single attempt at the ritual, and she would effectively damn herself if it were to fail. She couldn't imagine the God of Death taking lightly to his attempted disempowerment.

There were only two potential outcomes. Succeed... or all would be ash.

The sequence had played out in her imagination for decades, and for the first time in nearly fifty years, she became overwhelmed by genuine childhood giddiness as the moment of execution drew near. So far, things had gone as smoothly as she could have asked. The watchers from the forest were admittedly unexpected, not that she was fully sure of what to expect in the first place.

The one thing that gave her pause was Masau'u's general passivity up to this point. She was confident that, one way or another, Masau'u must be aware of her intentions. And yet, he had yet to stop her from committing her murders and making her preparations. Not even a deer to block her path and slow her pace. He had just watched and let the collection grow. That suggested one of two things, both of which were slightly unsettling. Either he was willing to let the ritual happen, or he wasn't powerful enough to stop it. If he knew but chose to do nothing, perhaps her actions might not be as effective as she hoped them to be. On the other hand, if he hadn't the power to stop her, was he powerful enough to energize the Mortalization spell that she intended to cast upon herself?

They were questions that she had left unanswered, as she had no other choice. The ritual was her best chance at interrupting her slow approach toward a fate she deemed worse than any hell otherwise. Most nights, her sleep brought nightmares of floating in space for durations of time that felt more like decades than the hours that truly passed. The white eyes of the indifferent galaxies that surrounded seemed to gaze upon her with fiery malice as she squirmed in place, without effect, to evade their observation. So realistic and recurrent were her nightmares that she had come to conclude their presence to be a warning of a fate that would inevitably come to pass if no other action was taken. She feared and simultaneously accepted that if she were to remain eternal, that the Earth would eventually decay and leave her behind in a universe unimaginably vast, empty, and indifferent to her endless perception of it. She would become a wraith floating forever in blackness, abandoned by gods real and imagined to go utterly mad without any possibility of respite.

Furthermore, she had long forgotten the joys of human existence and cared for nothing in the world but her *Tome of Instruction*. That was all that mattered to her anymore; the rest was just noise. Humans were never meant to suffer immortality. Their brains thrived in short bursts, not straying far from the clay from which they were molded. They were but snowflakes in the void, developing a rapid half-comprehension before a slow descent into nothingness once again. Their minds weren't built for the long haul. If Alan Watts was right, and we are all just the universe pretending to be players in a play for the entertainment of the former, what happens when an eye of perception refuses to blink? Mae was learning that it becomes dry, and eventually blind, as it drifts slowly further and further from the shores of eternity, lost to the sands of a desert never intended to be perceived for more than a handful of decades at a time.

She was only 124 years old, but everything was already so heavy and irrelevant. Society, politics, culture, wars, sports, family, even friends. All constructs of temporary things for temporary things. None of it mattered to her, nor was it designed with her in mind. She was a construct of a world now gone, and she longed to join it in death, in the dirt.

Yet she was forced to engage in society despite her incongruity. She would much rather spend her days rotting alone, of course. Years were spent upon mountaintops. A whole decade was spent lying at the bottom of the ocean. She passed years between bodies where her spirit simply roamed the Earth unbound to flesh and routine. It was nice from time to time, a vacation of sorts, but her mind decayed faster when she did. It was comfortable to be alone, but it melted her heart and mind into an abomination that could neither live nor die. It was better to roll about in society's muck and mingle with the actors as it seemed to slow the cascading entropy of her soul.

And every once in a great while, the rabble would remind her of the joys that she had lost, the people she had loved, and the late world that would never return. Those little serendipities and melancholic joys would almost conjure feelings of *it* once again.

And then it would be gone.

The only thing that came to entertain her was the tome that Malaki had left in her possession so many years before. It was the only thing in the world that was meant for her and not for the transient, as it seemed to require a dedication of time, patience, and moral flexibility that few short-lived humans could dedicate. Malaki was an exception, in more ways than one.

Given that it possessed within its pages the instructions for mortalization, it just so happened that it was also her only means of escape. It was ironic that the only thing seemingly made for her in this world was the only tool she had at her disposal to erase her prerequisite of its use and understanding. She ran her palm across its face.

The sounds of nails being hammered into wood roused Mae from her musings.

Sawyer had begun nailing the corners of long, heavy, black blankets over the windows and doors of the room. After a few short minutes, the room was fully engulfed in darkness. So absolute was the resulting darkness that Mae was compelled to light three candles that she had prepared nearby and position them about the room. She would require the darkness before long, but first, she required light to read her instructions and begin the ritual.

When the final blanket was nailed to the wall, Sawyer turned to Mae, letting the hammer drop unceremoniously to the floor. "What else do you need?" he asked somewhat begrudgingly.

It was a good thing that she hadn't decided to kill him earlier that day. The appearance of Masau'u's ghouls was something that she wouldn't be able to keep an eye on while performing her incantations.

"Go watch the friends of our friend. Don't let them get too close," she said.

His eyebrows shot to the sky while a high-pitched jolt of laughter leaked from his lips. "Umm, what am I supposed to do? Shoot them?" he asked between the giggles that rose from the comedy that apparently played before his imagination.

It was true. He wouldn't put up much of a fight. "You're right," she said. "Stay here. I have an idea." She left the room quickly, heading for the kitchen, where she found a large pot and combined in it as much salt as she could find and a half gallon of vinegar. She left the pot on the counter and jogged outside, returning with two dead geese dangling from her hands. She plopped the geese on the countertop and, after some nifty knife work, dropped each of their hearts into the pot. With the help of an electric mixer, the concoction was thoroughly combined.

She reentered the master bedroom carrying the pot and a large wooden spoon. She placed the pot on the floor and asked Sawyer to inspect its contents for taste. As he came near, got a whiff and recoiled in disgust, Mae dragged the dagger's serrated blade across his neck before stabbing it into his chest. She held his neck over the pot and ensured that at least a few pints of blood contributed to the mixture before allowing the body to collapse completely to the floor. When she was confident that she had collected enough, she dragged the body into the hallway and returned to stir the contents a final time.

She carried the pot outside. The cloaked watchers were within the tree line now, walking slowly towards her. With haste, she began pouring a line of the liquid in a semi-circle around the entrance of the corner bedroom. She hadn't enough liquid nor time to surround the entire house, and was forced to accept that the ward would only extend around the room itself. She walked inside and poured the liquid across the entrance of the room that connected to the hallway beyond.

But before she reentered the blanket-enclosed space where the ritual was to unfold, she walked back outside with the pot still in hand. The cloaked figures were now legion. Thousands upon thousands of cloaked shrouded faces glided toward her. The up-and-down bounce of human gait was absent: they floated in unison directly towards her.

Mae looked up to the moon and, for the first time in many years, thought of her mother and the way they would dance together in this very meadow on nights when the moon was full and bright. A tear tumbled down her cheek as she raised the pot above her head and poured the remainder of its contents upon herself. She released a guttural scream into the night as the metal pot clattered to the floor. It was a scream of fury. A scream of foreboding. A war cry that she hoped Masau'u and his friends would understand.

And when her scream finally lost air, she turned and lifted the blankets that shrouded what was once the master bedroom. She lowered her head, and entered the room.

10

Cacophony

Sawyer had given Sam a list of "expectations" to adhere by and lavishly paid him a thousand dollars a week to do so. The list was as follows:

1. Be prepared to receive the owner of the estate, Ms. Shawmaker, at any time (this includes maintaining a fully stocked kitchen, bar, cellar, and linen collection)

2. Reasonably monitor security systems and maintain a general security of the estate

3. Provide general maintenance (leaks, electrical problems, etc.)

4. Don't let the plants die

5. Don't let the rats live (in the cellar)

6. Maintain a dust-free environment in the gallery

All in all, the "expectations" weren't too burdensome for Sam. They gave his days a certain cadence and routine that he roundly enjoyed.

He began his days by waking in the guest bedroom at the back of the house, as the master bedroom was kept ready to receive Ms. Shawmaker at the drop of a hat if she were to arrive unexpectedly. Plus, the guest bedroom had floor-to-ceiling windows overlooking the meadow behind the house, making for cinematic sunrises to begin each day.

The room also had some more subtle touches that called to Sam. The carpet was a long-haired blue shag that his toes enjoyed sinking into, and along the wall stood a wide wooden desk where he placed his laptop and occasionally read. On the desktop were some knickknacks that he left undisturbed, including a small lawn gnome who appeared intoxicated, a well-crafted oak keepsake box filled with rings of various sizes, and a well-worn adventurer's guide to walking the Pacific Crest Trail.

The downside of the room was that the tall windows had no curtains, which made for some unnerving nights trying to fall asleep with the forest staring un-blinkingly into the bedroom. But after a few short days, he became acquainted with the trees mostly due to the early morning runs that he took around the property first thing every morning.

He would first jog toward the gate, then, turning right into the forest, he'd circumnavigate the meadow. After a few runs he figured that the clearing was approximately five acres in all, and that the woods were mostly a collection of ponderosa pine littered by the occasional boulder and modest granite deposit rising out of the moist earth. The jogs provided Sam with a familiarity of the forest, dulling its menace when darkness came to surround him each night.

Upon his return to the house, he'd rinse off in the outdoor shower, a roomy stall of smoky glass under an arched showerhead extending out from the at-tached main building. He'd then make himself a breakfast in the roomy kitchen which overlooked the pond through the towering bay windows that surrounded a circular glass table. The windows faded impressively from clear to stained glass as they ascended, a transition that made Sam wonder how it could have possibly been achieved.

To the left of the bay windows, a floating shelf displayed a diorama of the property. Sam was thoroughly impressed at how the display managed to mimic even the smallest details of the estate, from the peeling red paint of the barn to the tiny geese lounging around the frozen pond. It even had a miniature tree line surrounding the meadow, all under a sheer glass dome casing.

Immediately after breakfast, Sam would catalog the ingredients he had used and which ingredients in the kitchen were approaching their expiration. He'd then add these items to a running list of groceries that were promptly delivered every Monday morning at 8AM by a fulfilment service that monitored the list. The list was typically extensive, as the kitchen held only ingredients, and not a single processed or frozen meal could be found within it despite the gaudy walk-in freezer which contained exclusively venison.

Sam would then descend the narrow spiral stairs to the basement where he checked the rat traps in the cellar and the operating integrity of the security system across the hall. The latter was found within a small room that housed a three-monitor computer system overseeing the entire estate. Sawyer had provided Sam with an in-depth explanation of how to troubleshoot and diagnose issues with the system if any were to arise, however he had yet to experience any trouble, and the diagnostic self-check he ran every morning returned positive results without fail. The system was connected to his phone, as well, if he ever needed to check in on a camera from afar.

From time to time, he acknowledged the shotgun above the mantle. He was well aware that it was loaded, and he was well aware of how to use it. He sometimes had daydreams of burglars breaking into the house in the middle of the night and imagined the various ways in which he might respond. In more than one such vision, he saw himself holding the shotgun, and in some, he fired it. But the resulting feeling was not a masculine pride, but a hollow dread. The thought of killing conjured nightmares. Nightmares of running in the desert. Nightmares in which he couldn't find his rifle. Nothing but dust, and then Private Lively emerging from beyond the veil and into his arms, mumbling incoherently. Then screams. The screams were more often than not his own, mercifully waking him, drenched in sweat while the darkness of the forest watched him indifferently through the tall windows of the guest bedroom.

He removed the shotgun from the mantle and let it rest against the stony wall of the cellar. He'd rather be caught defenseless than routinely reminded of the smell of gunpowder and other things.

Sam would water the plants and dust the paintings and sculptures of the gallery twice a week. He'd play Black Sabbath, Electric Wizard, and King Buffalo loudly over the intercom system to reduce the looming feelings of domestic servitude that the chores induced.

His favorite piece in the gallery was a dark Renaissance painting of young David wielding a sword swung lazily behind his back while presenting the decapitated head of Goliath in his outstretched left hand. The head hung by the hair it was held by.

But beyond these routines, Sam had more than enough time to mill about the property at the whim of his leisure. He would sit and watch the geese for hours from the elevated perspective of the hunting stand, taking careful notes of the way they interacted with one another. He found that they had routines all their own, and he grew envious of their ever-present careless demeanor.

He poked around the house and enjoyed examining the oddities that he found. The bookshelf in the living room held an odd selection of books, including everything from instruction guides for the raising of cattle, Danielewski's *House of Leaves*, *Lonesome Dove*, and even the *Farmer's Almanac*. He eventually came across an aged hardback copy of *Walden* and read it from cover to cover over the course of several days. Its pages were logged with ancient water damage and its face was frayed by time, but Sam thought it only fitting, considering the themes that the novel expressed.

But when he had first pulled it from the shelf, a small, folded note tucked into its pages had come tumbling out. He unfolded the note and read the single word scribbled hastily upon its face: *Run*. The handwriting was crude and likely that of a child's. He considered the note for a short while with a vague interest, but eventually folded it back up and placed it into a random page of the *Farmer's Almanac*.

What a odd bookmark, he thought.

Typically, he wasn't much of a reader, but while passing the days in the house, he had a strange and overwhelming urge to consume as many books as he possibly could. He read for hours and alternated between a growing list of favorite spots to do so. He would sit in the hunting stand with his legs dangling over the edge. On clear days, he would lie on his back in the meadow and use the book to block the sun while he read. Most often, however, he would ramble into the forest and find a good tree to lean against while soaking in the gentle sounds of rustling branches above as they danced in the soft breeze, often twisting pine needles between his fingers while he read.

He also spent long afternoons just thinking in the quiet of the estate's isolation. He thought of the Marine Corps, the people he'd known, and the mistakes he'd made. He thought of the things he'd never forget and some of the things that he would never share. Mostly, he thought of his friends.

He thought of a few that were indeed with him now, in the breeze, and the smell of the pine.

Walking carelessly through the property one day, Sam decided to finally explore the barn near the front of the property. As he peeked inside, he found it to be a well-constructed building, albeit quite old and empty, save for the interior supporting beams that had kept it stable for so many years. The rectangular scars on the floor made it apparent that there had once been stalls erected within, likely housing horses. Sam was curious as to why the barn remained if it served no purpose and nothing called it home beside a few barn cats he'd spied running to and from it.

He assumed that Ms. Shawmaker preserved the barn for its aesthetic appeal, as it indeed conjured feelings of a world beyond Wi-Fi, one that we may never see again, at least until things reset one day. As all things do, he thought.

As he took a step into the building to investigate the structure further, he heard a loud twig snap somewhere in the forest. He whipped his head past the barn door to look into the brush, but saw nothing in the tree line. It was likely nothing, but reluctantly decided that it was worthy of further investigation. He approached the forest's edge cautiously and scanned its nearest stretch. Rays of sunshine dangled into the underbrush and the bushes near the forest floor made a comprehensive search challenging, but he saw no movement and heard no further sounds other than the wind worrying the branches above. Then, some thirty meters into the trees, a deer suddenly leaped from its hiding position and bounded deeper into the forest.

On the solstice, the night sky was clear and the moon was full, so Sam retrieved a well-aged cabernet from the cellar and drank it on the open meadow between the house and the woods. There was a grassless circle not 40 feet from the back door that had obviously been scarred by fires in the past, so he dragged some branches and bark from the tree line and had himself a modest bonfire on the spot.

Once the embers reached a self-sustaining glow, he went inside and turned off all the interior and exterior lights of the house and returned to the fire to lounge comfortably on his back, gazing at the constellations above him. Embers floated upwards in his periphery like willow wisps dancing in the cool night air. He pulled occasionally from the bottle, which surely cost more than his monthly wage, and thought of the waitress he had met at Macy's and the lone strand of hair caressing her rosy cheeks. He thought of her at Sawyer's party, and daydreamed of what might have been if he had approached her then.

A light illuminated his nose from the opposite side of the fire. He sat up abruptly, and turned to see that the overhead light of the guest bedroom, his bedroom, was on. Terror clenched him. Someone was in the house. He scrambled to his feet and sprinted away from the fire's light and into the nearest sanctuary of trees. It was a thoughtless reaction. Among the primary rules of combat, as he had been taught, was to be above your enemy and see without being seen.

Once he reached the tree line, he peeked around a trunk and stared intently into the bedroom while trying to control his breathing. He almost chuckled. He was now the darkness of the forest spying into his bedroom, unblinking. Five minutes passed, and nothing appeared to change beside a bitter wind rising out of the woods behind him. It ruffled his hair and the leaves of the tall trees surrounding him.

As he watched, a high-pitched ringing rose in his ears and, with it, a familiar anxiety. Sam felt his pulse quicken, and he clenched his fists. His eyes darted about his entire field of vision and the skin on his shoulders prickled with subconscious awareness.

Then, without any further ado, the lights of the bedroom flipped off, and all was once again dark beyond the fire's embers casting a soft orange hue onto the surrounding grass. The sound of Sam's heavy breathing was an intruder upon the tinnitus that existed as an ever present backdrop to his shaking perspective.

A hand rested on his shoulder.

He swung around wildly, screaming into the darkness. His adrenaline took over, and his conscious mind released control, giving way to a malevolent creature intent on dismantling whatever flesh he found before him. He thought nothing, felt nothing, and knew nothing but the desire for destruction, and marched rabidly through the trees looking for whatever had touched him.

Despite his fervor, he found nothing; only darkness and trees received him. Moon-speckled remnants of snow clung to the earth among the ponderosas rising into the heavy breeze that lifted the unkempt hair from his forehead. The canopy above him sang its chorus in the wind.

A light snow began to fall, and his senses came back to him slowly and one at a time. First, he noticed the cold. Then he looked down and saw his hands clenched into tight fists. He heard the trees rustling above him and then acknowledged the smell of the nearby bonfire calling him back to something resembling calm. Though he had regained himself, a vague, uncertain fear and the ringing in his ears stubbornly persisted. He took a deep breath and turned toward the house, which remained doused in darkness.

After a long moment of passive observation, the tinnitus slowly left him, and he walked cautiously back toward the house.

When he finally considered the circumstance, Sam concluded that Ms. Shawmaker must have returned and had silently entered the house and turned on the light. However, upon circling around the front of the house, he found no vehicle, and when he entered the house and looked about, he saw no signs of any intrusion at all. Everything was exactly as he had left it.

Nothing else of note occurred that evening. Nonetheless, Sam decided to sleep on the couch, away from the tall windows overlooking the meadow and the trees beyond.

One day, while he was busy dusting the paintings in the gallery, a thought occurred to Sam. He realized that he had never asked Sawyer why the previous caretaker had quit. It startled him that such a basic question had passed him by, and he kicked himself for not having brought it up.

Sawyer had mentioned that he would be out of the country for Christmas, "to see a man about a horse," and wouldn't have cell service until the new year, so Sam made a mental note to inquire about it the next chance he got. Not that it would change his decision about taking the job or living at the house on Emerald Acres. The situation was an absolute dream without comparison, leading Sam to consider abandoning his initial plan of going to school and instead making a career out of the job. But the more he came to appreciate his circumstances, the more he began to wonder why the previous caretaker had left it at all.

Sam also began to feel uneasy in the house in ways that were both difficult to describe and to escape. Once, while descending the spiral staircase into the basement, for example, he thought he heard whispers mixed into the creaking sounds of the metal that echoed from the walls. He stopped to listen more closely, but the sounds dissipated with the reverb, and he heard no similar sounds when he resumed his descent. The sounds reminded him of a time years ago when he had eaten magic mushrooms and taken a shower at the peak of his hallucinations. The sound of water falling upon the porcelain disguised itself as a chorus of voices talking to him from just behind the shower curtain.

Sam didn't believe in ghosts. That's to say, he had long believed that the human brain was more than capable of conjuring images, sounds, and most commonly, ideas, when given enough leeway to do so. It wasn't that he doubted those that shared their experiences of the paranormal. In fact, he found stories of phantoms, hauntings, and even aliens to be endlessly fascinating. He just believed that the brain itself conjured these things. For one reason or another, those that saw what wasn't there unknowingly conjured such things to compensate for something else, typically subconsciously.

When pressed on his beliefs, he would point out that hauntings and paranormal experiences were often congruent with challenging circumstances. Solitude. Grief. Stress. Fear. The brain is awfully good at filling in the gaps when pushed to its limits. He likened it to a metaphor that his therapist had told him years ago when explaining anxiety.

"Our brains are more or less the same as they were ten thousand years ago," she had said during one of their sessions. "They're designed to spot tigers in the jungle. In the modern world, by contrast, there are no tigers, but that doesn't stop our brains from vigilantly searching for them. That's anxiety, when we ourselves become the tigers we're searching for."

Despite the strangeness that occurred on the solstice, the voices in the stairwell, and the rising uneasiness that Sam experienced in the house, he had no true fear of ghouls or entities stalking him in the shadows of Emerald Acres. He feared heart disease, shotguns, and thieves with nothing to lose.

All the rest were just tigers.

On Christmas Day, Sam recalled the brush on the road sign at the turn-off, and resolved to trim it back. While going through the tools in the garage in search of shears, he also came across some paint cans and brushes and figured he could give the sign a sprucing up while he was out that way. He collected the tools into a wheelbarrow he found under a large black blanket and wheeled the supplies down the aspen-covered drive toward the turn-off.

The snow had largely melted off the path revealing a grey gravel road contrasting the brown mulch and pine needles of the forest floor that surrounding it.

When he arrived at the turn-off, Sam spent a few minutes trimming back the brush and another few carefully touching up its faded colors. It was only when he stepped back a good ways to mimic the vantage point of an approaching vehicle that he realized that the homestead depicted in the sign was a barn, and the barn looked an awful lot like the one on the property. The only thing, though, was that the sign's barn was blue rather than the peeling red of the one on the property.

Sam decided to add the history of the property to the list of questions that he would ask Sawyer when he spoke to him next. But just as he thought this, Sam heard the sounds of a vehicle approaching him from behind. He turned and saw in the medium distance an unremarkable black sedan driving along the road in his direction.

Sam leaned against a nearby tree and nodded to the vehicle as it approached. Assuming that it was Ms. Shawmaker, he was eager to be praised for his initiative in attending to the sign and the brush. But the vehicle only turned onto the pathway, and continued toward the house without slowing in the slightest or even rolling down its heavily tinted windows.

After days of feeling so carefree, the passing of the sedan did well to bring Sam back to earth. He collected the paint, shears, and brushes back into the wheelbarrow and followed the sedan that made its way along the pathway ahead of him.

By the time Sam arrived at the gate, he looked through the gate's black bars and saw a woman collecting items from the trunk of the vehicle that was now parked in the circular driveway. The woman wore a long corduroy robe with silver accents dancing along the edges of the fabric as it billowed in the afternoon breeze. Her long white hair was woven into a single braid that ran down her back.

"Let me help you with your things, miss!" he called out as the gate began to open once again. But she didn't acknowledge his distant call or so much as look at him. In fact, she seemed to hurry her rummaging. She closed the trunk with a slam and walked briskly towards the house. She punched the code into the keypad and closed the door definitively behind her.

Sam was perplexed. Sawyer hadn't shared much about Ms. Shawmaker, but Sam had envisioned a veneer of mutual respect between him and the owner of the property. In his daydreams, he had fantasized her being a jovial philanthropist overflowing with appreciation for the thoughtful care he had given the property. He had pictured friendly and open conversations between them, in which he could finally satisfy his curiosities of the home and its history.

He walked inside and stood in the foyer, burdened by the sense of being an intruder. He heard brisk footsteps moving along the hall toward the master bedroom, followed by the sharp thud of its door being slammed shut. Then nothing at all.

After a moment of hesitation, he decided to go to the kitchen to wait for Ms. Shawmaker to emerge. In all the instructions Sawyer had given him, none had involved anything specific regarding how to interact with Ms. Shawmaker or what he should expect. Sam poured himself a glass of water and racked his brain for anything that he might have mismanaged at the property that may have irritated her before she had arrived. Did she somehow have a remote inventory of the cellar, noticing that he drank her favorite Pinot Grigio? Did he get the wrong cilantro delivered? After some time, he decided that he was being silly, and even a little narcissistic. People were allowed to be rude and keep to themselves, especially in their own homes. Double that privilege if they're rich, he thought.

Eventually, he returned to the sink to refill his glass when something caught his eye in the diorama of the estate on the floating shelf nearby. He stepped closer, and nearly dropped his glass. In the diorama's meadow stood a kachina doll. What appeared to be antlers rose from its head above red bulging eyes. Its mouth was open, brandishing sharp teeth within. It held a scepter in one hand and a flame in another.

Sam had never noticed the doll before. It hadn't even been among the home's various oddities, let alone in the meticulously crafted diorama under the glass dome casing. He concluded that Ms. Shawmaker must have placed it in the diorama as she had entered the building. It was an odd action for her to take, but he couldn't think of a better explanation.

An hour passed with Sam at first pacing, then sitting indecisively in the kitchen. It was getting late, and he would soon need to attend to his evening duties. He thought it would be odd to go about his business without at least introducing himself to Ms. Shawmaker, so he finally decided to walk down the hall and knock on the door of the master bedroom.

"Ms. Shawmaker? My name is Sam; I'm the new property manager."

Silence was the response. He thought back to watching her unload the sedan in the driveway. He wasn't close enough then to see her face or determine much about her, but he would have guessed her to be relatively old, gauging by her wiry frame and the whiteness of her hair.

He knocked again, louder. "Miss Shawmaker?!" he called out.

As the silence drew on, his mind's eye suddenly conjured an image of the old woman lying unconscious on the floor, just beyond the door. His heart began to race. Again, he knocked, this time with authority. "Miss Shawmaker! I'm going to come in... I'm coming in!" The door was unlocked. He walked inside the room.

But Ms. Shawmaker wasn't there. The comforter on the bed was undisturbed. The dresser clear. The connected bathroom and closets were empty, and the windows were locked.

Sam marched out the front door and found the circular driveway empty as well. He paced around the dry fountain, his eyes diligently scanning the ground. To his dismay, he saw no tire marks indented into the gravel.

Exasperated, he sat on the edge of the fountain, gazing listlessly into the forest, searching for tigers.

11

Corduroy and Broken Glass

As winter faded into spring, Mae relished three routines in her weekly calendar that were beyond the rigors of her studies.

The first was that every Sunday, her father had arranged for a buggy to pick her up from the curb outside her dormitory to transport her back to the cabin in the woods for lunch with her parents. When she arrived, Mae, Edith, and John would share in a pleasant gathering around the kitchen table while the buggy driver waited patiently outside, or quietly in the foyer on colder winter days.

Mae would share with her parents how her studies were progressing and the various scuttlebutts traversing the city. For their part, her parents would share updates on the new hobbies they had embraced now that the home was empty of children. Edith had taken to candle making while John had grown fond of whittling and small woodworking projects to fill his time beyond the needs of his cattle business. He had recently hired some hands to assist with the latter as his knees were beginning to lose their durability.

Mae looked forward to her Sunday lunches with her family, and especially appreciated the long buggy ride to and from the cabin. While bumping along in the wagon, she would peer lazily out the windows and into the woods, imagining what curiosities the trees obscured from her. Her mind lapped at the stories she imagined playing out behind the wide green curtain, and occasionally thought back to the times that she and her father had travelled into town together.

The second routine that she embraced was a weekly visit to the Lowell Observatory just northwest of town. She had taken an astronomy class the semester before and had found the lookout at the top of the hill to be an extraordinary place filled with not only telescopes and associated studies, but also wide-open meadows and cleverly masoned walkways. And so, every Wednesday afternoon, Mae would place whatever book she was reading into a small backpack and summit the low peak to meander through the often-snowy grounds and peer in through the windows of the building-sized telescopes. During her visits, she befriended more than a few of the astronomy students and even a couple of the department's professors. She became a fixture of the place, and it was often joked openly that astronomy was but a poorly hidden paramour of young Mae Barrett's.

The third routine that Mae attended to on a weekly basis occurred every Friday evening after dusk. On such occasions, Mae would cross the railroad tracks and head north into the city to approach a relatively unassuming red-brick office building in the financial district. Oftentimes when she'd arrive, she'd pass late-night employees trickling out. Most headed home, while some turned left to the taverns.

Mae paid them no mind. She'd simply walk down the alleyway on the right side of the building and descend the narrow stairs that hugged its periphery. At the bottom, she'd knock on the red wooden door of Malaki Umber's flat.

So immediately charmed was she by the old man that she had had no hesitation when he initially invited her to join him in his basement home. He had expressed to her, in no uncertain terms, that he saw tremendous promise in her, and she believed him. She saw nothing but genuine inspiration in the man, and she felt trusted and empowered in his presence.

"You've been touched, child," he had said in his sly Cockney tone as the snow fell about them on the first night they met. "By what, I know not. But you've been given abilities that only few of this world can comprehend. Let me help you nurture them. Let me be your guide."

She had known the answer to be yes before he had finished asking the question.

His flat was murky and smelled of earth, cinnamon, and myrrh. It was less than tidy, though a single corner remained exquisitely organized and well-lit beneath a galaxy of votive candles hung individually and precariously on strings.

Beneath the lights lay a sprawling desk occupied by a myriad of open books and glass jars containing herbs and liquids that spanned the spectrum of color.

In this space, Malaki introduced Mae to a series of topics far from the narrow-minded intellectual lectures of her university education. Where the university's teachings implored its students to rehearse information it deemed to be worthy of their understanding, Malaki's lessons imparted to Mae a realization that true knowledge was gained by experimentation, the embracing of failure, and most of all, a respect for the most natural of all actions: play.

Late into the night the two would huddle under the hanging votive candles as Malaki listened to Mae read from his prescribed texts. After reading and discussing the texts at length, they would experiment with ingredients and processes to see what they could create.

It was a dance in a dark room, she once thought, regarding the process.

In one such experiment, she combined sulfur, rat blood, and hemlock into an ebony mortar before using a pestle to grind the concoction into a muddy paste. She dipped her fingers into the bowl, smeared the goo across her face, pulled a book of incantation near to her, and read from its pages in the flickering candlelight.

"Vox mea vocat oves, et ego fata ero eorum," she proclaimed.

As the final words of the incantation escaped her lips, the paste upon her face suddenly caught flame. Mae burst into laughter.

"It tickles!" she shouted with childish amusement.

On other nights, they practiced scrying upon one another. Malaki would walk out the door and up the stairs to do something odd and unexpected. He would then return and ask Mae what it was that he had done. When successful, Mae would watch, listen, or even smell what the he had done, observing from a powerful meditative state from inside the flat. After some practice, she could do all three at once. Not even Malaki could do that, he told her after she relayed his acts to him in vivid detail.

There were lessons on other topics, too. Sigil magic, astral projection, warding, and eventually, when Malaki thought her sufficiently invested to not be offput by its stench... necromancy.

"The taboo of death is a dull ache of the ego," Malaki said once, mid-lesson. "Are we not ourselves but between dusts? To me, I say that death is but a reminder of the very connection of hereditary dust between you and I. The subconscious fear of ego death is the ultimate answer to the question of why we turn our heads from decay and rot. No. I choose to fear not what lies within the Earth's dirt, just as I do not fear the dirt within my very being."

At first, the practice didn't bother Mae tremendously. Her father was a transcendentalist and her mother theistically apathetic, therefore, she was unburdened by the connotations of monotheism that haunted the subconscious narratives of those raised in the common traditions of western theology. She feared no hell and expected no heaven, as she knew enough examples of both in the world around her to satiate her natural inclinations toward fear and desire.

But the act of necromancy, as she gradually discovered, often required the taking of life. It was as simple as that, and there was little getting around it. Malaki did his best to dress up the dirty business, but no amount of diversional discussion or showmanship prevented Mae's inevitable flinch as he contributed small deaths to the spells that demanded them.

But by the time that Autumn came to pass, Mae had become so accustomed to the act, and its fantastic results, that she no longer squirmed or felt nauseous in death's presence. Come November, she would twist the necks of ravens without ceremony.

When the spring semester arrived, Mae attended to her studies at the university less and less. The Friday night visits to Malaki's flat became weekend-long dives into the occult, then week-long adventures into advanced ritual and incantation. She visited the observatory only on rare occasions, and when she did, it was typically only to experiment with specific spells of which Lowell's grounds provided an advantageous location.

She lost track of the days, and left the buggy driver unemployed after she left his back seat empty on so many occasions that her father decided that the price of his retainer was no longer worth the cost.

***

In March, after two months without a word from their youngest daughter, John and Edith Barrett rode into town to call upon Mae. They inquired at her dormitory and discovered, to their dismay, that Mae had abandoned the room two months prior. When they followed up at the university, they learned that Mae had stopped coming to her classes around the same time.

"She just sort of... faded into the background," said one of her professors. He was busy attending to a tall stack of papers to be marked, but relented and shared some of his observations when he noticed the concern contorting their faces. "She was always warming the seats of the front row, that one. Then one day, she started coming in late with bags under her eyes, always scribbling in her notebook with a suspicious gaze that darted about. I figure she lost the plot... A lot of kids just lose the plot."

The Barretts ultimately uncovered no answers on their trip into town, and returned home the next day utterly deflated. Edith felt the sudden pressing of old age, and again slid into bouts of sleeping for days on end, while John tended to the chores about the property in stoic dejection. Time seemed to crawl past with less and less joy by the day.

The months went by slowly.

Until one day, under a heavy August sun, Mae approached the homestead with bare feet and an airy disposition. Her eyes were vivid and attentive, and she wore a long corduroy robe that grazed the ground. It's hem muddy, faded, and slightly torn.

When her parents came outside to greet her, there was a standoff. Edith's jaw trembled with alternating anger and joy, while Mae's father just glared with a long and arching frown. Mae raised her eyebrows, stretched out her arms, and stepped forward to melt into her parents, giving each a long and warm hug that dissolved their anger.

It was a sweltering day, and the scent of the cattle pens made itself readily known, leading the three to quickly huddle inside and share a modest lunch of sandwiches and lemonade.

"I want to thank you both," said Mae. "I've learned a tremendous amount over the past couple of years. I've learned things about myself, about this world, and... what it really comes down to." She spoke in a tone that seemed both frail and confident, as if the former were a spade in the hand of the latter.

John began to suspect that Mae had been indoctrinated into a cult. After all, she had disappeared without a trace, and now, she had returned to rant about a newfound understanding of things. He had read stories of similar things happening in distant places.

He was inclined to ask her the name of her new church when she said something that made him forget his train of thought entirely.

"May I take some of your cattle?" she asked nonchalantly.

John was perplexed. "What... what would you want cows for?" he asked.

She leaned across the table and grasped his hand gently. Several dirty strands of blonde hair tumbled from a loose bun atop her head.

"I want to bring William back," she said softly, not batting an eyelash. "I found a way, but it requires..."

John ripped his hand from Mae's grasp and stood with such a start that it frightened Edith even more than Mae's words had.

He breathed heavily and pointed a shaking finger in his daughter's direction. "How dare you..." His lips quivered. "How dare you abandon us. First, to your books... and then you abandon even those... You abandon us without quarter, then arrive on my doorstep, out of God's blue sky, speaking of William? What devils have you consorted with, daughter?"

"You don't believe in devils, father," said Mae coolly.

John thought that his rage might escape his waning grasp.

"Get out," he muttered, jowls shaking.

"JOHN!" Edith called out to her husband.

"Quiet!" he responded without taking his eyes off of Mae. "Forsaker. Recreant. Be gone and leave us in peace." A tear fell from his cheek.

At first, Mae didn't budge, and only turned toward her brittle mother as if to speak a soft word, when John reached under the table and flung it across the room, shattering the glassware atop it.

He pointed toward the door.

"GET OUT!" he screamed.

Mae had never once heard her father scream.

She stood slowly, bowed lightly, and obliged calmly without a further word. She didn't turn back as she walked down the long gravel pathway out of the estate.

The following morning, John awoke to find that fifteen of his cattle were gone.

12

The Room of Burning Ghosts

Mae entered the room and surveyed the scene. The pentagram of bodies lay before her, ready to fulfil its role. They've each waited so long, she thought. So patient. The periphery of the room was draped with the long black blankets that Sawyer had hung, and there was not a sliver of light except for that which emitted from the three lit candles that flickered about the room. The rising smoke burnt her esophagus and stung her eyes, and with each inhalation of her lungs and blink of her eyelids, she knew that, at last, that the time had come to meet a quiet and definitive end. It was time to die.

She walked to the dresser and opened the *Tome of Instruction* to the bookmarked page: *Material Bounding and Mortalization*. She grasped the kachina doll, placed it inside the keepsake box, and closed the lid. She indented the point of the nail upon the box's oaken face and used the nearby hammer to send it straight through the box with a single precise strike.

She then carefully replaced the impaled box back onto the dresser, consulted the tome, and began to wrap the mandrake roots with hawk feathers. Once all three roots were tightly wrapped and restrained by hemp string, she set each atop the open face of a burning candle. Within seconds, each root caught flame, prompting Mae to then center herself within the pentagram of bodies, kneel, lower her chin, and close her eyes.

She brought her attention to her breathing.

In....

Out...

In...

Out...

The flickering orange upon her eyelids began to dissipate, and soon, the crackling of the lapping flames muted. She returned her focus to the rhythm of her lungs.

In....

Out...

In...

Out...

In...

Out...

In...

Out...

In...

As subtly as one slips into a dream, she soon experienced a flickering scrapbook of emotion and experiences; not one of which was hers. Each fluttered along her perception in a bokeh blur. Images, feelings, sounds, and even smells cascaded past her awareness like individual snowflakes riding a blizzard's howl. All at once, she seemingly embodied them all. The plants we take responsibility for. Dictionaries. Road rage. Grade-school valentines. The wind rustling the hair of a street cat. The fatigue built up from a day of work felt only when finally at home. The adhesive that holds skin to the muscles beneath it. Pavlov. Capitalism. Propaganda. Corn flakes. Glittering scales in sunlight under shallow water. Exaggerations of impact. Hydrogen bonds. Alloy wheels coated in brake dust. Wrestling. Feelings caught between high schoolers. Social security. Blue suede shoes. Flagstone steps with burn marks on their underbelly. Rogue waves. Xenophobia. Gelatin. Valium. Fears of disease that are discovered to be only gas. Satellite TV subscriptions. Expectations of obligation to family. Returns on risky investments. Gold. Minuteman missile silos. Bibles in hotel rooms. Paper boys. Dancing. The word "almost." Fellatio. Verdicts in trials of child support. Sea urchins. Blood. Emails asking for your feedback. Cambodia. Yellow-tailed foxes. The Santa Cruz Islands. F-16 fighter jets. Eternity. The overuse of punctuation. Gas station cigarette displays. Sonder. Road trips and the gasoline burned. Humidity. Graduated cylinders filled with sand. Tamagotchi. Xylophones. Federer's racket. Spreadsheets. Master Chief of the *Halo* series. Valley girl accents. Ulysses Grant. Every half dream you'll never remember. Cold cases. The Jackson Five. Inside horses. Melody. Procrastination. A hug at the airport. Red tape. Stallions riding west at dusk somewhere in Nevada. Falling leaves. The sound of air conditioning. Peter Pan. Neosporin pre-applied to band aids. Clowns. July. Streamers. Vincent Van Gogh. Armistice Day. National flowers. Ghosts. The loss of a friend. Symbols that take the place of what they symbolize. Queen bees. Symmetry. Love. Other things...

She opened her eyes, and found herself standing in a dark snowy field but a few feet from Malaki. His eyes blazed with orange flame and a tall crown of thorns rose from his head. A reprise of *Der Doppelgänger* played somewhere far off, carried on the wind, and a liminal blackness surrounded everything beyond the immediate vicinity.

"He corrupted you..." the visage whispered.

Mae snarled. "And what could I have become, blackguard? A long, silent witness of the wickedness of this world? No. I refuse and I damn you, ghost. Wicked beast. Speak not of the mage, for he taught me the only things... the *only* things... that have ever supplemented the curse that you've hexed me with anything resembling redemption."

Seconds passed. The wind tossed flurries of snow about them. Masau'u stood motionless, while Mae trembled with unexpected anger.

"I thought I saw something in you," the flame-eyed specter whispered. The wind carried its words unnaturally far. "I thought I saw perseverance." He shook his head slowly. "I only wanted for you to see all that was redeeming in this world... I only wanted you to see its meaning."

"There is no such thing as objective meaning in life," she exclaimed, taking a step towards him. "There is only the meaning we create for ourselves."

She continued forward, patiently closing the gap between them.

"So much anger," he replied in a carrying whisper. "Can you not see the forest for the trees?"

"Enough," Mae retorted bitterly, stopping only a step from the visage. The creature's eyes burned wildly with flame as it stared back into her own. "I'm not here to be lectured," she proclaimed.

"I know why you're here," he said, suddenly changing his appearance to that of the Indian she had met in the woods so many years before. Simultaneously, their surroundings changed to the very scene of their initial meeting. They stood beside the felled tree in the woods beside the clearing. In the nearby meadow, her mother called her name.

"I still believe in you, young Mae. There's still time," Masau'u pleaded.

Mae had not been expecting the change in surroundings and was shaken by the sound of her mother's voice.

Be unmoving, she told herself to steady her intention. She raised a flower of nightshade from her pocket and pierced its stem into the cloth of Masau'u's purple cloak before razing her gaze to look into his eyes.

"Don't abandon what I have given you," he said. "I swear to you... there is still time."

But Mae wouldn't have it. Not now.

"I prey to every god but you that there is not," she said coldly. She placed the palm of her hand onto his forehead, leaned in close, and whispered into his ear.

"Don't be afraid."

She awoke still kneeling on the hard concrete floor of the master bedroom. All ten of the bodies surrounding her in the dreadful pentagram burnt with vibrant blue flames. She raised her head to see that Masau'u was now floating supine, face up, in the thin air before her.

She shuddered with excitement.

"It worked," she muttered.

Realizing that time was of consequence, she darted to the dresser and scanned the text in the *Tome of Instruction*, double-checking the procedures that she had read and rehearsed a thousand times. She collected the vial of liquified nightshade, the dagger, and coddled the Tome while carrying each to the floating body at the center of the burning pentagram.

After placing the Tome on the ground, she lifted the vial and ever so slowly poured the liquid upon the torso of the god. When the vial was empty and the clothes were thoroughly soaked in its red liquid, she discarded the vial and jabbed the dagger into Masau'u's back from underneath. She pushed on the grip with all her might, and at first was met by a tremendous resistance. Upon the initial resistance, she feared that she might be unable to pierce his body, until, at last, the flesh gave way, and the tip of the blade erupted from the center of Masau'u's chest.

Mae stepped back with a heavy breath and knelt to collect the Tome. She rose with her face buried in its pages and quickly read aloud into the flickering hue of the room:

"Umbram quam negavi, nunc voco.Fons aeternus, occlude viam tuam—fiam aquae morientis flumen.Sanguis noxius, pretium Icaro solutum, madet in ferro siletur.Revolvitur rota, fati vincla fracta sunt.Mortalis iterum ero, et mors me comitabitur."

As she spoke, the liquid that had soaked into the clothes began creeping along the fibers toward the blade that absorbed it thirstily. By the time that the final words of the incantation were uttered, the blade was a uniform crimson without a hint of a glimmer.

She ripped the blade from Masau'u's chest and held it in her hands. It felt substantially heavier than before. As she stared at the matte metal, a tear dripped down her cheek and onto the floor.

The blue flames of the corpses flickered, and she saw a finger of the body before her twitch.

She knew that the time had come. All that she had sacrificed now resided in the blade that she held in her trembling hands. The grip of the blade itself pulsated, as if eager to drain the eternity from within her.

And yet, despite all that had gone into her designs: the murders, the thousand preparations, the stolen corpses, the toleration of society, the empty days, the endless nightmares, and the rotting emptiness that had come to call her soul home, she experienced the unexpected presence of hesitation within her. Her fingers trembled.

She raised the blade to her neck, but her muscles slackened and she feared she might drop the knife to the floor. Had she come all this way only to lack the fortitude to finish the job.

"Cowardice haveth a name and it is Mae," she whimpered.

Something in her peripheral vision caught her attention. She looked up and saw the blankets surrounding the room ripple unnaturally. It appeared that hands were pressing upon the blankets from the outside. At first she saw only a few, but before she could fully comprehend what was happening, a thousand hands began to pound upon the blanket walls while a chorus of high-pitched shrieks erupted in hellish accompaniment. The watchers had arrived.

Mae returned her gaze to the blade in her hand just as the blankets tore from the walls and a legion of cloaked and faceless ghouls collapsed into the room and upon her. She grabbed the dagger's hilt with both hands and, before she could think, plunged its crimson metal into her stomach.

Blackness became all.

13

Castles of Sand

Mae trailed behind the herd of cattle, tending to its tracks by means of illusion.

For hours, she and the cows pushed toward what was initially an impenetrably black and moonless eastern horizon, until at last, the sky began shifting gently into a deep-sea blue, periwinkle, turquoise, then bright blue.

As the horizon softened, Mae likened herself to a disoriented anglerfish floating upward toward the light of the sun. Death, disguised in light. Indeed, she knew that it was death that she approached, but it wasn't to be hers this day, but rather a long-sought rendezvous with another's. She thought of William's face as he greeted guests at his farewell party. Maybe, she thought, a better metaphor might be that *she* was the light, reeling her disoriented brother from the depths of death to speak with him once again.

She knew exactly the words she would say when she brought him back for but a split moment of golden time. They would justify whatever lengths such an encounter would demand.

The ends would justify the means.

She muttered the verbal incantation of a cloaking illusion as she walked. "Viae abscondite, terra dormiat, ventus ducat," she repeated, over and over, while throwing sand upon the tracks of the herd. The spell was a simple but effective one that cloaked the path of the cows, undoing the heavy prints that the hooves left upon the earth. When the bag grew empty, as it routinely did, she'd kneel to the forest floor and collect more, careful not to scoop up more pine needles than soil.

Occasionally, she'd catch a glimpse of the translucent sheepdog familiars that she had conjured to guide the cattle. They darted through the trees, turning back head that strayed too far from the path assigned.

As they crested a ridge, she made a point to approach a striking Rocky Mountain juniper that she had come to name the Rising Cartographer. Its gnarled trunk seemed to tell stories of an older, more worthy world, while its bushy limbs rose uncharacteristically high above the rocky soil.

"Hello again," she said, taking a welcome break from her Latin incantations. The Cartographer meant that they were getting close. Only a few hundred more meters and they would arrive at the well.

As Mae resumed her muttering and throwing of sand, she thought back on what Malaki had told her when they had spoken last. Over the previous months, their relationship had grown from that of teacher and student to pupil and pupil, leading to Mae's confidence growing wildly, like the limbs of the Rising Cartographer itself. She had decided that he was right to see something special in her, and she meant to do remarkable things in this life using the gifts that she had been given. The Latin she had learned came easy; it rolled from her tongue like sugar. The meditations had become second nature once the intricacies of the act were simplified, and the detailed steps of alchemy and their applications seemed increasingly like a well-rehearsed dance with each new rendition.

The world was a beach, and she was constructing wonders from its sand.

But when she mentioned to Malaki her intention to bring her brother back from the dead, only for a short, innocent conversation, his reaction was sober, to say the least.

She had referred to it in passing while they were strolling side by side through the cleverly laid brick walkways of the Lowell Observatory. She visited the grounds frequently now that the aperture of her focus had expanded once again, after the novelty of the arcane world had at last waned. Rivers of tourists poured all around them on the narrow pathways as they walked at their own patient pace. They didn't bother to lower their voices as they spoke.

"You said it yourself, Mal," Mae said defensively. "The taboo of death is but a dull ache of the ego."

Malaki narrowed his eyes and eyed her suspiciously. He was impressed with her decision to recite his words back to him in such a context.

"Mae, you are endlessly clever and creative in your conjurations, and attentive to the subtleties that your work demands. I believe in you, and I support you. I swear this to be true, darling. But I must insist... what you speak of... it demands respect to forces that even I dare not approach. To be perfectly frank, dear, I'd suggest you abandoned this idea and let both it and your brother rest behind us."

"Is the world not ours to contort?" she asked in rising excitement. "Again, your words, Mal. And to quote you again, 'There is nothing to fear in magic if sufficient respect is given where respect is due.' Is this not true?"

"I wouldn't say such things if they were untrue. But do not twist my words in my face when I am..." He stopped his quickening speech by stopping his rising volume with abruptness before closing his eyes in an impressive display of both self-awareness and control. "I am trying to help you. The extent of... respect... that is required here... it may not be worth the..."

"Anything is worth my brother," she replied curtly. Frustration seemed to catch flame from deep within herself, something that she had never before experienced in the company of Malaki. It felt like a coal that was a part of her innermost being now caught by the wind of his resistance and roused to a resounding smolder.

"Have you not lost someone?" she asked. "Have you not cared enough for them to try to bring them back, or are you not as capable as you pretend to be?"

The second she released the words she regretted them. Both her and Malaki had stopped walking while packs of tourists and students spilled around them as if they were lodged boulders in a shallow river. "I..." she hesitated. "I'm sorry... I didn't mean that."

Malaki looked downward sullenly. She had never once seen him even remotely so. He opened his mouth as if to speak, then closed it as if considering exactly what he wished to say. He tried again. "Just... know that what you are dealing with here... typically doesn't play nice. Even if you're playing by the rules, it might choose not to."

The conversation turned to other matters, and neither brought the subject up again.

But the words were recalled often by Mae, and they were indeed conjured as she trailed the herd of cattle approaching their destination. The cows came to rest in a small clearing in the woods. The translucent sheepdogs, having fulfilled their purpose, flickered, and fluttered out of existence.

In the clearing, a cement foundation of what was once a building lay below a red-brick fireplace rising into the pre-dawn sky. Plaster and charred wood was scattered about, and a cobblestone well stood only a stone's throw from the chimney. A few feet from the well was a tall and wide pile of freshly dug dirt, in which the mouth of a spade was shoved into the heap, its wooden handle extending upright.

It was reservation land. Hopi. Years ago, affluent white families became enamored with the area and thought they'd build their vacation homes on the land without consulting the tribe. After several lawsuits and appeals to the Bureau of Indian Affairs, the Federal government finally sided with the tribe and forced the families to abandon the properties. The families, true to their character, figured that if they couldn't enjoy the homes, they would rather burn the buildings to the ground.

And so they did.

Mae counted the cows grazing about the clearing. Fifteen head. The same number with which she had departed. She dropped her pack upon the concrete slab and rummaged through its pockets before removing the *Tome of Instruction*. It was a gift that Malaki had given her the week before. It had been a year and a half since their shared endeavors had begun, and he had given it to her as a token of celebration.

"I've got it all up here," he had joked, pointing to his head as he handed her the Tome wrapped in a delicate string.

She flipped to a page near the back of the book, in a chapter titled *Demonology*. This chapter was categorized differently than the rest, in that instead of titling each page by spell or intended result, it was instead headed by the names of various demons and their various associations, connotations, strengths, and weaknesses.

The page that Mae landed on displayed the name *Gamaliel, the Eater of Roots.* She ran her fingers across the raised lettering of the page. She carefully scanned the creature's description once again.

Inhabitant of things forgotten; Puller of souls buried; Capricious; Liar; Feeds upon deep deaths; Has multiple known forms, but most commonly appears as a twisted and gnarled tree trunk with hollow, sunken, black eyes dripping ebony tears; A suffocating air is known to surround the creature and is oft accompanied by the smell of decay and old earth; Can only be called by summoning spells spoken both under the earth and pronounced backwards; Powerful; It is advised that the summoner be of a masterful ability and supported by multiple peers of equal ability.

In a red scribble at the bottom of the page, the words *Do not summon* were written in bold across the final words of the formal description. When Mae had first noticed the page, weeks ago, she had asked Malaki why hadn't whoever had written the added words simply torn the page from the book entirely?

His response was to caution her on spending too much time studying such a chapter, then he suggested that she try to rip the page out herself. To her surprise, no matter how hard she tugged at its fibers, the page refused to tear even the slightest bit and held firm to the spine that bound it.

"It's a way to preserve the work from the capriciousness of its owner," said Malaki as he steeped his tea. "Sometimes, in old age, one regrets things one has written. Things one has created. You see, the ward upon the book prevents our ever-inflatable uncertainty from destroying objective knowledge. It is the deal we make with the thing. We share with it our knowledge, and it shares with us its memory."

Mae closed the book and carefully returned it to her bag as the cows milled about her. The first step in her intended ritual that day was one that required no nuance. She walked to a nearby pile of rubble and dragged the burnt remains of the house's front door to the edge of the well. She lifted its top and rested it against the circular cobblestone wall.

Climbing hallway up the plank, she jumped up and down with the entirety of her weight until she was satisfied that it was sturdy enough to not break while fulfilling its purpose.

A rustle in the trees broke her concentration.

She peered into the woods, and at first thought she saw the darting of a translucent sheepdog between the trees, but no further evidence supported that impression. No more sounds arose, and after patient observation, she returned her attention to her preparations

The soft and deliberate voice of Malaki came from behind her.

"You know you shouldn't be here, Mae," he said. He must have followed her in a manner of invisibility with which she was unfamiliar, as she could typically detect him when he attempted similar stunts on other occasions. She was more disappointed in herself than anything, for not noticing his trail.

"I figured you'd try. I didn't think it would be this soon," he continued. He walked to the foundation of the late house nearby, dragged his foot through a pile of soot and burnt wood while sighing as if familiar with the history of the entropy before him. "Gamaliel is not the answer you seek."

Mae wished to respond as sharply as she had on the Lowell grounds, but instead chose to hold her tongue after recollecting the regret that had followed her words the last time she had let them loose upon him. She was exasperated at being unable to protest too strongly, lest she hurt the old man's feelings. The coal within her chest remained smoldering still.

"Then what is the answer, Malaki?" she said, huffing and throwing her hands into the air. "Walk away? Let go? Let him disappear into the wind like everything else?"

"Such is the way of the world, child," he responded in a paternal tone.

She turned from him and walked a few steps toward the cattle before turning about in a flourish. Tears welled in her eyes.

"Then what's the point of all this," she gestured about her, "if we can't fix... things?" She dropped to the floor and sat looking into the trees, defeated.

Malaki approached and slowly sat down beside her. His cloak was dirty from his long trek, and his feet appeared scarred and bruised beneath the straps of his sandals. He too stared emptily into the trees while the cows milled about them.

"Sometimes, letting go is the best thing we can do," he said finally. "Do you know how pearls are formed? They're the result of pain. You see, when sand gets stuck within an oyster's shell, the rough grain rubs against the creature's skin and causes it tremendous agony. To dull the uncomfortable sensation, the mollusk coats the sand in layers of something called nacre, and over time, the layers grow, and the thing that was once an abrasive irritant to the creature has become something as elegant and pristine as a pearl. The creature's most cherished feature is something that was at first a terrible struggle, but given enough time and patience, has been transformed into something uniquely beautiful... My point is... that our pain, our loss, it doesn't go away. It becomes an unalienable part of us, and we can either dig at it and attempt to carve it from our skin, or we can coat it, and adorn it as something valuable, as it is, and will continue to be..."

She considered his words, and for several minutes nothing was said between them. Mae knew that he was right. Even if she could summon her brother, the act would be temporary, and afterwards, the loss would be no less painful.

But her stubbornness, a character flaw that she had inherited from her mother and something that she recalled seeing in her brother as well, latched onto her plans, resulting in a tunnel vision that refused to relinquish its claws; a lump of coal burning away at her skin.

If she was more honest with herself, she might have acknowledged that her desire to fulfill this plan had more to do with fulfilling a growing sense of self-aggrandizing glory than it was about saying goodbye to her brother at all.

But she wasn't.

"I have to try. I just... I just have to try," she whispered.

Malaki sighed heavily. "Theres nothing I can do to dissuade you, then?" he asked in a pessimistic tone.

She shook her head. Malaki frowned.

"Very well, then," he said. "But I can't let you do it alone."

Mae raised her eyes, glancing at him thankfully, before resting her head gently on his shoulder. He had become her best friend in the world. Quite possibly her only friend, she acknowledged.

"Thank you, Mal," she whispered.

"My only condition, though, is that I am given creative input into the *how*." He gestured to the cattle that grazed about them. "Let these poor cows go. There are more humane ways to summon a demon."

14

Things Would be Different if the Whiskey Were Gone

Sam spent the next few days resting, eating well, and giving respite to his mind. He took care to ensure that his obligations to the house were addressed, but retreated to his bedroom to sleep long into each day.

He was beginning to suspect that his mind needed a holiday, and he did what he could to give it one.

He decided to erect a makeshift curtain over the windows of the guest bedroom using PVC pipe and a long black blanket that he had found in the garage. The blanket rose only six feet, but it did its job in mitigating his apprehensions of the forest staring at him throughout the night. He had previously made peace with the forest's gaze into his room; however, he had recently begun experiencing bouts of tinnitus that erupted while he was lying in bed prompting the erection of the barrier.

The tinnitus had become such a regular occurrence that he had begun to wonder if he should speak with a doctor about it, but to his relief, it subsided when he erected the curtain, so he simply chalked it up to stress.

The kachina doll's appearance in the estate diorama, too, elicited his curiosity and unease. Despite his intellectual perspectives on hauntings and the supernatural, he had no desire to touch the doll. He likened it to a fear of bugs. A caterpillar is small and unlikely to pose any danger, but it still gives you the heebie-jeebies when it crawls across your leg.

Finally, he decided to simply throw a white sheet over the entire diorama and call it even. At least he wouldn't have to look at it any longer while making breakfast each morning.

A few days passed, and by the 31st he was beginning to feel well again. He realized he missed the comforts of society. He had expected that he would happily enjoy the prolonged solitude of living within the estate, and he had, but now he longed for the conversation and presence of others, if only to refresh his mind. He would sometimes talk to the geese by the lake or the squirrels that ran across the forest path, but that did little to dissipate his longing for casual banter and the simple human interactions that inspire in unexpected ways. Playing 9-ball in an empty dive bar, or people-watching in the park, now represented his highest aspirations.

He recalled the men hanging the pinecone atop the Weatherford Hotel in downtown Flagstaff: the Great Pinecone Drop would be happening that very night. Sawyer had given him permission to leave the estate for a couple of days, if the need arose, and Sam figured the time away would do him some good. His mind flashed to a pair of rosy cheeks below a strand of blonde hair.

With a sudden inspiration, Sam packed a bag and began prepping the house to be without him for a day or two. He set the security system to its "away" mode, watered the neediest of the plants, and set out extra rat traps in the cellar. He performed a quick dusting in the gallery, just in the off chance that Ms. Shawmaker happened to arrive while he was away. He informed David, still holding Goliath's head by its hair, that he was to be in charge while he was gone.

With that, he stepped outside.

But before he could enter the cab of his truck, he noticed a man walking along the path toward the gate. Sam paused and studied the man, who wore a white and purple striped collared shirt tucked into his distressed jeans. He appeared relatively harmless, but nonetheless, Sam approached the gate with a slightly cautious demeaner.

"Can I help you?" he hollered through the bars of the gate. The man was old and Native American. His face was sunburnt and he walked barefoot along the gravel of the path.

"Potentially," the man said slowly. "Are you Sam?"

"I am," he responded, raising his apprehension. "But I'm only the caretaker here. I don't own the place, so if you're looking to…"

"I'm not looking for the owner. I'm looking for Sam," the man said decisively.

Sam wasn't sure of what to make of the statement. "Well... what do you want?" he asked.

The man scanned Sam up and down critically before sighing deeply, frowning, and raising his eyes to the sky. "It's going to snow," he said, then without another word, turned and walked back up the path away from the estate.

How did he know my name, Sam pondered. The only way, he figured, was that the man must have been a friend of Sawyer's, sent to check in on him. The thought irked Sam.

He turned and walked back toward the truck. He considered what the man had said about it snowing. But when he looked up, he saw a clear sky sliding toward dusk, and his phone's weather app indicated nothing but the same for the next three days.

He got in the truck, moved through the gate, and drove down the pathway that the man had walked only minutes before. When he reached the turn-off, he looked in both directions, searching for any sign of the man, but saw nothing and no one.

He turned toward town, bumped up the heater, and lowered the windows to relish in a flux of varied temperature. He flipped on the radio as "Comfortably Numb" played from the speakers while the wind from the open window lapped at his skin.

He directed the truck through the trees, onto the highway, and by the time he turned off the interstate and into Flagstaff proper, night had begun to descend upon the mountain-top city.

The streets of the city were strangled with Christmas lights and mobs of people. Sam decided to first check into his room before adventuring into the bars and crowds and parked beneath the towering neon Hotel Monte Vista sign and made his way into the lobby.

The sounds of a saxophone echoed through the glass-plated lobby in which an impeccably dressed attendant stood behind an ornate wooden countertop. He spoke on a wired brass phone while rolling his eyes, unmoved by Sam's presence. To the left of the counter was an elegant old-timey caged elevator, the semi-hemispherical dial atop it lay motionless. A sign strung across the door stated, *Out of Order. Use West Elevator.*

A short hallway to the right connected the lobby to a dimly lit jazz bar from which the saxophone's notes were apparently escaping. Just as Sam meandered toward the doorway to examine the lounge, a woman wearing a flapper dress emerged and walked through the lobby with a confident strut. Her braided red hair struck him as somehow familiar.

"Yes?" asked the smartly dressed attendant from behind the counter.

"Oh." Sam turned back to the man. "Checking in. Yellowstone."

The attendant clacked at his keyboard before clicking the mouse decisively. He looked up to meet Sam's gaze. "Six hundred and one," he said, lowering his chin as if saying something dirty. He turned to rummage within a cabinet of keys that rattled against one another. He returned with an iron key that he placed delicately upon the countertop. "Breakfast goes til nine."

Minutes later, Sam emerged from the west elevator and onto the sixth floor above. The hallway extended in both directions, concluding at ragged window frames decorated with sheer floral drapes. He took the path to the right, as the room numbers descended in that direction. On every second or third door was a framed photograph of a celebrity from yesteryear, hung just below the peephole. Marilyn Monroe adorned room 614. Humphrey Bogart 611. Paul Newman 607. Clark Gable 603. Sam stopped at the end of the hallway to examine the door of room 601, on which a black and white Howard Hughes grinned back at him.

The room was quaint. A small mahogany table stood beside a mattress draped in a plush outdated comforter. On the table, a laminated sheet of paper explained that Howard Hughes had once stayed in the room in 1964. It stated that Mr. Hughes had rented out the entire sixth floor, but passersby looking up from the street had noted that he was commonly seen smoking from the window of 601 more often than any other window during his stay.

Bold red text lined the bottom of the sheet, reminding the guest of the hotel's strict non-smoking policy. All the same, Sam was happy to find the window's security bolt broken. He slid the glass pane upward to allow in a gentle breeze.

The curtains billowed into the room as he extended his head out and into the night's clean air. The view was fantastic. He watched the crowds congeal and break apart on the sidewalks beneath him, like oil and vinegar in the pan. Sounds equal parts laughter and jeering echoed off the tall brick building across from him, and the fragrance of cinnamon and pine demanded his attention.

After a quick shower, Sam descended to the street and set off with no particular destination in mind. He figured that come midnight he would make his way to the corner of Aspen and Leroux for the pinecone drop, but he had a few hours to kill. As he passed a bar with a crowd loudly milling about its entrance, he thought of the girl from Macy's coffee shop. He figured the shop would likely be closed by now, and she probably wouldn't even be working if it *was* open, but he decided the crisp stroll would be enjoyable. And you never know, he thought. He wished he had gotten her name.

Before he crossed the tracks, a brick building just off San Francisco Street caught his eye. The sign above the heavily stickered door read, *The Beagle Room*. Sam might have assumed the building to be empty, or at least closed, had he not heard loud rock and roll music emanating from inside. His curiosity overtook him. He opened the door and walked inside.

Within the quaint, smoky foyer stood a sleepy box-office attendant with long bleached- blonde hair, resting her elbows upon a tall wooden pedestal. The screen of a Gameboy illuminated her face. Without raising her eyes, she held out a translucent plastic box with the printed text, *Cover if you're cool*. Seven one-dollar bills lined the box, and Sam contributed a crumpled twenty-dollar bill that had miraculously made it through the washing machine twice over the past month. As he inserted the bill into the thin slot, he decided that the bill's durability was a sure sign that he was exactly where he was supposed to be at that moment. The thought warmed him.

Sam pushed through a doorway of draped beads into a small yet tastefully lit bar with no tender nor patrons in sight. Loud rock music continued from beyond. To his left was a modest merch stand with band T-shirts crudely fixed to the wall with masking tape. On a small folding table in front of the shirts were stickers and CDs. The name of the band was written in bold text across the face of the table: *THINGS WOULD BE DIFFERENT IF THE WHISKEY WERE GONE.*

Beyond a parted set of red silk curtains, the room opened into a wide, dark, and practically empty room in which a four-piece rock band played upon a wooden stage. Three black silhouettes stood awkwardly on the dance floor.

Sam noticed an elevated booth to his far left, where a sound engineer moved dials in a disinterested fashion, randomly spinning the stage lights about the band as they played.

As Sam leaned against the back wall and watched the band, he discreetly pulled from the flask taken from his jacket pocket. The band was okay. Probably worse than okay, but they appeared to be authentically invested in their craft, and for Sam, that was enough. There were two guitar players, one of which sang, and a bassist and a drummer. The guitarist on the right wore a Metallica shirt, shredding leads that were unquestionably inspired by Slash and Van Halen, while the other was centered upon the stage and simply held power chords while screaming into the microphone.

An honest cacophony, Sam thought, yet with each tug from the flask it sounded that much better.

After a few songs, the fact that the grand finale of the set had been reached was evident as each instrument was played as loud as possible without finesse or concern for timing for thirty uninterrupted seconds of noise. At last, the drum set mercifully emitted its final vibrations and its operator departed stage right, his skin glistening under the still spinning lights. Sam looked to the sound booth and saw the engineer flirting with a silhouette while his left hand still spun his dials thoughtlessly.

After the drummer left the stage, the guitar players rested their guitars beside their amplifiers, producing an ascending and coalescing wall of feedback.

The bassist was last to leave, and when he finally departed the stage, the engineer waited a full two seconds before unceremoniously cutting the power to the amplifiers while simultaneously flipping on the overhead lights. Just like that, the facade of the performance vanished like an exorcized phantom and after a long moment of awkward silence, *The Strokes* began to play from the PA speakers.

Sam was about to turn to leave when the singer of the band approached him. The singer had long black hair and was surprisingly well toned under a cutoff grey T-shirt displaying a unicorn rearing before a fiery explosion.

"Thanks for coming out! Can I get you a free shirt?" he asked.

Sam walked to the merch stand with the sweaty man and insisted on paying full price for both a shirt and a sticker. While he wasn't a fan of the group's music, his younger brother had played drums in a band while in college and Sam respected the grind. He knew it entailed hard work and empty rooms.

"Are you guys local?" he asked the singer. The man had a square jaw that jutted sharply while his eyes were bright blue and thoughtful.

"Nahhhh," he said, waving Sam's question away. "We're ramblin', man. Hitting San Jose tomorrow if the snow don't snow."

"I see you've, uhh, met the talent!" slurred a burly, bearded man who quickly inserted himself physically between the two of them. He wore a blue and grey flannel shirt, and his beard was dense all the way up his face until it stopped only a few millimeters from his eyes. He smelled like pickles, and he was unquestionably drunk.

"You look familiar," he said to Sam. He was much taller than latter, but still raised his chin and squinted his eyes as if it might help jog his memory. "Are you Melton's kid?" he asked.

"Nooo," Sam replied slowly. A twinge of playful spontaneity rose within him. He hadn't a clue who the man was, but the musician was undeterred by his presence and even chuckled at his brazen drunkenness. "I'm Sulley's boy. Graduated this past semester."

The large man nodded and shook Sam's hand excitedly. "So, so proud. So, so proud. Now out into the world you go. If you're looking for work, you know, between things, or, before things get going and all, you've always got a job here if you ever want one." He burped. "Always looking for help." Sam and the man shared a look of understanding that Sam wasn't actually Sulley's boy. Not that it really mattered.

A young woman in a sundress beneath a long black duster approached the singer with a coy wink and a kiss on the cheek before engaging in a twisting embrace. When they at last separated, the woman produced a joint, holding it between her thumb and forefinger ceremoniously. She raised her eyebrows to the singer in a questioning manner, prompting the singer to then turn to Sam and the apparent owner of the establishment.

"Y'all cool?" he asked.

Both men responded that they were, and Sam followed the group outside and up a metal stairwell that led to a second-story apartment above.

15

Held to the Flame

Mae was suspended in blackness. She felt nothing, saw nothing, smelled nothing, and heard nothing. Slowly, she grew aware of her thoughts.

"What is this?" she asked herself. Her awareness stood without context, and yet her thoughts existed in a blackness that seemed all encompassing.

"You are not who I had hoped you to be," a voice echoed in the darkness, as if she were in a colossal and empty cave. "You twisted my intentions and fed me flawed assumptions. You feared for only yourself, and closed your eyes to all other things. You spilled blood and wreaked havoc upon the world to save yourself from an imagined hell. A hell of your own creation, Mae. Well... isn't it funny how we create prisons for ourselves?"

As the voice faded, the blackness began to fill with tiny dots, miniscule and bright. More and more appeared, and before long, Mae came to realize what each dot was: a star. A thousand billion stars gazing endlessly upon her.

She would have screamed, had she a mouth, yet the urge to do so remained horribly unquenched without a means of quelling the terrible sensation. Had she a heart, it would have been tachycardic as panic flooded her awareness. She was convinced that she might blip out of existence itself from the sheer overwhelming terror that overwhelmed her, yet her perspective remained, and the long, dreadful moments continued to pass.

And they passed.

And they passed.

And they passed.

And they passed.

And then, just as she had begun to fear that anything left to resemble stoicism might itself shatter into the debris of what was once an ego, the stars began to fade, and soon pure blackness again reigned, and the echoing voice returned.

"You win, young one. I am relinquishing you of my blessing. It was something that I had hoped to do upon the completion of your... assistance. But as I said... I see now that you are not who I had hoped you to be. For that, I take responsibility, and I will not hold you to my flame just yet. But you have spilled blood upon this earth and must be held accountable. You have taken and not giveth in return. You have spat in the face of justice; of balance. Rotten thing. You have demanded mortality. You now have it. But hear me, child. You must right what you have wronged before death calls, lest you find what waits for you afterward to be an unending rot in a bed that you have made for yourself...

"Be afraid, Mae."

16

Midnight Pearl

Mae was awakened by an aching numbness in her limbs, the sound of a roaring fire somewhere nearby, and the terrible sensation of something lodged in her throat. She rolled onto her side and tried to cough, but the object pressed tightly against her esophagus and she found that she couldn't breathe. She raised herself onto all fours and violently convulsed her diaphragm in a desperate attempt to dislodge whatever was obstructing her airway. At last, she rocked onto her knees and thrust her fists into her stomach. A pressurized wave of bile spilled out of her mouth and onto the snowy ground, dislodging the object in the process.

Her gaze was glassy and disoriented as she picked up the object, a matte-black pearl. She would have examined it further, but her stomach continued to convulse and for another minute she heaved into the snow.

When her retching finally ceased, she looked up to find that the house on Emerald Acres aflame in the darkness of the night surrounding. From each window, tall tongues of fire whipped into the sky and the sickly scent of burning plastics, wood, paint, chemicals, and metals stung her nostrils. She stumbled to her feet in the middle of the meadow.

Memories flooded in. The ritual. The watchers. The dagger. Her time in space... Masau'u's echoing voice in the darkness. She lifted her shirt and saw a thick linear scar where she had plunged the crimson blade into her stomach.

With a sudden, overwhelming sensation of being watched, she spun about clumsily. In the tree line at the edge of the meadow, Masau'u was illuminated by the orange glow of the flames. Apparently satisfied with her awareness of his presence, he turned about and walked slowly into the darkness of the forest.

Mae's vision blurred. Before she could lower herself gently to the snowy ground, she vaguely felt herself collapsing in a heap to the floor.

Streaks of brightly illuminated dust stretched across her field of vision in long shimmering lines. She was looking upward at the underside of the barn's rafters. A flash of light, and a change of perspective. She saw the forest from a top-down perspective. The pines danced wildly in the wind and long green grass swayed underneath the canopy's cover in the pockets between the trees. Her vision changed to a view of the pond in the meadow, frozen over and with heavy snow falling all about. *Crack!* In the center of the small pond, the ice appeared to be impacted by something underneath it. Spiderweb splintering appeared near the impact spot. *Crack!* A pale fist burst through the ice. Mae's perspective shifted. She was looking across the meadow, toward the house, from within the tree line in the dead of night. Every light in the house appeared to be on. However, as she watched, the lights turned off slowly, and one at a time. The final lit room was the guest bedroom. A figure walked into the room just before its light extinguished. Her perspective changed once again; now she was looking straight up into a clear blue sky, a white haze slowly drifting past.

A raven crossed her vision. After a period of time strikingly longer than the other visions, she felt a gentle breeze upon her cheek and came to realize that she was conscious. As she sat up gingerly, she found that she was sitting in the snowy meadow, the sun kissing only the tips of the trees. She was cold, but wore a thick jacket that she did not recall donning.

A mixture of acrid smoke, burnt plastic, and damp ash lingered about her. When she turned, she saw that the charred remains of the house seethed plumes of white smoke. Only the chimney still rose above the heaped piles of rubble.

When she went to stand, piercing pain made itself known in her core and in her throat. She recalled a half-recollection of waking during the night. The house aflame. Retching violently into the snow. A black pearl... She obliged a sudden and unexpected urge to reach into her jacket pocket and produced the very same object.

The matte black pearl rolled gently within her palm as she gazed down at it. Something within its appearance made her queasy, and she quickly replaced it back into her pocket.

She stood and slowly approached the smoldering rubble that sent a homing beacon into the sky. She had yet to consider her next steps, but no matter what they were, police or fire fighters arriving to discover the remains of nearly a dozen humans within the burning building would surely be counterproductive.

She stumbled toward what was once the master bedroom and picked up a charred two by four to assist in poking through the smoldering ash. The smoke burned her eyes as she worked, and twice had to remove herself to breathe clean air in the meadow.

But to her incredulity, she found no bodies in the rubble. No bones. Not even chalk marks on the concrete below. Nothing that gave the slightest indication of the occult happenings that had occurred in the room just hours before.

She circumnavigated the building and found that the barn too had burnt to the ground. In a similar fashion, she poked through its debris and discovered that the ground beneath it was uniform; no open graves littered the dirt underneath.

She walked toward the pond and sat on the raised ledge of the fountain, which was one of the only objects left untouched by the fire. Even the tree-stand appeared to have caught a floating ember and collapsed into a pile of smoking rubble. Abruptly, laughter rose from her as she realized that both Sam and Sawyer's vehicles had gone and vanished. *The bastard has a sense of humor*, she thought.

She began to contemplate what it all meant. Things hadn't exactly gone to plan, that was for sure. But, in the end, she had to admit that she had got what she wanted.

As far as she knew, she was mortal.

"But why not just kill me?" she whispered. "Why not just burn me up with the house?"

She recalled the echoing voice of Masau'u in the cavernous blackness of her dream.

"You must right what you have wronged," he had said.

But how was she to do that? Her murders were final. There weren't even bodies to ask forgiveness from any longer. Was she to join the Red Cross? Donate to soup kitchens? Apologize to the families of those she had killed? She pictured herself standing on a stoop, holding a bushel of flowers.

A flash of anger overcame her. Why couldn't the bastard, for once, just tell her what he wanted her to do? If he had come out with what he wanted from her in the first place, back in the woods when he first cursed her with "perspective," all of this could have been avoided. If he wanted her to be his voice box preaching natural homogeny and respect for nature, why didn't he simply say that? And then he had the gall to blame her when she didn't properly decipher his cryptic instructions. She had been but a child when he bestowed upon her that terrible responsibility, and he left her without even a hint of help or instruction. Then, he had simply stood by and watched as she did what she did, in a grasping response to the suffocating circumstances he had unsympathetically placed her in. And that wasn't even the end of it! Now, she acknowledged, he *at last* absolves her from her flailing, reprimands her for her efforts, and prescribes *another* impossibly vague directive with the overt threat of eternal damnation should she not oblige. What does it even mean to right a wrong as ghastly as murder? Even with her magical intuition and abilities, such spells would be complex and harrowing. Even with substantial luck on her side, atoning for murder wasn't exactly simple alchemy. There were chapters in the Tome that...

The book.

Where was the book?

She sprinted back to the smoldering ash of the master bedroom and dug furiously through the pile. Her boots began to heat and her feet protested in pain as she flung debris to and fro, but she didn't care. It was too important. She had to find it. There was no other option. It was either find the book or she would collapse into the smoldering pile and accept what may come.

But after nearly an hour of searching, when the rubber of her boots began to melt and she found it hard to see from the smoke pouring nonstop into her eyes, she at last relented.

Sobbing, she stumbled into the meadow and collapsed in utter sorrow.

The Tome meant more to her than she could admit. It represented not only Malaki's faith in her, but her faith in herself. Through it, she had come to understand who she truly was. Long ago, she had abandoned any semblance of identity outside of the acts she could manifest while using it. She was the spells she cast, and the book represented who she was: an arcanist, and little more.

She wrapped her head in her arms and wept into the snow.

When she was at last empty of tears, a thought occurred to her. She was now bound to the life of Melody Shilawea. It had been so long since she had last been irrevocably tied to a single human body, without the backup plan of simply transferring to another if things went south.

It wasn't the plan, of course. Mae had put all of her eggs into the idea that her consciousness would be dissolved by the time the ritual was complete. But thankfully, she had burned few bridges in the lead-up to her planned departure, and the basic supports that Melody Shilawea had relied upon over the past several years still stood intact: her shop remained back in town, as did her apartment. No matter what her next move would be, she figured she ought to head back to Flagstaff and go from there.

She hadn't her cell phone, so she had no choice but to walk out of the forest and to the highway. She could catch a ride into town after that.

As she meandered toward the gate, she spun around and looked about the smoldering ruins that lay within the meadow. She anxiously fiddled with the ebony pearl in her pocket that she couldn't, for some reason, bring herself to cast away. She wondered if this was the last that she might see of the meadow, and decided that it was likely that it was. By now, she could only vaguely recall where the cattle pens used to stand and thought of the tent that she, her mother, and her sister had slept in while her father and the workers finished the cabin over a hundred years before. In the smoldering heap of its most modern rendition, she could almost see it still. She thought of her mother, and how she would call to Mae and Susy when it was time for them to come back inside when dusk approached. She imagined her father whistling as he chopped wood nearby.

Her eyes watered and she again desired for the long sleep. She wished to be at her parents' side, in whatever blackness that may be. With a helpless gasp, she cursed Masau'u for making that most natural and essential facet of life a feat that she could only fruitlessly desire. Without the prospect of a natural death after death, she was hardly human at all. She was other and formless.

Could something so utterly inhuman come to bear a human's toll? What virtue could be expected from the void?

She studied the smoke still rising from the house. If the fire service had been alerted, it would have already come. The estate had few neighbors, and the nearest fire lookout station was several miles south. With any luck, the heap would simply burn to nothing over the course of a day or two, and someday people would approach the meadow with only harmless curiosity as to what had happened here.

A smile formed on Mae's face as she considered the stories they might conjure. They'd wonder who had lived in the house. What they had eaten. What games they had played. What had mattered to them as they went about their days. Mae thought it wonderful that no one would ever know the full story. It was among the few consolations that she carried with her as she turned and walked out the gate and began the long walk back toward the interstate.

The path was familiar; however, it was an undeniably different experience on foot than it was in the comfort of a vehicle. Much longer, too. It wasn't until she was well into her journey when she finally felt the exhaustion that had built up within her over the course of the past several hours. It was as if she had been up all-night drinking, running a marathon, and burying her best friend. Her body had been compensating well, until at last it allowed her to experience the burden that it had been carrying all this time. Her ribs ached, her throat throbbed, and her head was cloudy. Her feet protested, and the next thing Mae knew, she found herself in the ditch vomiting into the dirt.

From her knees, she concluded her convulsions and raised her head. Motionless, she gazed intently into the forest. Eli "Lucky" Duval stared back at her through the trees. Mae shook at the sight. Her arms trembled as they held her aloft. Her inclination was to run, but all she could manage was to rock back onto her knees and retain a watchful eye upon the ghastly sight before her.

Lucky stood on the hillside between the trees and stared at her piercingly with muddy black eyes. His head was cocked to the left and his body hovered an inch off the ground. Slowly, the specter began to float directly toward her, its limbs dangling loosely at its sides.

His head rocked back as the forward momentum carried his body towards her. It was as if he had no control of his appendages, his head included, yet the body remained perfectly vertical as it floated directly toward her.

A bloody scream erupted from Mae's mouth. She rose to her feet in a fury and bolted down the road in the direction of the still distant Interstate 40. She turned back as she ran, and to her utter horror, saw that Lucky's specter trailed closely behind her.

The memory of her past with the man flashed before her eyes. Lucky was a drifter, a low-life gambler infamous for growing debts then skipping town in the late 1970s. He was in the process of fleeing Flagstaff when Mae rubbed elbows with him in an alleyway outside of the Rendezvous bar. She asked him for a cigarette and eventually invited him to play poker with her at the estate that night; she was expecting some friends for a game. He, of course, obliged, but when he arrived, found that he was the first. Mae handed him a drink in the foyer and asked him to make himself comfortable as he waited for the others to arrive. Within an hour, she was dragging his lifeless body into the grave already dug for him in the barn.

As Mae's sprint hastened along the pathway, she recollected his voice calling to her from the living room while she sat patiently in the bedroom, smoking a cigarette. "Are we playing hold 'em or 21, ya suppose?" he had asked.

"Yes!" she replied cordially. It wasn't a minute later that Lucky began to choke and claw at the door behind which she listened indifferently. The claw marks drug upon the grain of the wood were so deep that she was forced to replace the door in its entirety the next day.

As she sprinted through the forest, she again turned to see if he was still close behind, but Lucky was nowhere to be seen, which was lucky for her, as she was at the limit of her physical exhaustion. She gasped and doubled over to catch her breath. She coughed sloppily into the dirt, then, despite the objections of her limbs, dutifully resumed her stumble toward the interstate.

As she continued on, she heard a sorrowful violin playing up ahead. She immediately recognized the sound, and knew the instrument's player, but had no choice but to continue towards it, as she was too close the highway now to turn back, and who knew what worse things might be lurking behind her?

What did you expect? she asked herself abrasively. One cannot haunt a wood for a century and not expect to be haunted as well once mortal and vulnerable too. That axe had two faces.

When she came around the next of the winding road's bends, she saw pitiful Pauline Windsor playing a violin at the side of the road. A black instrument case rested on the floor before her translucent figure. The sound of her mournfully slow violin echoed all around.

Mae walked carefully past the woman, whose eyes were shut as she mournfully drug the bow across her strings. The case had a few single-dollar bills within it, and when Mae's gaze returned to meet Pauline's, the woman's midnight-black eyes stared back at her. Several long red marks lined her neck.

"Ya spare but a quarter, miss?" she asked in a southern drawl that immediately brought Mae back to the day she had offered Pauline room and board at the estate, on the understanding that she'd play her violin whenever Mae requested.

She walked past the woman with a quickening stride, her face contorted to hamper the tears that streamed from her eyes. Her lips quivered as a moan of anguish came from her lips. From somewhere deep within the trees, she heard the unmistakable voice of Reverend Holmes emphatically preaching an unholy sermon.

"Fickle art our designs upon salvation, Rip me from thy talons, oh Lord, and cast thee into the fire! Transcend thy skin, and devour thy soul! Ensnare our pride and deliver us unto thou's vile caress!"

The yelling conjured more terrible memories. Only after he had begun to lose his mind had Mae attended one of his sermons, mere days before the town insisted upon his removal. TO the townspeople's relief, Mae arrived to philanthropically take him with her to the Northern Arizona Rehabilitation Center and Asylum, which of course was only a hole within the earth of the barn.

She quickened her pace and dropped her gaze to the ground in an attempt to avoid any further confrontations with ghosts from her past.

As the reverend's booming exhalations mercifully faded into a dull echo behind her, she rounded a final bend of the road to reveal the crossing highway at long last. Tears streamed down her cheeks, and as she crossed the highway and walked along the westbound shoulder of the 40 with her left thumb protruding into the air, she thought of William and cried.

17

In The Wake

"All I'm saying is that time isn't as big of a deal as you're making it out to be," said Teddy, sitting with his legs crossed on the floor, the head of his girlfriend, Roxanne, resting on his lap. Teddy, Sam had discovered, was the name of the singer of Things Would Be Different If The Whiskey Were Gone. Roxanne lay on her back while crocheting a cloth figurine. Whenever anyone asked what she was making, she'd say "voodoo doll" without a hint of sarcasm or another word of explanation.

Teddy continued, "Neither is death. Everything is just one thing and everyone is the same. There's no future or past or this or that. It just *is*, man. And I think that's pretty fuckin cool."

"That's pretty fuckin fucked, if you ask me," said Blane, who lounged on a couch cushion nearby. His long blonde hair hung over his face like an old English sheepdog, and he twirled drumsticks between his fingers as he spoke. "I'm not the same as no Nazi. I'm not the same as the fucking moon, dude."

Sam chuckled at this statement, and couldn't stop no matter how hard he tried.

Teddy responded despite Sam's breathless cackling. "You're missing the point, man. Everything is just different perspectives of the universe, okay? The universe, everything that's ever been everything, is tired of being everything. Maybe one day it decided to pretend to be something close to nothing for a while. Maybe it wanted to play pretend, for fun, or something. And we're just everything pretending we're space dust."

He leaned forward and gestured wildly with his hands. "Maybe the moon is just the universe pretending to be a giant fucking space rock hanging out nearby and keeping an eye on us."

"Sounds like the moon is a fucking pervert, if you ask me," said Blane, not giving an inch.

Sam's laughter grew inconsolable. He excused himself to the landing outside to get some fresh air and regain his composure.

It had been a long time since he'd smoked weed. Five years, to be exact, and his inexperience was on full display. He marveled at his breath emanating from him with each exhalation. He found himself thinking of Sawyer and the morning hike they took back in Phoenix. What a day that was, he thought. He wondered what that walking enigma was up to. Probably seeing a man about a horse, he figured.

A fluffy snowflake landed on Sam's arm, and he looked up to find a galaxy of snow falling towards him. He squinted his eyes so that it looked like he was taking the Millennium Falcon to light speed. He was enveloped in the thought when he heard footsteps and banter echoing from the alleyway below. He looked down and saw Chester, the burly and inebriated owner of the Beagle Room, striding alongside an unknown figure. They approached the stairwell, each carrying a case of beer on their shoulders.

"Ahoy!" shouted Sam, before bursting into hysterics at the sound of his own voice.

The evening continued, with Sam finally levelling off after a couple of beers to offset, or at least numb, the sharper effects of the marijuana. The figure that had walked alongside Chester in the alleyway turned out to be Melody, a friend of his. Melody was a confident redhead dressed in all black, who owned an occult bookstore down the street. When Chester introduced her to the group, he explained that he and her had become allies at the chamber of commerce meetings as of late, where they'd closed ranks against the affronted family-friendly businesses appealing to affluent tourists and puritans.

Melody handed everyone a sticker of a pentagram with the words *Dark Shadows Bookstore: The Front Lines of The First Amendment* lining its perimeter.

Sam considered the freckled young woman a harmless, albeit expressive, contrarian. She seemed to say whatever she felt, and it was obvious that she was highly intelligent. He watched her casually debate Teddy into intellectual corners, gutting his philosophical assumptions as if they were Build-A-Bears being separated from their stuffing.

He liked her, although she didn't seem to care for him in the slightest.

"So how many babies did you kill?" she asked when they were alone while the rest of the group went outside to smoke.

"Sixteen," he replied with a wink. He wasn't typically so bold, but the social lubricants were doing their job exceedingly well.

Melody didn't appear impressed. "For real, though," she said. "You know you were just a cog, right? In a bloody machine."

Sam sobered a bit. Thoughtfully, he responded, "No... I mean, it wasn't black and white. Good and evil, like you think it's going to be. Staring down the devil in your sights and pulling the trigger. It definitely wasn't that. But we were just kids trying to get along, ya know?"

"Kids in a cogwheel," she said.

"Maybe," said Sam. "But even if so, the kids around me made the cog irrelevant in the first place."

"Just don't start going on about freedom and shit." She at last smiled, to Sam's tremendous relief. He was beginning to think that she might shank him with a cross when he turned his back on her. "People don't think about what that word means anymore. Nowadays, it's just a buzzword to sell gold to baby boomers watching Fox News at 2am."

The group barged back inside, shedding snow from their jackets and smelling of cigarettes. "We've got fifteen minutes until midnight strikes, ladies," announced Chester. "Get your leggings on and let's go see that pinecone hit the dirt."

And so they did. Chester, Melody, Sam, Teddy, and Blane swayed through the streets, joining a similarly swaying crowd marching toward the Weatherford Hotel where the pinecone was hung.

"Where's Tommy and Sean?" Sam asked Teddy.

"Ohh, they're optimists," he said mockingly. "They're back at the apartment getting their beauty rest, 'cause they think the snow's going to stop and that we're going to be driving to California tomorrow." He chuckled and pointed upward at the heavy snow now coating the excursion. "We're not going anywhere tomorrow."

Suddenly, Sam realized that he wouldn't be going anywhere either. He had planned to stay away from the estate for only a night, but he now feared that if he did in fact get snowed in, his stay might get extended a day or two. The remaining influence of THC in his system stirred his initial anxiety, but after a moment of contemplation he determined that if he wouldn't be able to drive to the estate, neither could Ms. Shawmaker. *Unless she had a snowmobile... or a helicopter*, the marijuana argued.

They turned the corner of Aspen, where they became fully absorbed by a sprawling crowd that faced the glittering pinecone strung high on the corner of the hotel's balcony. Above each bundled head rose puffs of vapor. The energy was rising, as the countdown clock behind the pinecone had dipped below three minutes just as they had arrived.

Sam sensed Melody standing beside him, pressing up against his arm. "Do you believe in new year's resolutions, baby killer?" She spoke in a monotone voice and stared straight ahead, but the heavy lean into his shoulder sent a message that was difficult to misinterpret.

"I believe in setting goals. I'm not sure I've ever followed through with a new year's resolution before, but I can appreciate the spirit," he said, suddenly careful with his words.

"Well... maybe this is the year. Why don't we choose something easy? I resolve to not commit grand larceny this year. You?" she asked flatly, now looking at him.

"I'll be holding you to that," he said, smiling. "This year, I resolve to be more present... and to not kill any babies."

The clock hit midnight, and amidst the exploding cheers and faraway thump of fireworks, Sam turned toward her, intending to kiss her in a bout of spontaneity. But instead, as he turned, he found her standing contently still with her eyes closed, and he decided to leave her be.

He felt silly. It seemed that he would fall in love with every girl he spoke with. As he stood surrounded by the cheering crowds celebrating another year gone by, he acknowledged a heavy loneliness billow up inside of him, like a kiln turning his clay into pottery.

In response to a quick vibration in his pocket, he pulled out his phone. There was a notification from the security system back at the estate. His eyes widened and anxiety gripped him, erasing his loneliness. He hurriedly entered his passcode and opened the application. Motion had been detected in the meadow behind the house. He flipped to the camera overlooking the clearing, hoping to see deer grazing in the grass, but instead he saw something else entirely. In the grainy night vision, he saw what appeared to be a figure standing in the dead patch of grass where Sam had made his fire on the solstice. Antlers rose out of the figure's head, and it held a long stick in its right hand, and a flame danced in its upturned left palm.

It stared at the camera with glowing eyes. Motionless.

In his terror, Sam didn't notice the phone slipping from his frozen fingers until it fell into the snow at his feet. He lunged for it, and after clumsily wiping the ice from the screen, saw that the security camera's view of the meadow was now empty. He flipped wildly through the other cameras of the house, and saw nothing out of the ordinary until the screen abruptly flickered and froze into a white screen with text reading: *Water exposure. Please shut off power to prevent damage to device.*

"Motherfucker," he whispered angrily as he held the power button of the phone. Melody seemed to notice his change of demeanor and leaned into him. Sam was furiously blowing into the charging port of the phone and didn't immediately acknowledge her attention.

"What's up?" she asked compassionately.

Sam looked up, slightly embarrassed at being so frazzled.

"I..." He wasn't sure of how much he wanted to share, given the uncertainty and strangeness of his circumstances. But after seeing what appeared to be genuine compassion in her eyes, he relented. "I'm a caretaker of an estate just outside of town. I think I... I think I saw something on the security cameras just now." Sam held out his phone. "But I dropped this fucker in the snow and... now it's bugging out on me."

"What did you see?" she asked, intrigued. "A band of robbers? Mothman?"

"To be honest, I don't know what I saw." He hesitated. He wanted to tell her about the kachina doll. He even thought of mentioning the other peculiarities of the house, but worried she might dismiss him as losing it. But as he plunged his phone back into his pocket, his fingers grazed the sticker that she had given him earlier, and he recalled her appreciation of the occult. A few stories of vague oddities weren't going to send her running in the opposite direction.

"I want to tell you about where I'm staying," he said at last. "About some things I'm... noticing there. Is your shop nearby?" He preferred not to talk about such things amongst the others. He could assume with certainty what their reactions would be.

She cocked her head in growing curiosity. "Are you seeing ghosts, Sam?" she asked in an amused tone.

"I'm not sure if I'd use that word," he replied. "But I'm starting to wonder myself."

18

Veins of Stone

Malaki led the way as he and Mae trekked through rolling thickets of ponderosa pine. They walked with ponchos covering their heads and heavy packs on their backs as the sky let loose a steady torrent of rain.

That morning, tall cumulonimbus clouds had towered overhead as they packed up the remnants of their camp and set off on the second leg of their journey. The day prior, they had traversed what Malaki estimated to be twelve miles of forest. He warned that although the second day's hike would be shorter, it would include a consistent rise in altitude that would make it just as difficult, if not more so, than the first day. The rain wouldn't help, either.

Not long after they ate modest breakfasts of granola and set off, the grey clouds above them opened up, as if on cue. It seemed that the sky carried an entire ocean in its belly and the ground quickly became a sludge.

Throughout the hike not much was spoken, a notable oddity in itself. Mae had always been astonished at how seamlessly she and Malaki communicated, often only sharing filler words and half thoughts as they knew what the other already understood. But on the hike through the dripping forest, Malaki's stoic demeanor was hard to interpret. It was likely due to him being uneasy at the prospect of their journey, and their intentions upon its conclusion, Mae decided.

Her own thoughts relied upon an optimism that she refused to relinquish. The thought of speaking with her brother, even just once, ignited a swelling of hope that warmly coddled her outlook, keeping it dry despite the rain.

She knew the attempt would be precarious. Despite Malaki's lecturing, she understood the dangers of summoning demons. She'd read the anecdotes of survivors of rituals gone wrong. She had read the transcripts of the ravings of the possessed.

But the irony was that Malaki's own words drove her onward despite the dangers that lurked ahead of them. The particular words that drove her forward were words that he had spoken as they had rested lazily within his flat after a particularly exhausting alchemic misadventure in the early days of their partnership. Her and Malaki had attempted to combine a pair of ingredients that were stubbornly disinterested in dancing with one another, and the flat nearly caught fire. The inadvertent combustion was only avoided when Malaki recognized the accelerating catalyzation of the reaction and doused the table in a large pot of water that he kept nearby for that very reason. Evidently, it wasn't the first time that such a thing had happened.

After the dousing, Mae rested on the couch with her legs crossed and protruding into the air while Malaki lay on the floor, staring at the ceiling in dejected manner. When he turned his gaze to discern the demeanor of his apprentice and found Mae's expression to be overtly apprehensive, he spoke an impromptu line of encouragement to douse her unsettled nerves.

"The thin line between success and failure is one's relationship with fear and how much influence one allows it to have on their decisions," he said. "Long ago, I made a promise to myself to never let fear dictate the choices I make. Fear offers a valid perspective, don't get me wrong, but its suggestions are to be taken with a grain of salt, and it hasn't a seat in the cabinet of my influence."

Mae had twiddled with the string of her jacket as she considered the statement. "Who sits in your cabinet, then?" she asked.

"Mostly just my stubborn reluctance to be told how to live life in any particular manner. That sits atop the highest-backed throne, and at times, I am under the impression that I might be in *its* cabinet and not the other way around. What about you, young Mae? What gives you council?" he asked.

At the time, Mae hadn't been sure what to say, and as she hiked through the muddy forest, she still hadn't settled on an answer. But she was confident in one thing: she didn't wish to give fear a seat in her cabinet, either.

Deep down, she had to admit that this pursuit of conjuring William was, in a way, a means of convincing herself that she was free from fear's sticky influence. Trial by fire, she thought. Potentially literally. Before she could cross-examine this concept, she leaned her weight forward and lifted her heavy boots to ascend a particularly steep incline, an act that erased her contemplation due to the strain of physical exertion. By the time she had reached the ridge, her train of thought had shifted.

"We're nearly there!" Malaki called out from up ahead. "You're doing splendid, young one." Then he turned and was off, apparently eager to arrive at the mouth of the cave.

"We're travelling to an old lava tube,' he had explained the night before while sitting on a felled log across the fire from Mae. He hadn't previously shared what their destination was, and she hadn't asked. She trusted him when he said he had a better idea for summoning Gamaliel; only suggesting that she pack for a four-day hike through the woods.

She had considered asking why they hiked instead of taking horses, but she had long ago forgone doubting the man and his sometimes-subtle reasons. Without fail, there always seemed to be one.

He continued, "Some seven hundred thousand years ago, a river of lava flowed down this mountain, fed by a volcanic cinder cone near the peak. The outer edges of the flow cooled and hardened as it made contact with the air, but the inside current kept the river warm, liquid, and moving. While it flowed, the lava dug into the earth like a river of water carving a canyon. When the eruption stopped and the flow of lava finally ceased, the exterior of the river remained while the inside drained, leaving a long, hollow tube running for nearly a mile under the forest floor."

"Was your last apprentice a Geology major?" she asked playfully.

"No, no, no," he laughed. "I only know of it through a friend of a friend. You see, lumbermen stumbled onto the entrance back in 1915 and, being too afraid to venture far into the cave themselves, passed the location to my secondhand acquaintance, who just so happens to be a fan of rocks and lava and those sorts of things. He took me to it last summer, and we hiked almost the entire thing.

When we got nearly a mile inside, I feigned chest pains and asked that we turn back, which we did. The truth is, though, that I had noticed something in the darkness that disturbed me; something that was not quite pleased with our presence. I was in no position to deal with it at the time. I hadn't the resources, and my friend—Shea Collins is his name, by the way—hadn't exactly received the full story regarding my dealings with the occult. I had no choice but to retreat from the cave and act out a mild medical emergency, which of course, resolved itself with fresh air upon our exit. But I remember well the impression that the creature lurking in the darkness had made on me. I felt its gaze piercing my movement and the stench of rotten death nearly overcame me the farther into the cave we went. Shea explained away the scent as being nothing more than a result of the volcanic basalt rock, but I'm no fool. I know the difference between natural sulfur and other things. It left a sour taste in my mouth for weeks afterwards."

His thoughts seemed to drift, and both him and Mae were silent for a long while. An owl's hoot came from somewhere in the distance, audible over the crackling of the fire.

"If I am to be to be frank with you, Mae, and I know that I can be, I never intended to return to that place. In fact, I am quite terrified at the prospect. But your stubbornness..." he noticed her brow furrow and corrected himself, "*determination,* regarding this matter of yours, compels me to join you. To support your learning, if nothing else, as I have truly enjoyed doing over the past several months. And if this is what we are to do, I believe that the lava tubes, which are now only a few short miles away from here, present our best chance at something resembling success."

Mae recited his own words. "The thin line between success and..."

"There are more lines than one that demand respect when it comes to the arcane, young Mae," said Malaki, cutting her off. "We must be careful." His seriousness struck her as sincere and deliberate, and Mae adopted his candor. He was helping her, after all, and she owed him a sincere demeanor.

The rain was an ever-present deluge as the pair approached a scattering of boulders rising from the floor of a ponderosa grove. A deep and wide hole accepted the falling rain into its yawning portal. Frigid air poured from the cave's mouth, prompting both to adorn their heavy jackets.

Malaki dropped his bag to the dirt, undid its straps, and removed an old miner's helmet with a carbide lamp attached to its front. He twisted the lamp open, poured dry carbide into the chamber, and resealed the device, careful to shield the compound from the rain. He then pulled out his water skin and poured a small amount of liquid into the lamp's upper chamber. He held a hand over the lamp to allow the acetylene gas to accumulate, then ripped his hand to one side to spark it. A strong flame burst from the wick, and Malaki put the helmet on his head.

Mae couldn't help but laugh at the sight of her magical mentor adorning the clothing of a blue-collar worker. "Where's your pasty, pitman?" she asked, giggling.

Malaki shook his head but couldn't prevent a smile from crawling across his weathered face. "I do love me a Cornish pasty," he said, before repeating the process and handing Mae a headlamp helmet of her own.

Are you confident with your warding spells?" he asked.

She nodded. He mimicked the action while looking past her anxiously. It was obvious that he was uncomfortable being in this place once again.

"Just... be ready to cast one without much warning," he said. "I don't antic-ipate being outright attacked by this thing... whatever it is... but... just be ready, okay?"

"I will," she replied, suddenly aware of fear loudly protesting at her council of influence.

"Then we shall succeed," he said, patting the top of her helmet playfully. "Let's go."

Malaki picked up his pack and carefully led Mae downward into the mouth of the cave. A stream of water cascaded from the rocky entrance in a water-fall, making the descent slow and treacherous. The frigid air that had seeped from the entrance turned out to be a reliable omen, for as they descended, the temperature dropped at least forty degrees, and the sweat and rain that had accumulated inside Mae's clothing throughout the day made itself known.

After the initial short descent, the cave's entrance levelled off into a natural foyer that opened into a wide and fairly uniform fifteen-foot-high and twenty-foot-wide tunnel that extended beyond. The ceiling was domed, and it reminded Mae of newspaper clippings she'd seen showing the subway tunnels in New York City. Their headlamps took turns dancing along the tall arching ceiling and occasionally down the length of the tube, which stretched far into the shivering darkness.

Nearby, a pile of branches and driftwood had accumulated against a wall. It was the result of flooding, Mae assumed, and she suddenly became anxious of the possibility of being drowned in the cave. Malaki's subsequent words did little to quell her worry.

"We need to go as deep as the tunnel allows," he said, his voice echoing in reverb. "The further we get from the open air, the better chance we have at this."

The ground was covered in jagged rocks of various sizes and textures. Most were uneven ebony rocks and gritty boulders, but the occasional slick face of a rippling sheet of shale made each step unpredictable and dangerous, especially due to the weight of the bags they carried.

Other than the smell of damp earth and sulfur, nothing overtly malicious made itself known. As Mae raised her gaze to examine the tall arching ceiling, she nearly lost her footing and abruptly spun about to keep from falling.

When she regained her balance, she looked up to see a massive shadow rising upon the relief of the wall before her. Panic threatened to overwhelm her before she realized that she had been startled by nothing more than her own shadow cast by the light of Malaki's headlamp behind her.

"Easssyyy, child," he said gently. "Easy."

"Sorry," she replied. "Just... nerves."

"I know. I've got them too, although I've yet to notice anything too... off, just yet... Have you?" he asked.

In all honesty, Mae felt doused in an unshakeable dread of a variety that she was inexperienced. She hadn't seen anything supernatural, beside the trick that the headlamp had played on her eyes. She smelled only the expected sulfur of the rock, and she heard only Malaki's and her own echoing voices and sounds of clumsy movement. And yet, with each step deeper into the cave, a fear seemed to build within her chest. She knew that there was only 50 to 75 feet between them and the surface above them, but the suffocating blackness that evaded their lamps seemed to leech at her skin as if it were darkness from legions below. Darkness that had never known the sky nor the air of the living.

She sensed it when she inhaled, and when she lowered her lamp to illuminate safe places to place her next step. She felt it staring at her from far ahead in the tunnel, above her lamp's tunneled gaze.

But alas, "No," was all she said.

The difficult terrain made their progress slow and deliberate, but after an hour of careful navigation, the pair arrived at a massive wall of fallen rocks and boulders. For all Mae knew, the cave might continue on for many miles beyond the collapse, but this was the end for their journey. In a way, it seemed a mercy in that it forced them to go no further into the depths of the earth's darkness.

A small trickle of water bled from under the rocks of the collapse. It pooled into a murky sump in the middle of the space before escaping in a thin stream that squeezed under a nearby wall.

"End of the line," said Malaki with a sigh of exhaustion. He removed his helmet and let it rest on a Volkswagen-sized boulder nearby. The helmet's lamp faced upward and illuminated the rocky ceiling. They dropped their bags and sat with their backs against the boulder on which Malaki had rested his helmet.

They breathed heavily, and Mae sensed that both dwelled on individual thoughts of trepidation that neither shared aloud. She assumed that both, at least to some degree, were telepathically aware of the stormy seas that raged in the other's mind. She was plenty aware of his, at least.

It wasn't always clear, telepathy. Sometimes it was like reading Braille engraved in the sand. But regardless of its often-vague nature, it was nonetheless impossible for Mae to misinterpret the emanating sensation that thoroughly overcame her mentor sitting beside her.

It was fear that shrouded him.

He wasn't alone in his affliction.

19

Orbis Conclusus Est

"How do we start?" asked Mae, eager both to speak with her brother and to escape the darkness of the cave.

Like Malaki, she rested her helmet upon a nearby boulder. In contrast with the light of his helmet, which illuminated the ceiling, she aligned hers to shine upon the darkness of the tunnel from whence they had emerged.

Malaki deeply inhaled the thick cave air before responding to her question. "The Tome," he said. "We start with the Tome."

When she produced the book, Malaki flipped to its center and stopped between two unremarkable spells of simple prestidigitations intended for the novice mage. Mae was confused. How could magic tricks suitable for a child's birthday party be relevant in a situation like this?

Malaki reached into his pocket and produced a small vial of turquoise liquid. He then popped the vial's cork and poured the liquid liberally upon each of his hands. After discarding the vial and ensuring that the liquid coated all ten of his fingers, he carefully lifted a single page and turned it over. The page that was then exposed was one that Mae had never seen within the book. At the top of the page, the words were written the words, *Summoning Further Entities*.

Malaki noticed Mae's incredulity. "Like I've said... the pages can never be destroyed. But no one said anything about pages being hidden." His voice then lowered in tone and volume. "Listen, I brought us here because I believe the depth will be helpful in capturing Gamaliel's attention. But we may still be forced to contend with whatever it was that I saw here on my initial visit, years ago. I haven't noticed its presence yet, and with any luck it has departed, but in the unfortunate circumstance where both entities decide to appear at once, we will have to split our attention. I can likely conjure and hold Gamaliel on my own, for a brief time at least, but when it appears, you will need to take over, as I haven't the context of William to request of it that which you seek. Whoever among us that is not conferring with the demon should keep a watchful eye on the darkness, lest the other entity decides to join us."

With that, the pair read the Tome's instructions and began their preparations. Malaki produced a large pouch of salt from his bag and with it drew a six-foot-diameter circle upon the floor. Simultaneously, Mae walked about the perimeter of the area making sigils with her hands by tracing shapes in the air while repeating Latin incantations of warding. Malaki produced a stake and a large wooden mallet, and drove the stake into the earth at the center of the circle of salt that he had spilled. He removed from his bag a round linen-wrapped object. He unwrapped the package carefully, revealing a human heart, which he quickly impaled upon the stake.

Malaki noticed Mae watching him apprehensively. "I have a friend in the anatomy department at the university," he said in an apparent attempt to cool her uneasiness. "He allows me access to his cadavers in exchange for vials of vitality, which, if I'm being honest," he said, laughing, "are just suspensions of whiskey, ginger, and cornmeal."

Mae too found humor in the story, but the sight of the heart still disturbed her slightly. In their previous pursuits of magic, Malaki had yet to suggest using any materials of such consequence. She began to understand the weight that he had placed upon the endeavor in which they were now irrevocably engaged. She returned to her sigils for the next several minutes, deciding it best, if only for the sake of her growing anxiety, that she not observe the rest of the ritual to which he attended nearby.

"Mae," Malaki said when his preparations were complete. "Three things..."

She stood nervously against a boulder. She had been confident until they had descended into the cave. Now her confidence was being sucked away by the humid darkness.

"Number one," Malaki continued. "Trust yourself. You can do this. Number two, make no contract with this thing. No matter what it says, it will lie to you.

Anticipate that. Number three, and most importantly, if you wish to conclude the ritual for any reason, you can do so by saying the following words: 'Orbis conclusus est.' Now repeat it back to me."

"Orbis conclusus est," she replied.

"Very good... Are you ready?" he asked.

She hesitated, then stated that she was. Malaki nodded, not unlike how he had when they had first entered the cave.

"Keep an eye on the tunnel and be ready," he said. "I'll let you know when it's time for you to take over." Slowly, he approached the circle of salt. He knelt before it and lowered his head in quiet meditation.

Minutes passed without even the movement of the wind to mark the seconds. Mae kept her gaze on the long, tall cave beyond them. The light of her headlamp soaked into the ground, walls, and ceiling of the tunnel beyond, after which darkness swallowed all.

"Mae," said Malaki abruptly after several minutes of silence. His head remained lowered and his eyes were shut. "We have arrived at the ultimate step of this terrible matter. I need to whisper an incantation that cannot be spoken in the light. I need you to extinguish the flames of our headlamps."

Mae was hesitant. "I... I'd be afraid to, Mal," she stammered. She suddenly felt like she was a little girl watching the cattle being led away by the traders that came to call.

"Do it!" he muttered between gritted teeth. Mae had never heard a tone so malicious come from his lips, giving her pause. He continued, noticing her reluctance. "Mae, if you don't extinguish those flames, I will be unable to bring back your brother." His voice gurgle, and there was something else... a Bostonian twist, whereas his voice was normally dignified and posh. She looked closely at the man and quietly gasped as she saw faint blue veins scattered like lightning beneath his pale skin. She became aware of a rancid smell suddenly assaulting her nostrils. She fought back the urge to vomit and stepped slowly toward the *Tome of Instruction* resting nearby.

Banishment, she recalled, was on page 134.

"Yes, Mal," she said, trying to disguise her intentions. "I'm going to shut them off now."

The Tome lay open upon a nearby boulder, but when she lifted its body, her shaking hands scattered several loose rocks to the floor that had being lying beside the book. Malaki rose to his feet slowly and clumsily turned to face Mae. His eyes remained closed and his body moved awkwardly as if it was the first time its controller had moved a bipedal skeleton with intention. He seemed taller than he had been minutes before.

Mae grasped the book tightly and stood, transfixed on whatever it was that loomed before her. Malaki stood before her, but for reasons found in the uncanny valley of observation, it was clearly not so.

"Orbis conclusus est," she yelled with an air of desperate authority.

A wide smirk grew on Malaki's face, while his eyelids remained tightly sealed. The voice that came from him now abandoned any attempt of mimicking Malaki's voice, instead shifting to a gargled sound like rock grinding heavily upon rock. "Arrogant creatures of light." It gasped and growled. "Wastrels, beckoning others beyond thy warrant." The creature turned and began walking toward Malaki's headlamp, which illuminated the ceiling above them. When it reached the device, it began to slowly twist the knob of its water regulation valve. After a few twists, the lamp began to flicker, then fully extinguished. Mae's lamp, which rested against a boulder adjacent, was now the only source of light amongst them.

"One is gone, one remains, then no more light shall haunt thy veins," the creature gurgled.

Mae flipped frantically through the pages and found the spell of banishment. She was relatively familiar with the spell, which was simple, but she required a reminder of some nuanced pronunciations of the Latin. She scanned the page in haste as the creature began to twist the knob of her headlamp's water valve. "Now, suffer me," it growled.

She had rapidly read all but the last sentence of the incantation when the light flickered out. In the darkness, she looked up, and saw a pair of green glowing eyes with black slitted pupils staring back at her.

"Excidat haec praesens tenebra, in aeternum damnata. Per ignem, per lucem, abscede nunc!" she bellowed with a shake in her larynx.

The eyes drifted nearer.

"Excidat haec praesens tenebra, in aeternum damnata. Per ignem, per lucem, abscede nunc!" she repeated, this time in a distressed wail.

Nothing changed, despite the ever-approaching gaze of the lizard green eyes and the growing pace of her fearful breathing. She must have pronounced something incorrectly. Even a single syllable pronounced incorrectly would have left the spell impotent.

The eyes drew nearer. Mae turned to run, but immediately tripped on a boulder and fell upon its jagged peak, gashing her flank and leaving her writhing in agony.

She spun about and looked up to see the creature's bright eyes peering down at her.

"Die," it gurgled, falling upon her body with a splash. It devoured her flesh piece by piece while the sounds of her bones snapping echoed through the narrow, dark cave.

But despite its intention, it didn't inhale all, as Mae's ego remained. After moments of unimaginable suffering, her awareness drifted softly upward, as if she were being brought to the surface of the Dead Sea by salty buoyancy. She saw everything about her, heard the terrible sounds of her body being mutilated, but felt nothing but the welcome comfort of nothingness as she floated upward and through the rocky ceiling. Her perspective rose through the rock, higher and higher, until at last she rose out of the ground to float gently above the forest floor high above the cave.

Once above the ground, her momentum shifted, and she began floating through the trunks of the trees like a balloon being carried by a soft breeze. The rain persisted, and she shifted her gaze in the direction that she was now moving. Upon doing so, she became aware of what was pulling her: squarely in the direction of her momentum was a muscular young man hiking alone through the trees. A daypack clung to his shoulders and he moved with a spry gait.

Mae, without any semblance of control, careened directly into his chest.

Immediately, she acknowledged that she possessed the faculties of the young man. His skeleton collapsed to the ground.

As she opened her newly acquired eyelids to stare at the wet forest floor beneath her, something twisted and squirmed deep within her. Before she could investigate the sensation, it ceased its movement, and Mae, for reasons that were utterly mysterious to her, was confident that it was dead.

20

The Ghosts of Old Coconino

Sam and Melody Irish goodbyed from the rest of the group and began walking toward Dark Shadows Bookstore. It wasn't far, but the chilly air seemed to carry a sharper bite than it had on the way to the pinecone drop. As they approached the storefront, Sam saw that the glass to the left of the central entrance displayed an array of books, a large split geode, a propped-up mammalian spine, and a taxidermied skunk. To the right of the door, plywood covered what was obviously once glass.

"Brick," Melody explained before Sam could even ask. She gestured toward the spray-painted *FUCK YOU* scrawled across the plywood. "Although *that* was me."

She unlocked the door and led Sam through a series of tall and winding rows of bookshelves, each categorized and labeled efficiently. He wasn't sure what he had expected, exactly, but he was surprised by the cleanliness and organization of the store. They passed handmade directory signs reading *Tarot*, *Mythology*, *Folklore*, *Alchemy*, *Astrology*, *Crystals*, *Eastern Religions*, *Demonology*, *Paranormal Studies*, and on and on. They finally reached the apparent rear of the store and walked down a long narrow corridor flanked by tall bookshelves. A red directory sign on the left side read *Left Hand Magic*, while a blue sign on the right read *Right Hand Magic*.

At the end of the corridor was a black door with a sign that read, *Danger. Death Beyond*, and again Sam thought back to Sawyer and the house at the end of Tequila Lane. Melody pulled out a keyring, unlocked, and opened the door, leading to a surprisingly ordinary office.

"I was expecting a witch's lair," said Sam cheekily.

"Yah, the insurance company didn't want to cover my Nganga," she replied.

"Your what?" Sam asked, perplexed.

"Never mind," she said, falling upon the leather couch against the back wall of the room. In all, the office contained the couch, a desk holding old blue MacBook, a tall filing cabinet, and a couple of cushioned chairs beside an end table with a stained-glass light fixture upon it.

Sam took a seat in one of the chairs and looked down at the floor. It was old hardwood sealed with a bourbon hue. "You can't be older than twenty-five," he said cautiously. "How'd you come to own a place like this so young?"

Melody just stared at him flatly, pointedly refraining from entertaining his question.

"Gotcha... So..." he began.

He proceeded to tell her everything regarding the oddities that he had been experiencing. The bouts of sudden tinnitus and anxiety paired with peering darknesses. The solstice night, when the lights of the house had come on unexpectantly, and the hand on his shoulder in the woods. Ms. Shawmaker arriving, but not actually arriving. The kachina doll. The general eeriness and the whispers he half-heard in the stairwell. Finally, he shared what he had seen on the security camera that very night.

As he spoke, he began to regret his decision to share at all. He felt he was rambling about nothing, with no hard evidence, only anxiety and hallucinations. She's going to laugh me out the door, he thought. But as he continued, he studied her face for any indication of apprehension and saw nothing but growing curiosity and attentiveness to his words.

When he finished, she paused for a long time, staring at the hardwood floor. She then stood and walked out the door without saying a word. Sam was sure she intended to lead him to the front door to show him out, and he even stood to begin his walk of shame. But when he walked to the doorway of the office, he instead found her returning down the long corridor with a large leather-bound book in her hands.

"Where did you say this property was?" she asked. "The one you're looking after?" She plopped the book down onto the desk and pulled an office chair out before producing a pair of reading glasses from one of the desk's drawers nearby. Sam thought the glasses gave her an air of unexpected elegance. As she cracked the book's spine, he looked at its title: *Notable Early Homesteads of Coconino Forest and Northern Arizona.*

She opened to a fold-out map of the area, and Sam pointed to the general location where Emerald Acres was located—which was easy, as an icon was located on the map at that spot. Melody moved to a table and turned to a page halfway through the book.

She began to read in a transatlantic accent:

"In the late 1890s the railways to northern Arizona were thoroughly established, enticing ambitious settlers from the east out west. In the mid 1890s, one of those families, the Barretts, took that journey and ventured to Arizona in search of land to call their own. This was, of course, possible due to the Homestead Act that President Abraham Lincoln signed into law in 1862, allowing for heads of households to claim up to 160 acres of land, in accordance with blah blah blah." Melody skipped ahead in the text. "The Barrett family elected to claim a parcel of land that had previously been hotly contested by the Hopi Indian tribe. During the many years of surveying prior, government surveyors were forced to call in the army on multiple occasions to disperse the Hopi from the area. From the few interpreted exchanges with the tribe regarding the land that the Barretts eventually chose to call their own, it seemed that the tribe had claimed the land as dangerous and that no man should reside there. The surveyors were not deterred by the red man's tricks, and the Barretts came to reside upon the idyllic land in late 1898." Melody rolled her eyes and shook her head. "Racist ass white people." She continued, "Over the next several years, the Barretts raised cattle, sheep, and various livestock on the land and had tremendous success in their associated businesses in trade. Eventually, in 1927, one of the daughters of the settling Barretts, Susy Childers, inherited and sold the land to Wells Fargo Bank to settle a gambling debt of her husband's..."

She read ahead silently as if to ensure that nothing else of value could be gained from the text, then closed the book with a thud and looked decisively up at Sam while removing her glasses. "You're living on some cursed land, dude."

"C'mon," he said, chuckling. "That's a leap, right? Sure, it used to be Indian land, but everything out here used to be Indian land. Plus, it sounds like the family that homesteaded there did just fine." He was grasping at anything the least bit logical besides ancient native curses and the supernatural.

"Not all bad things in this world are as immediate in their maliciousness as radiation," she replied. "Some dark things... take time."

"Fair," admitted Sam, "but what about my tinnitus and those episodes? I started getting those before I even got there."

"That, my friend—and this is going to sound a lot less sexy—sounds like stress. I used to get these terrible migraine headaches back in the day, where..."

"This wasn't a migraine," said Sam abruptly.

She seemed to recognize his offense and extended her hands in apology. "You're right. I'm sorry. It wasn't a migraine. But from my vantage point, given your history, and with me being completely objective here, abrupt bouts of tinnitus mixed with strong uneasiness sounds like symptoms of anxiety. I could be wrong, but I doubt that has anything to do with the supernatural, as much as I might want it to be." Her eyebrows rose abruptly and excitement replaced her sensitivity. "But this Hopi shit," she pointed at the book, "That kachina doll. The FUCKING WOMAN ARRIVING AND THEN VANISHING?! That sounds pretty wild. Combine that with what we just learned about the history of the land... I think we might have something there."

Sam hadn't seen this type of vigor in her before. She appeared genuinely excited about the possibility of stumbling upon a Native American paranormal encounter. He stood on the precipice of either being terrified by her words, or being over the moon at being the one to have given her something that excited her so. He decided to choose the latter, and relished in her beaming smile.

"Okay, okay," he conceded. "So, what do we do now? Get a priest or something?"

She laughed. "No. I don't think the Pope knows much about the Hopi gods. I, however, have a friend that might. If you can hold off going back there for one more day, I bet I can get him to meet us."

"The snow might not give me a choice. Who's your friend?" he asked.

"Name's yao. Reserved old man, but he runs the Native American Studies department over at the university. A few weeks ago, I came across some books that were of interest to him, so he owes me a favor."

Sam didn't have any plans for the rest of his stay, and the prospect of spending more time with Melody appealed to him. He longed to turn the conversation to more lighthearted matters and potentially get to know her better more on a personal level, but her darting eyes suddenly suggested that she was considering other matters and that she might be eager to conclude their evening. He was always cautious to not overstay a welcome, as his midwestern parents implemented in him a social awareness that flirted with neuroticism.

"Thank you, Melody. Really," he said as he rose to his feet. Melody just smiled and nodded in response. "I'll come back in the morning."

As he opened the office door, he gestured toward the corridor beyond and the signs that hovered above the bookshelves along its sides. "What's the difference between left and right-hand magic?" he asked.

Melody smirked mischievously. "Whether you want to follow the rules or not."

Sam trudged through the heavy snow back to the hotel. The snow was accumulating quickly on the streets. He figured there was at least already half a foot on the ground. It was a windless night, so the snow fell straight down in vertical lines upon his hood and shoulders. He had always hated the wind, and was glad that the snow was easy to keep out of his eyes.

He thought of Melody, and wrestled with an urge to romanticize his new friend. She had been kind to him, and her directness was a welcome contrast to his passivity. But that didn't necessarily imply romance, and he chided himself for constantly tumbling down stairwells of imagined love. He tried his best to minimize his imaginings of his hand in hers, but had little success. Her ginger hair danced freely in his mind as he walked through the snow.

His phone was still off, as he wanted to ensure the battery was fully dried before he turned it back on. He wondered what time it was, and figured it was at least two in the morning. He realized he hadn't passed a single other human, or car, for that matter, and all was silent, muted by the snow, except for his heavy breath and his boots crunching the powder.

It was exhausting work, especially as he was still acclimating to the altitude of the mountain.

He had only a couple blocks left to go, but stopped on the corner of Cherry and Leroux to catch his breath. As he looked about the scene, he could at last appreciate the utter, and almost eerie silence that replaced the sounds of his walking. Most of the businesses had left their Christmas lights on, the sidewalk lamps were brightly lit, and the snow fell all around him, but the muted silence and isolation of the scene made for an uncanny juxtaposition between the sights that he saw and the lack of sound.

Then, just like that, it was no longer silent. A sharp ringing began in his ears, and with it, his heart began to race. He spun around with a pressing need to scan his surroundings. He hadn't need search long, as his gaze quickly locked upon a dense pocket of darkness at the end of Cherry St. It was distant, two full blocks away, but where the streetlamps ended, where the businesses ceased, existed a thick blackness with immense gravity that seemed to claw at Sam's sight. He again had the overwhelming urge to sprint away from its gaze. It was the very same sensation he had experienced behind the gas station while he waited for AAA to arrive.

His surprise and angst toward the dark specter, if that's what it was, turned from anxiety to anger. "It's just a tiger in the forest," he muttered to himself. His voice quivered and primal fear began to rise in his guts. His vision became vignetted and as he glared into the darkness, he clenched his fists. "Tigers," he muttered again, and began trudging toward the absence of light at the end of the road.

His instincts screamed at him to stop, but his anger wouldn't hear it. He was going to show his rattled nerves that there was nothing in the darkness to be feared. There was nothing to fear but his own hypervigilance. He felt a tear roll down his cheek. He moved his arms to rack back the charging handle to make sure that there was brass in the chamber, but found his arms empty. No rifle.

He slapped his face and quickened his pace toward the edge of the streetlamp's illumination.

He stopped before he entered the darkness. He felt as if he were standing at the edge of a cliff, looking directly into the void. Of course, the unlit streets beyond were not pitch black. He could still see the muted snow-covered street and sidewalks in the glow of the streetlights and Christmas ornamentations of the city streets behind him. But what called to his attention was the humanoid-sized blackness that stood in the empty road not fifty feet ahead of him. It was a floating impenetrable blackness that hugged to the uncanny valley of Sam's perception. The sight, whatever it was, was not overtly menacing or objectively dangerous, although it's appearance suggested to some long-ago forgotten defense mechanism within him that he should run from its presence while the tinnitus in his ears rose and reached a grotesque fever pitch.

The pitch began to warble in his ears.

"Sam," it seemed to say, in a high-pitched flutter.

That was enough to convince Sam's conscious mind to agree with the subconscious. He turned to run, but his legs wouldn't move. His arms trembled. He was stuck. It was similar to a bout of sleep paralysis, a sensation that he truly despised. Another tear fell down his cheek as the figure began suddenly walking toward him.

Sam tried everything he could to move, but the effort was useless. His nerves were locked and he hadn't the key. He tried to yell out, but all that he mustered was a long, labored groan that seeped from his gaping mouth.

The figure continued toward him. Sam had been abandoned by all that was good in the world. His bones suddenly felt like they were whittled out of old, dead trees, and he smelled nothing but moist earth. He managed a slow blink and, and when his eyes again opened, the pocket of blackness stood before him, not two feet away.

The void incarnate. Black as midnight oil. It had no features but for its outline that whisked in and out of itself like a black mist gently contained by some innate force of the world. The sound of a crackling fire accompanied the high-pitched ringing now.

A low gurgling sound then rumbled in his ears, accompanied by a harmonizing scream that lay a whole octave above it. If an old tree, from which many a man had hung, could speak, it would make a similar sound.

It repeated itself twice, and on the second repetition, Sam's vaguely conscious mind came to comprehend the words that it spoke.

"Wake up," it seemed to say.

"You okay, mister?" asked a voice.

The blackness was gone, as was the curdling in his stomach, the burning of his skin, the void within his lungs, and everything else that accompanied its presence. Sam spun to his right to find a gruff old man pulling a sled full of supplies, staring at him curiously.

"Ya look like ya saw a ghost or sumpin'," he said in a thick Appalachian accent. "Ya got a dollar?"

Sam quickly groped at his limbs to confirm that he could move them once again before looking back into the muted streets beyond to confirm that the blackness was gone. When he was confident of this fact, he hastily trudged away in the direction of his hotel without saying a word. He lacked anything meaningful to say.

"Well fuck you too, buddy! I hope ya freeze ta death," yelled the old man, well behind him now.

21

Whispers of Undoing

Mae's walk along the shoulder of Interstate 40 was short-lived, as a sky-blue Ford Bronco pulled off after only five minutes of thumbing. A sticker on the back window read: *PEACE, LOVE, AND DEATH TO NAZIS*.

Mae approached the open passenger-side window and discovered a leather-faced woman tipping her hat upward with a thumb while leaning across the center console.

"Get on in if cigarette smoke don't bother ya," she said in a gruff Texas accent, unlatching the door. "How far ya headin'?"

"Just to town," said Mae, getting in and closing the door behind her. She had done her best to dry her eyes before entering the vehicle, but her face surely remained scarred by the cold. She tried to keep her eyes directed out the passenger side window in an attempt to avoid the questions that were sure to come.

"To town it is, then. Name's Wendy. Yours?" asked the driver.

"Mae," she replied quietly, unaware of the slip. She was lost in memories in which Mae was still the only name she possessed.

The Bronco smelled heavily of incense and burnt tobacco, and the winding melodies of a sitar bleeding from the speakers made for a slightly nauseating experience. But it was a ride, nonetheless. All Mae needed was to get to the bed of her apartment and all would be easier; she could approach navigating the labyrinth of... everything, after that.

She noticed Wendy occasionally peeking in her direction as she brought the vehicle up to the speed of the highway.

"So... What's your story, hun?" she asked. Mae had been hoping she wouldn't. "Ya need a place to stay or somethin'?" Wendy's voice was bassy and tough, yet her face was kind. The lines about her eyes suggested she'd seen a thousand things. Her straw cowboy hat routinely dipped down over her eyes, requiring her to lift its brim.

"I got lost in the woods," Mae said. "I was hiking, and I lost my way. That's all."

Wendy snorted dismissively. "I'll tell you what, darlin', I ain't never seen someone hike in Doc Martens."

"Well, now you can tell all your friends," replied Mae in a monotone voice. She didn't want to be rude to the woman. She was being helpful in an existence otherwise doused in foes. Regardless, Mae felt her patience draining away with every word that was spoken.

"It's been a long day," she said after an awkward pause in the conversation. "I don't really feel like talking, if I can be frank."

"You just be Mae, now. Pretty country. We oughtta enjoy it." With that, Wendy lit a cigarette, and carried the Bronco onward toward flagstaff.

When they approached the curb outside of Mae's apartment, Mae paused and turned toward Wendy before exiting the vehicle. "Do you have any ghosts?" she asked, surprised by her own words.

"So *now* you wanna chat," Wendy said with a laugh, throwing her hands into the air in exasperation. "What do you mean? Like, do I have regrets?"

"Yes," said Mae bluntly.

Wendy observed Mae curiously and tipped the brim of her hat back above her eyes. "I guess I've made as many bad decisions as the next person out there."

"The worst ones... The ones that haunt you... How do you stop them from keeping you up at night?" asked Mae. Her question was not abstract. She was acutely worried of being kept awake when she finally lay down upon her mattress.

Wendy reached forward and turned off the radio before turning to face Mae. She cleared her throat. "I guess I just tell myself that I was plopped onto this Earth without my consent, and all I've ever been able to do is my best. Now, sometimes my best ain't as good as I might want it to be, but damnit, I don't have to justify my existence to anyone or anything."

She must have noticed a sadness suddenly billow in Mae's eyes, as her demeaner turned decisively consolatory, if not outright maternal.

"And neither do you, miss Mae. Now dear, you're so young. You've got your whole life ahead of you. No matter what you've done, I want you to remember one thing: life is a game of improv and all we can do is *'yes, and'*. You got me?"

She lifted Mae's chin just as she would lift the brim of her hat. Mae gave a half smile and looked upward and away as she exited the cab. "Thanks for the ride," she said softly.

Mae opened the door of her modest apartment, collapsed into the bed, and slept for a day and a half. Her dreams were null, to her relief, and she ceased to exist in any form that troubled her.

When she finally awoke, feeling spry and optimistic, she found that the day's rest had bestowed upon her an idea. She had always been astonished as to what a well-rested mind could accomplish. It seemed to be a superpower that humanity took for granted. We spend a third of our lives in a state of absent hibernation, our bodies recreating and processing things that our wakeful minds cannot, and yet we as a species have come to overlook this miracle as being mundane, if not an inconvenient stoppage in the meaningless production-line of our existence.

But sleep was a joy for Mae when her sleep wasn't rife with terrible nightmares of the stars, those infinite jesters. Its only other detriment was that it reminded her of an ultimate rest that mockingly avoided her. On this occasion, it had blessed her with a whisper of hope in her pursuit of the long nap that she so desired.

She departed hastily and walked to the bookstore nearby.

A small crowd of protesters milled outside the entrance holding picket signs and singing hymns. The group was comprised of members of the same evangelical church that had come to denounce the store on the same day of each month. It must be the fourth, she thought. They always came on the fourth.

The signs were varied but thematic, and Mae could tell that the group put plenty of time and effort into their creations. One of the signs even had glitter along its border. She thought that some of the sign holders might be in competition with one another, to see whose sign could denounce the store's evil with the most pizzazz.

One sign read, *Turn back, repent, be saved,* while another read, *Seek truth, not spirits!* Her favorite read, *Don't sell your soul for a paperback!*

During her monthly interactions with the group, she would typically mingle with them outside the store to rouse the fervor of the crowd as best she could. She got a bit of a kick out of it, and even looked forward to their monthly protests. It had become a game, and she figured that the attention that she gave them only encouraged their desire to return each month. On occasion, she would even dress up for their arrival, wearing Kiss makeup or arriving at the store doused in blood, which, of course, was only water with red food-coloring, as she wouldn't waste any real blood on their account.

Today, she hardly acknowledged the crowd. They shouted, hooted, and hollered, but Mae just lowered her head, unlocked the door, and entered the bookstore. She left the *Closed for the Day* sign still hanging on the doorknob.

She immediately began searching throughout the store for a book that she vaguely remembered coming across some months before, although she couldn't recall exactly where it had ended up. She remembered it being amongst a similar pile of donated books, and hoped that it hadn't yet been sold. The tricky thing, was that she didn't recall which section she had placed it in, and the ambiguity of the book's contents could have led her to place it in several different locations. She scanned the bookshelves dedicated to invocation magic without any luck. Next, she checked interdimensional studies, but again came up empty. The same was true for shadow magic, familiar conjuration, and even the ever-vague bookshelf dedicated to "miscellaneous oddities."

She was nearly ready to accept defeat and begin crafting a new plan when she had a sudden inspiration to look in the return bin. Sure enough, there it was. *The Codex of Ascendant Shadows and Familiar Dimensions.*

The text was dense, and Mae soon recalled why she had lost interest in the book when it had initially crossed her path. Its spine was four inches wide and its table of contents alone spanned three pages. Its author, Tacitus Kilgore III, was described on the back of the codex as being *an astute master of dark studies and manipulation of the fourth dimension and beyond!* His photo, once black and white, had faded into a shadowy blur.

Mae sat in the aisle between the bookshelves and scanned the text, hoping to find something that might promise the incredibly specific and esoteric purpose that she pursued. For when she had awoken from her stirless sleep, a course of action had come to her. If it was possible, she could theoretically undo her sins and relinquish herself of the punishment that Masau'u had promised to levy upon her.

Her idea was superficially simple: to find a way to undo the past and prevent her victims from crossing her path in the first place. If she could harness powerful enough magic, she could theoretically manipulate the paths of her victims to prevent them from dying at her hand.

But that sort of magic was beyond even the most studied of magicians. She considered herself to be among the best in most arcane engagements, but her knowledge was generalized, without much emphasis on any particular topic beyond alchemy, of which she was most certainly among the best in the world.

But what the codex seemed to suggest, at least in chapter titles and in the abstracts of its relevant sections, was that what she sought may be possible, with substantial effort and attention given to the many subtleties involved. Much digging within its heaping and layered texts would still be required before anything substantial could be discerned. Until she did, she could only wonder as to what energy and resources it might require, and she subtly feared that her new designs might demand as much, if not more, sacrifice than the sins she was hoping to annul.

She rose to her feet and carried the book to her office where she closed the door behind her, despite the store being empty. She placed the book atop her desktop, pulled up her chair, and commenced a long and uninterrupted bout of study. She had hoped for a quick resolution to her predicament, but the size and thickness of the book quickly humbled her impatience.

She would be required, it appeared, to earn via careful study the elusive and long sleep that she so desperately desired.

22

The Fogged Glass and The Left Hand Path

uted light spilled through the drapes of room 601 while the snow outside continued falling in a cold accompaniment to the approaching morning. Sam lay in bed with his gaze set emptily upon the ceiling. He had found no sleep throughout the night. Not with the terrible visage of the black void still burning its imprint into his memory; its voice still reverberating in his skull.

Terrifying as the experience was, he still grasped for logic to quell his uneasiness. It had been a long day, he reasoned, and he had gone about drinking and smoking without having dinner the night before. No wonder he was seeing things. The cold had likely played a part in impacting his nerves, as well. But more than anything, he finally, and for the first time fully, came to acknowledge that the trauma he had inherited in war was something that he by himself could not nullify. It was a clear and forgone conclusion now, no longer up for debate. He needed help, and he resolved to make an appointment with his doctor that week. He'd have called the office right then and there if it wasn't New Year's Day. The office was surely closed.

He intended to thank Melody for being so blunt with him about it. There was a lot that he hadn't yet processed from his time overseas. There were things he wanted to simply hide away in the drawers of his mind, but they proved to be clever things that constantly found ways to crawl out and dishevel ones hair. They wouldn't let him be.

But now, as he finally and deliberately stared the issue in the face, a sense of calm returned to his mind. The cliche was true: the hardest part of getting help was asking for it. And now that he'd made up his mind that he would, everything else seemed to rest lighter upon his shoulders.

He reached for his phone on the bedside table, and was glad to see it turn on without issue. When he looked at the security camera app, he saw that nothing appeared to be out of sorts at the property, and the view of the meadow showed only an empty and snowy field.

To his great relief and simultaneous apprehension, he discovered that the system saved camera footage for 24 hours. When he checked the reel from midnight the night before, a shiver traversed his body.. He rolled the footage back three times. There it was, exactly as he remembered it to be. The figure with antlers upon its head, glaring hauntingly into the camera's eye. Then, from one frame to the next, it was gone.

At least I didn't hallucinate that, he thought.

He had a missed call and a text from Melody. *Meet me at Building 4, room 413 at noon. Don't be late, and don't embarrass me.*

Sam just shook his head and got dressed.

Ten till midday, Sam walked down a long and impressive corridor in building four of the university, where he found Melody sitting on a wooden bench, reading. The hall was wide and its freshly waxed floor mimicked the glistening light of the stained-glass walls that culminated each end. His boots squeaked with each step, wet from the snow outside, so there was no sneaking up on her. However, she didn't look up until he stopped only a few feet away.

"Ready?" she asked without looking up from her book.

The two entered a wooden door with a foggy glass window embedded into it. A brass plate outside the door read:

Dr. Kyao Kwatoko Lomayaoma

Director of Native American Studies

Inside was a stuffy office in which a grey old man stood in the center of the room, putting golf balls down a long strip of artificial grass toward an elevated white plastic cup. In the corner of the room, a desk messily covered in papers stood before a chalkboard covered in tangents of thought.

"Hello friends," he said politely, abandoning the putt he had been aligning. "Come on in."

It didn't take long for Kyao to respond with curiosity to what Sam shared. He took particular interest in the kachina doll and the footage of the meadow. "That sounds a lot like Masau'u, the god of death, fire, and earth," he said.

Sam's eyebrows shot to the sky. Melody paced behind him, laughing. "Well," she said, "that doesn't sound very good."

Kyao chuckled. "No, if what you're telling me is true, it does not sound very good." He stifled his laughter and turned to look at Sam intently. "From what I know of this piece of land, is that my ancestors knew something about it that I do not. But whatever it was, they thought the land dangerous and avoided it at all costs. They settled widely and evenly throughout the forest, but left those few square miles of good, fertile land untouched."

He pointed to Sam's phone on the desk, still displaying the paused footage of the figure in the meadow. "Now that, like I said, seems to me to resemble Masau'u's personification. My people see Masau'u as representing the natural balance between life and death. Not in an inherently malevolent way, but as something to be respected. Much like the secular visage of the grim reaper, he helps spirits cross over to the afterlife, and he is the keeper of the underworld. He is also the guardian of the Earth, the Fourth World. He reminds us that the land is not ours to own or destroy, but something that demands respect and humble interaction."

His face grew stern. "If I were you, I would leave this land to itself, just as my ancestors did. Again, I don't know what they knew about the place or how it relates, if at all, to Masau'u, but I would take a cautious approach here." He walked back toward the putting green and picked up the putter. "In our belief system, Masau'u punishes those that disregard the natural balance of the world, and personally, I wouldn't want to be the one to be punished on behalf of all humanity. Not after all the terrible things that we have done to this world."

Sam and Melody walked side by side out the double doors and through the snow toward downtown Flagstaff. Neither said a word, each deep in their own thoughts. Sam was shaken by what the man had said. No wonder the previous caretaker had left. At the moment, he considered doing so himself. He opened his mouth to state his intention of leaving the property, so that it could be someone else's problem, when he was beaten to the punch by Melody.

"You asked me last night the difference between left and right hand magic," she said. "I didn't lie when I said that it's about whether or not you want to follow the rules, but it's also the difference between practicality and scholarly bureaucracy."

Sam hadn't any idea of what she was getting at, and remained silent.

She continued, now gesturing with her hands with enthusiasm. "I don't have enough time on my hands to read the libraries of texts required to practice right hand magic. Plus, most of those that do are just nerds that need an opportunity to dress up in cloaks and end up in prisons of the ego. I have, however, dabbled a bit on the left side of the aisle." She looked over at Sam, as if to gauge his reaction. "The best way I can describe it is that if right hand magic is the heavily guarded front door to the mansion, left hand magic is the long-forgotten sewer entrance built for bootlegging."

"Are you telling me that you're a witch?" Sam asked, smirking.

"I consider myself more of an arcanist," she replied confidently. "But what I'm getting at is..." She paused, seemingly deep in thought. "Maybe I can help you get rid of this thing. I've read about a spell of banishment, where all we..."

"Woah, woah, woah, woah, woah." Sam stopped walking and looked at Melody with a sudden air of seriousness. "Look. I'm no religious zealot. But from what I gathered from Doctor whatever-his-name-was back there, is that antagonizing this thing might be a bad idea."

"I didn't say we'd antagonize it," said Melody. "We'd just..."

"Kill it?" said Sam sarcastically.

"Send it back to where it came from," she continued without acknowledging Sam's wit. She turned and approached him. "Look. I can do this. Let's go there. Together." She reached out and held his hands gently, making Sam stifle a gasp at the softness of her touch. "Just for one night," she continued, "and that's all. Please... let me help you."

"I don't want to go back there," he said pensively. "With or without you."

She pulled from his grasp with a sullen and dejected demeaner. Did his words truly hurt her so?

It was blindingly true. He didn't want to go back. And he sure didn't want to be a part of some satanic banishment ritual, or whatever it was Melody had in mind. He wanted only to dust his hands of the whole thing and drive down the mountain back to Phoenix. He suddenly missed the valley city and regretted skipping the semester at Arizona State. He wished he had stayed and not taken to an adventure of whimsy to sit by himself in someone else's home.

But he knew that he had to at least go back once more to grab his things. He might as well go with Melody. He reached out and retrieved her hands and squeezed them gently to prevent her from pulling away again. He realized then that he hadn't held a woman's hand in quite some time. It warmed his heart in a way that he wasn't fully expecting nor prepared for, and when he looked up into her pleading eyes, he was all but undone.

He sighed breathily in surrender. "One night..."

She smiled succinctly and gave him a quick kiss on the cheek. He would have continued speaking, but was so rocked by the touch of her lips that he lost his train of thought entirely. She finished it for him. "And it will be gone. Money back guarantee," she said, and winked.

Despite her confidence, Sam was not looking forward to staying another night in the house. He was beginning to suspect that all of his rationalizations about ghosts and the supernatural were nothing but covers for deep-seated fears of such things. He felt confident brushing aside talk of phantoms and looming evils when their presence was theoretical, but now, his darting eyes gave him away.

Sam returned to his room at the Monte Vista and spent the rest of the day resting and appreciating the snowy view out the window that Howard Hughes had enjoyed so long ago. The snow had finally stopped, and he had high hopes of returning the following day once the streets were plowed to a relatively safe degree.

Since his room hadn't one, he asked for a coffee pot in the lobby, and, upon returning to his room, brewed pot after pot throughout the remainder of the day. He sat in an crude and uncomfortable wooden chair that he pulled near the window and contemplated the mess that he found himself in. He passively watched the tourists mill about the sidewalks below.

If he actually were to quit Emerald Acres, his relationship with Sawyer was surely over. But, on the other hand, Sawyer seemed to be open-minded. What if Sam were able to get a hold of him and explain everything that he and Melody had discovered? Surely he'd understand. Maybe he could convince Sawyer to abandon his contract with the property. Or even better, purchase it himself and demolish it. He could let Kyao explain, if it came to that.

He knew he was being optimistic, but decided that it was his best chance of salvaging his reputation with the enigmatic and affluent man. Sawyer was one of those people that you want to keep as a friend, so Sam pulled out his phone and gave him a call.

"Rocket!" Sawyer answered on the second ring.

"Sawyer! How you been?" asked Sam, his voice shaking slightly, suddenly awkward and terrified of broaching the subject at hand.

"I'm excellent, Sam. Thank you for asking. How's the property?"

"It's good, it's good… Listen…" Sam choked on his words. "What I'm about to say is going to sound a little crazy…"

Sam proceeded to describe everything he'd learned from Kyao and Melody over the past day. He described how the land was originally important to the Hopi tribe and was likely cursed by an ancient Hopi god. He raved about the security camera footage and even got Sawyer to look at the footage from his phone while on the line. He went into verbose detail regarding his eerie encounters while on the property, and spoke at length of the kachina doll and its mysterious appearance.

Just as Sam had felt the night before while relaying his fears to Melody, he waited for Sawyer to burst into laughter when his ravings concluded. But as he finished, he was instead met by a patient and receptive tone.

"I… I don't know what to say," said Sawyer gently. "I'm sorry I put you through all this, Sam. Listen. I wouldn't blame you if you wished to leave after all that. But do me the favor of at least seeing what this girl can do. Who knows, maybe she really can help. If she can, great. It'll save me a lot of hassle, and maybe you'll even be willing to stay. If not, you can take off the next day and I wouldn't hold it against you."

It was a striking relief to the culture of concrete objectivity that was prevalent in the Marine Corps, and for the first time, Sam suspected that his expectations of ridicule might be a result of the time he had spent in its ranks.

Sam promised to see it through for one more night. Rhey ended the call as Sawyer said that he had to go to "see a man about a horse" once again. The line didn't bring the smile to Sam's face as it had in the past. He would go back to the house for one more night, if only to respect the wishes of the man to whom he felt at least a bit of obligation. Sawyer had trusted him with the job, after all, and there was no way he could have known about the haunting. The least Sam could do was give him a day's notice before quitting.

And if in the process he were to spend a little more time with Melody, well, that would be just fine.

23

The Forest Weeps for Us All

The rain pelted the flimsy brim of the hat that now rested on Mae's head. She raised her trembling hands and saw that a thick bushel of hair covered her arms. She brought her fingers to her face and traced unfamiliar contours.

She had no words. Whatever had just happened to her, and what had unfolded far beneath her feet, rattled her terribly, and she could manage nothing but accelerating breaths. So recent had been the sensation of the creature's teeth shredding the skin from her cheek that she raised her fingers to her mouth to verify that the skin there now was in fact unharmed.

In the process of verifying this, she was again reminded that it was not the skin that she knew, and upon acknowledging this, she fell to her knees and sobbed uncontrollably into the wet dirt.

For nearly twenty minutes, she sat and unfurled her emotions into the earth. Malaki was gone. She, as she knew herself to be, was gone. And it was all her doing. She had insisted upon attempting the summoning, all along knowing it to be a wildly dangerous attempt at holding a castle of sand within her sieved hands. She had led herself and Malaki to their deaths and hadn't even the redemption of death itself to console her.

Maybe she *was* dead. She again raised her hands to examine her body. It certainly wasn't the body she knew to be hers. The additional organs were particularly difficult to wrap her head around. But everything seemed to work fine, as far as she could tell.

She rose to her feet slowly and wiped the mud from her hands and face. She undid the straps of the backpack that hugged her back and dug through its contents. In the main pouch she found a hardback copy of *Walden*, a fold-out laminated guide to harvesting fungi, a peanut butter and jelly sandwich whapped in kraft paper, and a canteen of water. In the small exterior pocket of the bag she found a wallet, a box of strike matches, and a set of keys. The wallet contained some small bills and a folded photo of a young man hugging a plump blonde woman whose smile raised her upper lip high above her top row of teeth.

They looked happy. On the back of the photograph, in a sloppy cursive hand, were the words, *I love you so, Matthew.*

Mae replaced the photo and returned the wallet to the bag with quivering fingers. She slung the bag back upon her shoulders and began walking aimlessly through the forest, for a lack of inspiration of what else to do. She hadn't any idea where she was, or even which direction was north. And even if she was to find her way to a highway or even a town, what then?

The rain was unending. It seemed fitting. Let it drench her and carry her away, for she was now nothing but a leaf upon the ocean, wishing only to be swallowed by its depths. She wanted nothing more than to disintegrate and become one with its dark currents.

Then, out of nowhere, and for the first time in many years, she recalled her interaction with the Indian, all those years before. It was a memory that she only rarely conjured, but it came to her as she racked her brain, trying desperately to untangle and make sense of the inexplicable experience that she had just endured.

The two main things that she remembered him saying were to not be afraid, and that he wished to "give her time and perspective." For years, whenever she had considered these words, she had assumed the man to be raving mad, and that her panic had driven her to pass out from fear as he touched her forehead. But given her spirit's Houdini act just minutes before, she now began to construct a new theory.

Was she... her ego... somehow unable to die? Did the Indian make her immortal somehow?

The concept left her spinning, and she was compelled to sit upon a nearby boulder as the world took to an accelerating spin. Was that how he intended to give her perspective? Let her rot upon the earth until she saw what he could have simply said to her in words? At once, a century's worth of searing anger toward the Indian and what he had done, overcame her, and she screamed bloodily into the moist forest until she grew lightheaded and saw spots.

Buit when the rage that muted her perspective at last came to dissolve, she began to consider the further implications of her circumstance. If she truly could not die and was destined to flutter from one body to the next when her flesh perished, then... her mind reeled at the consequences as she followed a long line of dominoes all the way to where dominos could no longer stand. The repercussions of the thought encompassed her imagination for several minutes while the rain fell unceasingly about her.

After some time, she had an urge to move her limbs, for the novelty of her vision if nothing else, and began rambling through the forest when providence struck. As she moved aimlessly through the rain and the trees, she stumbled upon a cascading clump of boulders rising out of the forest floor. The same clump of boulders that marked the entrance to the lava tubes.

She decided then and there that whether her shackles to the Earth were secure or not, she would venture back into the cave. She knew that it was unlikely that Malaki had survived his possession, but she knew equally well that she would be unable to tolerate her (potentially eternal) existence if she didn't at least attempt to save him. So numbed were her sensibilities that she didn't even fear the wrath of the beast within. Tears welled within her eyes once again, and she made straight for the entrance of the cave without concern.

She now knew what it felt like to be massacred piece by piece, and with this understanding, the uncertainty of the situation was gone, as was any instinct resembling self-preservation.

She descended the rocky boulders of the entrance, but not quite slowly enough, as her boot skid upon a moist boulder, sending Mae tumbling down the fifteen or so feet into the opening of the cave. From her unceremonious descent, she inherited some road rash, a nasty gash upon her arm, a slight limp in her left leg, and a laugh that rose from her throat as she giggled at the cascading misfortune that continued to find its way to her.

She stood and hobbled to a pile of branches against the right wall of the entrance as she produced the box of matches from her bag.

The logs were moist and required several matches and much patience, but eventually, she was able to ignite the end of a branch that she then held like a torch. She carried the branch with a surprisingly strong arm and placed three additional logs into her backpack before marching into the tunnel. The ends of the logs in her bag jutted awkwardly from the top as she tread deeper into the cave.

The hike was as long and haunting as she recalled it to be, but her unwavering sorrow carried her forward. Every moment she expected to see green eyes materializing from the darkness to devour her freshly delivered meat, but for the time being, she remained seemingly alone. The light of the torch was sufficient to illuminate her immediate surroundings, but unlike the headlamps that she and Malaki had worn on their initial descent, everything beyond a ten-foot circumference of the branch was enshrouded in utter blackness.

She wondered why the beast had allowed her to travel so far into the cave without suffering its consequence. Maybe it liked to play with its food, she thought. But with each step, miniscule branches grew upon her tree of hope. Just maybe, she would find Malaki alive at the end of the tunnel.

After some time, the torch's flame began to encroach upon her hand. She rested it upon the rocky ground and produced another branch from her bag and illuminated its end with the flame of the old. She left the old branch and advanced further into the blackness. Every so often, she looked back to see the first flame fading, until after several minutes it was gone.

She continued into the darkness. The hike seemed much longer this time around, it being darker and her lacking accompaniment. She began to suspect that she might walk forever into an unending cave. Maybe she was dead after all, and her limbo was one of regret, fear, and darkness. Her supply of branches would soon be exhausted, and she would be left to wander the cave in blindness for as long as her undying lungs drew air.

But then, at last, to her utter astonishment, she heard a voice call to her from the direction in which she was walking.

"Mae," the raspy voice echoed.

It was Malaki's voice. No question about it. She had good reason to suspect that the voice was nothing more than a malicious trap of some kind, but she was beyond caution. She hastened her pace and called out in return, "Malaki! I'm coming to get you!" while frantically jaunting over boulders. She was struck by the voice that bellowed from her larynx. It was a man's voice, and hearing her words manifested in such a foreign manner surprised her. It seemed that she would continue to be surprised by the change for quite some time, as one takes for granted the axioms of the self.

Soon, hints of the rockfall that concluded the cave were illuminated by the soft light of her torch. It was the fourth and final of her branches to be burnt, as she had found nothing combustible during her trek deep into the cave. Her return journey, if there was to be one, would be enshrouded in darkness.

"Mae," the voice called again. She was getting close. The voice was unmistakably Malaki's, albeit hoarse and weak.

"I'm coming, Malaki!" she responded emphatically, again quickening her pace. As she homed in on his voice, however, she noticed drops of red smattering the boulders over which she bound. Splash marks, She looked ahead to the perimeter of her torches light and saw a scene of splayed guts and bones littering the floor. It was a scene of primal destruction and undoing. Nature on full display. The smell of wet iron mixed roundly with the otherwise mossy humidity of the space. When she stepped closer, she saw it to be the bloody remains of Mae Barrett strewn violently about the floor of the cave.

Despite her newfound reckless abandon, she shivered at the sight and its gruesomeness. She wanted to both vomit and sob, and she unexpectedly thought of her mother. She walked directly to the left wall and hugged it to circumnavigate the scene and approach the voice that lay deeper still.

Malaki lay with his body half in the murky sump of water that had collected at the end of the cave. His legs were shredded and bled into the water, turning it a ghastly red.

Mae approached him solemnly and knelt beside his head. It was obvious that he was dying; her mentor; her only friend in the world.

"Mal," she sobbed, completely forgetting that her body was now another's. "I'm here, Mal."

"You sound different, child," Malaki whispered with great effort, forcing a smile. It was apparent that each word he produced required tremendous effort as bolts of pain shot through his face with every syllable.

"Wha... what happened? How are you still alive?" she asked with Matthew's mouth.

Malaki coughed and Mae noticed that he looked past her, evidently unable to see. "Let's just say that bastard didn't anticipate... me," he said. "When the lights went out, it discarded my body... and resumed its preferred form. It... attended to you... and I had a chance. I took it." He coughed. "I conjured Eclipsion, my trustiest blade, and diced that scaled beast back to oblivion. It got me too, though, as you can see." He gestured to the shreds of his legs marinating in the pool. "You came back for me. Why did you come back for me?"

Mae's eyes filled with tears. It was becoming clear that her friend's next words would be his last. She rested her palm gently upon his forehead. Beads of sweat moistened his skin. "Of course I came back for you, Mal... I don't know what's happened to me... It's almost like..."

"Like you're immortal?" he interrupted. "I've known it for as long as I've known you, young Mae."

She rocked back in astonishment. "...How?"

Malaki went to speak, but then abruptly pitched forward and coughed a ruthless cough. As he lay back down and caught his breath, Mae noticed a stream of blood trickling from his mouth.

"You've been blessed, Mae. Something, or someone, has made you immortal." He gestured in the direction of her scattered remains, mercifully shrouded in shadow. "As you can see, that doesn't always mean what you think it does."

"How di, did you know?" she stammered.

Malaki just smiled. "I knew you were special. I saw you from across the mall at the university. When someone has a gift like yours, it's hard to miss, when you're sensitive to such things, as I am." His breathing quickened. "I figured whatever gave you that must have thought you to be mighty special, Mae. I thought I'd help you be special... I wanted you to... Do you remember the field, Mae?"

"I do, Mal. I do. What about it?" she replied tearfully.

But Malaki did not respond, nor would he ever again.

For a long while, Mae simply stared into his face. He appeared content and mild, as if all the weight of everything that had ever burdened him had suddenly dissipated like a fog with the arrival of dawn.

Her final burning branch began to flicker, indicating that it was nearing the end of its illumination. In its light Mae caught a glimmer of the *Tome of Instruction* lying nearby, its pages open upon the earth, as if the dirt was reading its words. She picked up the book and quickly flipped to a page titled *Illuminarious*. In the fading light, she read the short incantation, produced a small cut in her hand with a blade from her original pack that laid nearby, and touched the strap of the backpack upon her back with the weeping finger. The bag immediately produced radiant white light that illuminated the cave's walls and ceiling.

Now, with the light surrounding the scene, she couldn't help but look closer upon the scene of her flesh's disarrangement. Gore was scattered about the rocks and blood seemingly touch everything within fifteen feet of the massacre, but between the limbs and human anatomy were the grotesque remains of the beast that Malaki, true to his word, had slaughtered. Thick, obsidian scales, long segments of coiled, ridged bones, and pools of black bile and blood lay on the floor of the cave.

As Mae turned away from the repugnant scene, she saw the flame of the burning branch extinguish nearby, emitting a puff of white smoke. A thought occurred to her. Why hadn't Malaki just used the Illuminarious spell when they first entered the cave? Why bother with the headlamps at all?

She placed the Tome of Instruction into her backpack and lifted what was left of Malaki onto her shoulders. She was surprised at how light his body was. As she carried the corpse back toward the cave's entrance, she noticed the hem of his shirt was meticulous and hand stitched with care. She could only assume that it was his own work, and it suddenly became obvious to her as to why the headlamps were used, and not the spell.

24

Esoterica

For three days and three nights Mae dug into the *Codex of Ascendant Shadows and Familiar Dimensions*. She took only short breaks to collect the delivery orders that were dropped outside the front door of the bookstore, but otherwise, all she did was read, attend to her body's requirements, and sleep for relatively short bursts when necessary.

The words of the Codex seemed to ramble, spin, and flip in ways that were both confounding and frustrating. She would refer back and forth between the pages in her efforts to define the abstract concepts the book elaborated upon, but felt as if the text was toying with her in some way. Sentences seemed to bend into self-referencing idiosyncrasies, and on more than one occasion she suspected that the words she had read on her first time through had changed subtly by the time she referenced them again.

Was she reading a book of nonsense? She considered it on more than one occasion. However, she had another theory. Maybe she hadn't paid the book its due toll. In her various occult studies over the years, she had heard whispers of books that only revealed their ultimate secrets to those that paid to play, or after a key of some kind was used to reveal the true nature of its text. Sometimes the key was a simple thing, like reading the text under moonlight or in a mirror. More often, though, it was not so simple. The trouble was, she hadn't a clue as to what the ticket to ride might be, as the key would often be deliberately obscured. It was a game that narcistic arcanists played with the world, as if it to say, "Here! Here lies all the secrets you so dearly desire. It is all before you—but good luck reading it."

She slammed the book shut, suddenly confident that this was the case. She had reread the chapter titled *Basics of Interdimensional Bounding* three times, and after each rendition, had come away with an entirely different understanding of the process. She flipped the Codex onto its face and stared into the image of the author, Tacitus Kilgore III. The image was but a washed away smear, blurred by time and friction. How she wished that she could look into his eyes so she could properly despise him.

Or maybe... Inspiration struck her. Maybe it wasn't time and friction that had worn away the man's face. After all, the rest of the book's leather cover appeared relatively unharmed. She touched her finger to the smeared image. Maybe it was a clue.

A faint, unintelligible whisper brushed against her ear like a voice on the wind. Years before, she might have jumped. A younger Mae might have even screamed at a phantom voice hovering about her, but on this day, she took encouragement from the encounter, as it surely meant that she was on to something.

"How does one see that which is blurred," she asked aloud, half expecting a response, though none came. Still, the question rang true. She stood and paced around the empty bookstore, considering the question. She held her hands behind her back and considered the questions with a wide aperture of mind. She picked random books from chance bookshelves and opened them to random pages. In situations such as this, one required assistance from the muses of inspiration and serendipity. She'd come to rely on their guidance on more than one occasion throughout her life.

She paused before a row of books titled *Chemical Mechanisms of Transcendence*. A small red sign was hung just below the title with writing in a nearly microscopic font. It read:

Dark Shadows Bookstore has been legally mandated to inform our patrons that we do not, in any way, endorse the use of illegal drugs or substances.

The words "do" and "drugs" were bolded. If Mae were to give honest advice to any well-intentioned young person regarding the use of drugs, specifically hallucinogens, it would be a suggestion to challenge the natural borders of their perception. It seemed to her that the western world had assumed its natural biological interpretations of the world to be the single true means of interacting with and understanding the universe. As she understood things, the answers people often sought within themselves sometimes come only from expanded perspectives.

Of course, like anything else, certain substances could easily become abused and she did not advocate for that. When drugs were used as a lazy and purposeless escape from reality, they became a vice that thoroughly outweighed the potential benefits. But if taken intentionally and carefully, she considered the expansions of one's mind through certain compounds to be a fruitful and worthy pursuit.

She pulled a book from the shelf: *The Doors of Perception*, by Aldous Huxley. She flipped to a random page and read a lengthy and uniquely beautiful passage that elaborated on the themes of escaping from our natural survival-driven perceptions of existence. In Huxley's definitive tone, the passage did well to separate reality from the language, labels, and concepts that we use to define it, and in doing so, proposed that we often miss the forest for the trees when seeking to understand our often-ambiguous existence.

She closed the book and her eyes mimicked the act by closing their lids. A theory manifested in the forefront of her mind. If she trusted the wisdom of serendipitous guidance, which she did, Huxley's words were a bread crumb trail that deserved to be entertained, if nothing else.

That wasn't to say that she was about to produce a bag of mescaline, LSD, or psilocybin. She no longer needed such mechanisms to expand her mind's eye. No, she required only a quiet, dark space in which to meditate and be unbothered for many hours. The meditation styles of the old sages produced an altered perspective that rivaled any drug peddled on the street, minus the troublesome side effects they produced. However, she only rarely engaged in even holistic meditative altered states, as they often conjured fearful interactions with higher beings which were generally less than enjoyable. It was a process that, although enlightening, seemed to expose one to presences beyond the peripheral existence of everyday human engagement; presences unconcerned with the squishy vulnerabilities of the human psyche.

But if the act gave her even a slight chance of unlocking the Codex and understanding its riddles, she would happily expose herself to such dangers.

In the center of the store was an open area where three leather couches surrounded a Himalayan throw rug embroidered with a gold endless knot. Mae wished to waste no time. She rested the Codex upon the cushion of one of the couches, lit a stick of copal incense, and sat in a Sukhasana pose in the center of the knot.

It had been a long time since she'd last dove into the depths of deep meditation. It was a simple process: deep, long breaths, and an unwavering focus upon them. The latter, combined with the patience that the process required, were the factors that restricted the process to the realm of esoterica and not the world at large.

If only the masses knew how much deeper the meditative method could take them. If they did, the number of enlightened individuals walking about on any given day would surely grow exponentially. Who knows, maybe our society would be more peaceful. Our existence less fearful.

On the other hand, the number of deeper beings in contact with those unprepared for such relations would make for treacherous and unexpected seas for our species to sail.

Maybe it was best that only the few utilized the practice.

Mae closed her eyes and, over the course of several hours, sank into a rhythm of breathing while thinking only of her breath. Her stomach protested with hunger and her muscles demanded movement to shake loose their stagnation, but Mae kept her attention upon her breathing and her breathing alone. It was an act of self-abandon, neglect, and rhythm. The more her body pleaded, like a puppy demanding its dinner or a child crying for attention, the more she forsake it. It was a practice that had taken many decades of failure before she had at last mastered its routine. It was a ritual in ascension, and as her consciousness began to flutter beyond the boundaries of her body's perception, she comprehended flashes of existence in a manner not unlike what many might consider omnipotence. Flittering perceptions danced past her like specks of sand in a desert monsoon.

A lifelong smoker lighting a match. Greyhound buses. The whistling of a teapot. Scurvy. Thunder on the high plains. Steering wheels. Microplastics. A child's first recognition of their eventual death. Klondike bars. Restaurant tables held for reservation. Grapefruit trees. Open bibles. Xylophones. Nursing homes. Translucent jellyfish. Larceny. Howitzers. Yosemite Valley. Long-married couples rubbing elbows on short flights. Child brides. Vindictive landlords. Killer whales in tanks. Muralists painting scenes of exaltation. Mirages. Water balloon fights. Foreign aid. Labradors jumping into pools. Turbulence. Tracks in the snow. Salt lamps. Teeth marks. Earrings. An old man learning to play the guitar. Flatulence while sitting alone. Value pack diapers. Refusing to answer the door. Fire's burning down the forest.

She opened her eyes and found herself still sitting upon the rug in the center of the bookstore, however, a soft pink hue seemed to encapsulate everything about her.

She felt light, as she always did upon successful ascension, and she considered the sensation similar to how it felt to glide between bodies, although she had developed more control in that matter. In this process, she was fickle in contrast to the capricious winds and wills that could blow her soul about at any time. If a heavy enough wind blew, or an unwelcome visitor wished it, she could be flung out of her trance in a flash. It was a realm of inhospitability, to most.

Through the thick pink nectar of the plane of existence she now inhabited, she moved slowly toward the Codex still resting upon the cushion of the couch. As she did, the air about her visibly rippled and curled back upon itself. She opened the book onto its back and saw, to her relief, that the portrait of Tacitus Kilgore III was now as clear as day. He smiled at her piercingly from beneath a crisp black top hat and through square eyeglasses. His mustache twirled neatly upon his lip, and he wore a three-piece tuxedo.

She returned the book to its upright position and cracked its spine. As she opened it to the first page, she discovered a new foreword greeting her. It read:

Hello, and congratulations upon revealing the Codex of Ascendant Shadows and Familiar Dimensions. My name is Tacitus Kilgore III, and I will be your guide upon this journey of exploration, enlightenment, and esoteric awareness. By revealing these words, you have shown at the very least a basic comprehension of magical manipulation, but what I ask of you is this, seeker of knowledge: put aside your assumptions and allow the text that follows to impress itself upon you in its own, patient time. Welcome to the Codex of Ascendent Shadows and Familiar Dimensions. May its knowledge both guide and humble you as you step onward in your journey. Bon voyage, and good luck.

As Mae continued reading, she discovered its contents were both engaging and intuitive, though its length still daunting. No longer did the text unravel in riddles that twisted back onto themselves. There now existed relatively straight-forward lessons to be learned.

She knew that her trance was fragile, so she read at as quick a pace as she could while still retaining the information. She wished she had the *Tome of Instruction* at her side. It was a useful accompaniment on excursions into unknown depths.

Mae felt herself abruptly missing Malaki. It'd been nearly a century since she'd last seen him, although she still thought of him often. He would have appreciated the playful nature of the Codex's hidden nature. She remembered how Malaki would disguise the appearance of various ingredients in his flat to play tricks on her during their short time together. She'd think she was concocting something mischievous, but would discover that the trick was on her, as the mixture she stirred would pop into a puff of glittering smoke or begin whispering incoherent gibberish, much to the amusement of her mentor.

After lingering with similar memories for a gentle moment, she let them drift off and away. She returned her attention to the Codex in the hopes that it contained the information that would ultimately set her soul loose and free to at last to join Malaki in the nothing and everything all at once.

Then, serendipitously, a familiar voice called out from behind her in a soft ethereal reverberation.

"Hello, darling," the voice said.

25

Thin Places

S am slowed his truck to a stop at the curb outside of Dark Shadows. On the business's doorknob hung a hand-written sign reading *Closed for the Day.* Mae sat patiently nearby, wearing exactly what she had been wearing the first two times he'd seen her: Doc Martens, black pants, and a black hoodie, although this time she sat upon a large green duffel bag stuffed to its absolute capacity. He'd known many seabags like it in his military tenure.

"Bodies?" he asked as he tossed the heavy bag into the bed of the truck.

"Tools," she replied, entering the cab.

Sam steered the truck toward Interstate 40. It was apparent that the snowplows had been busy over the past twelve hours, as the streets were finally cleared enough to safely navigate, although the sky remained grim. They took a cloverleaf onramp that led onto the interstate and headed east for a handful of miles before eventually taking the forest service road exit that would lead them toward to Emerald Acres. But before they entered the forest, Sam parked and installed the tire chains that he'd purchased the day before, as the road ahead was unplowed and lay under a thick layer of snow.

As he worked, a gust of wind blew at his back and a few snowflakes began to fall. The last thing he wanted was to be trapped on the property, even if Melody was with him, but he was in it now. No turning back. He could only hope that the sky was bluffing and that the clouds would eventually part.

Just wait one more day, he thought. Wait until tomorrow afternoon. Then it could snow for months on end, for all he cared.

Once the chains were installed, he reentered the cab and pulled the truck forward over the cattle guard to follow the dark winding path through the forest.

The trees were considerably more menacing this time around. They seemed to hang over him and watch with disdain as he drove. The darkness between the rising trunks was enveloping, and he felt a dull pressure in his throat, as if he had swallowed a pill that refused to descend the esophagus.

He suddenly thought that there was something he'd forgotten to do that day. Something that was classified in his brain as important, but he couldn't recall what it was despite several minutes of pulling at its slippery edges. Whatever it was, it eluded him, and he returned his focus to the gloomy, twisting drive through the woods.

He looked to Melody in passing glances hoping to find reassurance in her presence, but was reliably met by her contently closed and resting eyes, not unlike how she had looked when he had meant to kiss her on New Year's Eve. She seemed immaculate in her calmness, and he decided to leave her be. A hint of jealousy crossed him. She didn't seem the slightest bit shaken by the situation, and he both admired and wanted to admonish her for her indifference to the anxieties that pressed so heavily upon him. Surely she could sense his apprehension, yet she showed no signs of empathy and only retreated into herself as if in a preemptive defense to avoid any such conversations.

But after some thought, he decided he was selfish for thinking such things. She was allowed to be calm, even if he wasn't. His anxieties were his to bear, after all. Not hers.

Then, as he turned his attention back to the forest, he was struck by an encroaching feeling that the woods demanded his focus from him hungrily. For no concrete reason, his heart rate increased and he felt suddenly as if he were descending into a tight pine vessel intent upon squeezing him breathless. It was as if he was driving into a fish-eye lens. Sweat covered his brow. He somehow came to sense, as one perceives unseen and imagined specters, a portal of blackness erected behind him in the back seat, its tendrils ready to reach around the head rest and pull him into the void at any moment. A cold breath danced along the lobe of his ear.

He was in the process of summoning the courage to look into the rear-view mirror when he thought that he saw something dark and humanoid in his peripheral vision of the forest. He whipped his head to the left and gazed into the trees at his seven o'clock.

He saw something tall and dark moving through a thicket some fifty yards away.

"Stawhhpppppp!!" screeched Melody, clutching the bar above her. Sam slammed on the brakes, prompting the tires to slide agonizing close to a ditch overlooking a deep gulley. "Look where the fuck you're going!" she screamed.

"I thought I saw something back there," said Sam. "I'm sorry!"

"It's called a deer, Sam," she said angrily. "Do you need me to drive?"

"No, no, I'm good." he said, although he knew this might not be the truth. He looked into the thicket behind him and saw nothing. He reversed the truck away from the ledge and pulled hard to the right to resume the trek toward Emerald Acres.

The presence that he had sensed sitting behind him was now absent. "So many absences," he said aloud. "Sometimes I feel like I'm becoming one myself."

Melody didn't respond, and there was a long silence. Sam noticed that she was sitting contently once again with her eyes closed.

"Have you been out this way before?" he asked finally, grasping for a distraction from his thoughts.

She opened her eyes but took a moment to respond. "Not this way, exactly, but nearby... about seven years ago," she said. "Have you ever heard the story of Stephanie Matthews?"

He hadn't.

"I wouldn't expect you to, I guess. Stephanie Matthews was a hermit who lived not too far from here, a handful of miles further east, where the woods meet the high plains and the trees are thinner. Anyway, she lived by herself in a shack near a creek that flowed all the way from the San Francisco Peaks. She minded her own business. Kept to herself. But one day, in a small town a few miles from where she lived, a place called Pinesdale, some children went missing. Three, in fact, all below the age of nine. The police had few leads, but the townsfolk had their prejudices of Stephanie, and implored the police to follow up with her about the missing children. And so they did. They rolled up to her shack, kicked down the door, and guess what…"

Sam hadn't a clue.

"The townsfolk were right," she said, letting the words marinate.

"Okay. That's a pretty fucked-up story. What'd it have to do with you, though?" he asked.

"I was seventeen at the time, and I wanted to be a firefighter. I spent a lot of time at the station, mostly just cleaning the trucks and making coffee for the guys. My father was a captain on one of the engines, and he let me go on ride-alongs from time to time. Well, I went out with the crew one day to run some drills in the wildland truck out east. We were just about to head back into town when we got redirected to Stephanie's place. I distinctly remember hearing the 911 operator describing it over the truck's radio." She mimicked the formal voice of the operator. *Engine seven. Redirect to secluded structure, approximately three miles southeast of Forest Service Road 219. Code three. Look for the squad cars when nearby. Patient is reported to have sucking chest wound resulting from gunshot.*"

Sam was dumbstruck. She'd been through a hell of a lot more than he had understood and suddenly acknowledged that he'd grossly underestimating the woman this whole time. It couldn't be an easy thing to recall, let alone share, and he regretted bringing the subject up in the first place. Eventually, though, Sam's curiosity got the best of him; besides, simply hearing her speak was a consoling distraction as he drove through the sullen trees. As the snow continued to fall, he was trying his best to neglect the anxieties that lingered persistently within him.

"So, the police got her, then?" he asked finally.

"Yup. They put a couple bullet holes in her chest. They said in the report that she attacked them when they got there. But if you ask me, they saw what she'd done and decided to cheat the jury."

"Why do you say that?" he asked.

"Well. My dad told me to stay in the truck when we got there, but of course I didn't. I saw what she did to those kids. And if it were me, I'd have put some holes in her too if I got the chance."

Sam definitely regretted asking now. and nothing more was said for the remainder of the drive, which was mercifully short. Within five minutes they reached the turn-off sign in its newly painted glory. He turned the truck and began driving down the snow-covered pathway under the arching aspen trees.

At the gate Sam entered the code and pulled onto the property after the gate's lower limbs strained to pushed through the heavy snow at its base. Melody must have finally recognized Sam's anxiety, as she reached over and rested a hand on his shoulder. "It's going to be okay, Sam. Remember, it's not radiation. It's not all-powerful. And if something comes at us in the night, we'll cut its fucking head off." She smiled and Sam even managed a genuine laugh. "Deal?" she asked.

"Deal," he replied, and pulled the truck into the circular drive to let the engine rest at last.

Sam exited the cab and walked toward the pond, eyeing the meadow beyond expectantly. Between the trees beyond were dark inkwells, black holes between rising bark. Vertical slivers of the void that haunted his waking moments recurrently.

Six dead, bloody geese lay scattered near the pond.

He stood over the grisly scene, unable to form words that seemed worthy of his grief. His breath trembled and he fought back a wave of tears. The apprehension that he had temporarily muted again twisted his guts into ribbons. He turned back to the truck as Melody pulled her massive duffel bag from the bed, hoisting it onto her shoulder.

"We shouldn't have come," he said. "I shouldn't have come back here."

With the heavy bag resting on her back, she gazed downward toward the gravel beneath her, snowflakes falling lazily about them. She breathed in deeply and turned to him.

"What's the code to the door, Sam?"

26

The Black Between Trees

Sam sat for a long while in the kitchen, looking apprehensively at the floating shelf nearby still covered in a white sheet. He thought about pulling it away to see if the kachina doll remained within the diorama, but something held him back. The atmosphere of the room seemed dense and decisively different than his time there before. With his every movement, he was afraid of disturbing something lurking, as if he were putting a bloody finger into the ocean.

Melody, without hesitation, took her things down the hall toward the master bedroom, "to set up," as she had said. Sam wanted nothing to do with what she had planned, and decided to let her at it alone. He intended to gather his things and huddle up on the couch in the living room to wait out the night. The room had a tall fireplace that he intended to light and burn log after log while watching comedies on the elevated flat-screen TV that hung on the wall. As an added bonus, the room had no windows to speak of.

He remembered a time, years back, when he had taken acid with some friends, and after a bit of a bad trip, had thought that he was going to die. He did his best to make peace with God and wrestled with his impending doom, before his friend returned from the kitchen with pizza rolls and turned on a *SpongeBob* marathon.

From then on, he couldn't watch the cartoon without thinking of his mortality.

He wished that Melody would be that friend. He envisioned her returning from the long hallway, asking him to hold her. To comfort her and protect her from the fears and apprehensions that had finally come to her. He thought of what it might feel like to have her chin resting on his shoulder, wet from her tears.

But she didn't seem capable of fear. Or even empathy, perhaps. From the moment he had met her, she had displayed an unshakeable confidence wrapped in an impossible consistency. She was the opposite of a damsel in distress. She wasn't here for him either, he finally admitted to himself. He was her ticket to something incredible, that was all. He was her way inside the door, to reach something that beckoned to her while it cackled in his ear.

A shudder of embarrassment traversed him.

He mustered some gumption and began to walk toward the guest bedroom which contained his various effects. Momentarily, he considered checking in with Melody, but decided it best to leave her to her devices, a vague surliness toward her growing within him.

You'd fall in love with a rock if it held your hand, he scolded himself.

Through a series of wide windows that lined the hallway he saw that the snow had picked up considerably since he'd last checked. Chunks of puffy snow fell from the sky and spun about in the swirling gusts of a night that had come quickly.

From somewhere within the house, he heard the sound of the wind whistling through a loose vent or crevasse. The fear of a prolonged stay began to grip him. Deciding to do his best to leave the thought outside with the snow, he continued along the hall and into the guest bedroom.

The long black blanket still covered the arching window of the room, obscuring the meadow and the forest beyond. The portal was tall and the light bluish glow of the snow filtered in above it and filled the room. Sam pulled his bag from the closet and began stuffing it with clothes. He hadn't much to pack, which was a blessing. Once the bag was full, he turned about to leave the room, and found Melody standing in the doorway with a horrified expression upon her face.

One hand rose and covered her mouth while the other pointed toward the window.

"What is that?" she inquired softly.

Sam turned to the window and found the blanket entirely absent and the view uninterrupted. A thick fog obscured the meadow and all was silent, until abruptly, a man burst out of the fog and ran directly into the window with a tremendous, terrible thud that made Sam fear the window might shatter into a million pieces. It didn't, but the fact did nothing to ease Sam's horror as he noticed that the man wearing fatigues under a Kevlar vest and helmet.

"Lively," Sam whispered through sudden tears.

Private Lively recovered from the shock of running into the window and dropped his rifle to the ground. He flung off his vest and gingerly touched his chest where a crimson pool of blood began to expand on the fabric. He then fell dramatically to his knees, digging frantically into the dirt with a KA-BAR knife. With every two or three shovels of dirt he looked over his shoulder as if closely pursued. He turned and flung the knife into the mist, as if aiming it at something, before returning to dig frantically at the dirt with his hands, his fingers now bleeding as the nails peeled back upon repeated furious contact with the earth.

Sam approached the window and looked out at Private Lively through the tears that glittered his view. He touched the glass and his mouth twitched with short-circuiting despair. Just as he touched the glass, Private Lively stopped his digging and looked up to make calm eye contact with Sam. Lively stood and slowly approached the window, stopping when he stood only inches from Sam's face on the other side of the pane.

"You left me to die, Sam." His voice was unmuted by the glass.

Sam sobbed as he shook his head violently from side to side. "No," was all he managed to mutter.

"Yes," said Private Lively, nodding. "You could have carried me. You could have saved me. But instead, you left me to die… alone."

Sam fell to his knees, half leaning against the glass. "No," he sobbed again.

Private Lively looked up with a start, gazing past Sam and into the room. His expression suggested he had seen something terrible behind Sam. He stumbled backwards, the fabric at his chest now moist and red. He spun around and sprinted frantically into the mist.

Sam turned to see what Lively had seen, but the room was unremarkable and Melody was absent from the doorway. He turned back and found that he was kneeling inches from the black blanket still hanging from the PVC pipe archway that obstructed the view of the forest.

"Melody?" he whimpered, hoping to hear her voice from behind him.

No answer.

He collapsed, folding onto his knees to become thoroughly dismantled on the wooden floor. For a long while, he was far away and no longer thought of Emerald Acres. His bout of tinnitus was a different sort of ringing. It was a remembered one; one of those curious things forgotten for years, which then reemerge with a sudden triggering smell or sensation. He heard its ringing, smelt the acrid scent of gunpowder, and imagined sand pelting his cheeks.

When he finally collected himself, he wiped the tears and snot from his face and rotated himself to again face the door where he saw Melody sitting in the doorway, her back resting against its frame. She too sat on her butt, one knee bent, the other straight. In her hands, which rested in her lap, she fiddled with the oak keepsake box that she must have taken from the desk nearby. Her head hung low, but when he finally sat up from his groveling, she looked to him with a compassionate glance.

"Who's Lively?" she asked softly.

Sam didn't respond at first, eyeing her pensively. "Did you come here earlier? Ten minutes ago?" His voice was gruff. "You pointed at the window."

Her expression changed from compassion to curiosity. "No..." She shook her head. "I came out a few minutes ago to grab a drink when I heard you sobbing down here. I came over and there you were... What do you mean, I pointed at the window?" she asked.

Sam shook his head and said nothing more. Melody crawled beside him and let him rest his head on her shoulder for several minutes.

"I want to show you something," she said finally.

Sam didn't care about ghosts anymore. Masau'u evaded his thoughts, as did the blackness that seemed to follow him. The numbness within him blanketed concern for all else, and even his earlier disillusionment regarding Melody felt distant and irrelevant once again. He followed Melody down the hall with a glazed disposition, the heavy snow still falling heavily outside the wide, peering windows.

In the foyer, which was a primary intersection in the house, she spun about and stepped forward to grasp Sam's hands. "Listen to me. You've been exceedingly kind to bring me here and to trust me with this. I promise you, come tomorrow, everything is going to be fine. But… I need your help with something. It's a small—"

"No," he said curtly. "I don't even want to be here, Melody. I wish I was back in Howard Hughes's room, overlooking the tourists on the street, not playing Hogwarts in a haunted fucking house."

"*Howard Hughes*?" she repeated, confounded.

"*That*'s the part that bothers you?" Sam asked with a bite in his tone.

She crossed her arms defensively. "So, you don't believe I can do it, then?"

"I don't fucking know, Melody. I don't fucking care. Maybe you can and maybe you can't. But that doesn't change the fact that you practically dragged me back here, when you knew perfectly well that this place scares the shit out of me. You don't feel this?" he gestured about him.

"Let's get something straight right now," she snapped, ignoring his question. "I didn't force you to do anything. You came back here on your own agenda, and just because you can't say what you mean and you get pushed around like a fucking leaf in the wind by pretty faces and… what fuck are you looking at?" She had noticed Sam gazing past her shoulder. She turned to see what had captured his attention and saw, through the front windows and the falling snow, light flickering inside the barn.

Anger swelled up within Sam—the same anger that had led had him to approach the darkness in the streets of Flagstaff the night after leaving Dark Shadows. The same animalistic fury he had experienced in the woods the night something had touched his shoulder. He gritted his teeth. He was tired of letting unseen phantoms bash him against the rocks only to retreat into the darkness unscathed.

"What do you think it is?" Melody asked.

"You're the expert," said Sam sarcastically.

She looked at him, rolling her eyes and obviously done with his company. "Listen, motherfucker. Yes, there's something here. I can feel it. The moment I walked through that door I could feel it. But that's the reason we're here, okay? It's just something that we have to push through to achieve a worthy end. And let me tell you something else—"

"What *is* the end, Melody?" Sam interjected. "What's in it for you? I keep telling myself that you're here to help me, but sometimes I feel that you're here for something else entirely."

Melody closed her eyes and continued talking as if he'd said nothing. "And let me tell you something else... whatever it is that's here—Masau'u or otherwise—it should be afraid of *me*. Not the other way around."

She opened the front door and walked decisively out into the storm, toward the barn.

"Melody!" Sam screamed after her, but she didn't acknowledge his call, and only continued onward toward the structure still emitting a warm light from between its cracks and under its carriage doors.

"Melody!" he screamed again, with similar results. He gritted his teeth and meant to dart through the door after her, but to his surprise, he found that he couldn't move. He was locked, just as he had been in the dark streets of Flagstaff. His breath quivered and the familiar tinnitus rose like a tidal wave in his ears. His eyes darted and, abruptly sensing a now familiar heaviness from the tree line, saw the cloud of absolute blackness hovering between the trees.

"Wake up!" screeched the voice of a woman from the depths of Sam's head as his primitive fury returned in full sway. He was done being controlled. He was over being helpless. He thought back to the sleep paralysis he had suffered frequently when he was growing up, and how he had eventually managed to find a way to muscle out of the condition. He would pull upward from the sheets with everything he had, until finally, he would shoot up in bed in a damp sweat. Sam did the same now, pushing against the force that held him. A muted, prolonged groan emitted from his mouth as he struggled.

As he slowly regained the muscles in his face, he screamed a guttural scream into the night.

"Wake up!" the wretched voice responded, louder now. Sam pushed with all he had. He felt a twitch in his hands.

"WAAAKKKE UPPPP!" the voice bellowed.

Sam lunged forward, barely catching himself before falling face first through the open door and onto the welcome mat below. He looked up and found that the blackness in the tree line was gone. However, the barn door was now ajar, and a flickering warm light bled from it and into the storm.

He regained his composure and began trudging through the heavy wind and snow adding to the accumulation already piled upon the ground. He raised his arm to shield his eyes from the airborne projectiles, and for a split second felt it was sand being thrown into his face and not snow. The cold snapped him out of it, and he continued toward the barn, shivering. He was astonished at how quickly Melody had managed to traverse the distance, and he kept looking up in the hopes of seeing her emerge, but saw nothing but the open carriage door.

As he approached, the snow crossing his sight glowed softly in the light emitting from the barn. He sensed a strange etherealness from the structure that was not unlike like déjà vu.

Through the open door he could now see the interior walls of the barn being painted by a flickering light within, likely that of a lantern. The age of the wood was on brilliant display, amplified by the shadows cast by the light source, which seemed to come from a low vantage point.

At last, he reached the doorway. Inside the barn he indeed found a flickering lantern resting on the center of the floor. Melody was nowhere to be seen.

"Melody!" he shouted, but the only response was the howling wind that met the walls of the structure. He stepped inside slowly, trepidation rising within him. The wind grew softer as he walked cautiously toward the lantern.

The crack of a gunshot rang out, and abruptly Sam had an incredible urge to sit. He brought a hand to his chest, and when he brought it away, saw that his fingers were covered in blood. He turned his head, producing bright white pain in his chest, to see Melody standing in the doorway of the barn holding a shotgun. The estate's shotgun.

He coughed and began to see spots, small bubbles that obscured his vision. He turned and tried to run but the attempt was counterproductive, as the effort dropped him fully to the floor. As he reached forward and tried to crawl, the spots grew and merged until his vision was engulfed by darkness.

As Sam's consciousness began to slip away, his hands dug fruitlessly into the dirt, his fingernails snapping. The instinct of a dying creature, not fully forgotten by man.

27

A Vantage of Darkness

Malaki was buried under a rising ponderosa pine.

Mae sat by the grave for a long while until the grey of the afternoon bled into night.

There was too much to process. Her experienced death. Malaki in the dirt. The body switching. The eyes of the beast. She hadn't the capacity to confront any of these things, nonetheless each of them all at once. So, once the body was at last buried and any immediate danger had passed, she simply sat and stared into the dirt that held her friend's remains, for several hours.

The rain had made the digging easy, but she had feared that if it persisted for much longer, it might dig into Malaki's grave. Thankfully, it stopped shortly once the hole was filled.

As night embraced the saturated forest, Mae remained sitting and staring. Her body shook from the cold, but she did nothing to prevent it. The flame within herself flickered and threatened to cease entirely. She was rotting timber. A thinning cloud. She just sat and turned her brain into a sedentary thing. She was a boulder rising out of the forest floor, and she thought nothing of it. No thoughts arose at all. It was as close to death as she could be while still drawing breath.

At last, a thought pierced the veil of her nearly inanimate state as an owl began to *hoo* from somewhere in the forest. For the first time, Mae truly feared that this would be the closest that she would ever come to death. Would she ever know such soothing nonexistence? Would she forever be forced to exist, feel, process, remember, interact, opinionate, respond, trust, fear, believe, hope, share, love, give, grieve, and take, forever, without breaks? She was caming to orient herself towards death in a similar way that one might regard sleep after a long, exhausting day. It was not something to fear, but a welcome respite from the tiresome weight of being.

A respite that she had begun to fear would forever evade her.

When the sun rose, and not knowing what else to do, Mae wandered about the forest. No longer was her goal to find a road or civilization or even a meal, despite the twisting of her stomach. It was simply to move and be away and let whatever may come, be.

And so, she did.

Throughout the night she rambled through the still-soaked forest, until the sun rose to glisten the puddles and warm her skin. Despite everything, Mae had to admit that it was a glorious day. The fragrances once trapped in the soil were now released, and with each step she ruminated in a paradise of the olfactory.

The fragrance of the wet earth returned her to the cabin in the clearing. Her father tending to the cows and her mother singing inside. Susy running about and the paperback novels that captured Mae's curiosity. She remembered reading the stories a dozen times each, completely wearing out the structure of the books. By their final readthroughs, most had completely lost their faces and their spines threatened to separate entirely.

She had a core memory of her mother suggesting that she put the stories aside and spend more time in the present moment. "Go out and play with Susy!" she would say while Mae curled amongst her books in a quiet corner of the room.

She remembered rolling her eyes and returning to her grand odysseys of heroic cowboys and heroes tumbling across the virgin west of America. The tellings captured her so, that the very idea of enduring Susy's dull musings left Mae entirely uninspired to follow through with her mother's encouragement.

With this recollection, Mae felt more remorseful than she ever had ever before. Her mother was more right than she could have known. So wrapped up in her stories of elsewhere was Mae that she had abandoned stories of her own. She had been so concerned with engaging with the potentially magnificent that she had lost out on the good and assured, and as a result, the latter had passed her by.

Mae moved on through the forest, and by providence, saw that she approached a road crossing perpendicular to the direction that she walked. She moved onto the road's black gravel and stood in its center. A nearby sign read *Interstate 40 – 2 miles.*

Her initial reaction was, of course, to follow the road. It was the logical step toward survival. But a sudden wavering overwhelmed her, and she wondered if she wanted to follow it at all. What would she be going towards, besides playing the confusing role of Matthew, a poor man that had somehow acquired amnesia to his past and was now a different person entirely? And even if she were to abandon the body and take another, what then? The cycle seemed an exhausting trudge from one misfortune to another, and the thought alone tired her. Even the concepts of comfortable rest and food were little motivation, as her biological drives seemed inconsequential to the malignant apathy that had planted itself within her. An existential weight crushed her biological demands, and as her body's cells protested with every mechanism of their faculty, Mae crossed the road and reentered the forest on the other side.

She passed many small gurgling streams, but didn't stoop to fill her mouth, nor did she stop to rest when night returned. She just walked, and did what she could to ensure a blank state of mind, making it into but a thin sheet of metal incapable of absorbing anything at all. She required nothing. Enjoyed nothing. Felt nothing. Was nothing. And yet, her body stumbled on.

She was a wraith that slithered amongst the trees.

Until at last, on the fourth day, Matthew's body could slither no more. It collapsed into the mud of a riverbank and, after an extensive and stubborn hour of conclusion, died at last.

And just as had happened when she was devoured by the monster in the cave, Mae's soul floated slowly away from the corpse. As her vantage rose away from Matthew, she looked down at the man's body lying face down in the mud below her without sorrow.

Her soul then began to glide through the trees in a slow parade. It took no action to avoid the trunks, for when she careened into their rising ascents, she simply traversed the bark as if were fog.

For hours, her spirit flew through the forest without declaring its intention, but Mae was confident of its direction. Her floating perspective was all she was, and yet it carried her forward through the trees without consulting her on where she was going or why. The movement of her soul like that of a will-o'-the-wisp through the trees seemed to be thoroughly independent, like the beating of a heart. She assumed it to be homing in on whatever poor soul was nearest. Why hadn't she been sucked into Malaki's body when she died in the tunnel, she wondered.

She then began to wonder if she could manipulate the direction in which she travelled, and found that by simply pressing her will in a certain direction, as if leaning from side to side while riding a bicycle, that she could indeed steer her floating soul in whichever direction she pleased.

Well, that's something, she thought. She rose out of the trees and looked over the entirety of the forest from above. The rolling green hills spilled out endlessly and she saw that the forest expanded along the ridges of the nearby mountain. The San Francisco Peaks to the north relished the unobscured sun and towered over the entire area. She rose even further, and saw the cluster of civilization that was Flagstaff, teeming with buildings and roads and rising clouds of smoke. She rose higher still, and saw the curvature of the earth until even the most distant of landmarks began to dance along the unraveling horizon. She rose further still and traversed the tallest of clouds.

She looked up to see a blackness growing out of the deep blue of the sky directly above her. She turned towards it and moved upward in its direction, staring deeply into the void of eternity that blossomed overhead. As stars began to speckle her gaze by the thousands, then billions, then exponentially more so, she was immediately enraptured by the view. In all her experiences, even on the darkest and clearest of nights at Lowell's Observatory, she never once seen a sky as pristine and endless as the view that laid before her now. And as she stared into space, and slowly drifted towards it, time seemed to lose all meaning and she melted into a soothing nothingness that the silence beyond Earth's atmosphere provided.

The closer she drew to the beckoning stars beyond, the more she became enchanted with them. She sensed a profound nothingness surrounding her that mimicked the absence that she so desired.

If only the sun wasn't so bright and so near I could feel the emptiness even more so, she reasoned in a blind desire for desolation. She was growing quickly drunk upon the solitude that the endlessness of space provided.

And as even the sun's looming gaze drifted behind her, Mae at last thought not, felt not, processed not, remembered not, interacted not, opinionated not, responded not, trusted not, feared not, believed not, hoped not, shared not, loved not, gave not, grieved not, and took not. And yet she was, at least, as much as a floating soul in the vastness of space could be... She drifted towards the stars still, and as she did, lost all context for distance entirely.

After a long enough time that was impossible to measure, Mae turned her soul's perspective back toward the Earth, intending to return at last. It seemed that the long float in the deprivation chamber of space had done her well, as the silence and desolation had eventually blessed her with a fresh optimism that she hadn't experienced since before she had entered the cave with Malaki in the rain. It was like she had awoken from a long sleep after a tiresome day, and she felt refreshed and eager to embrace the challenges that, not too long before, felt all enveloping and insurmountable.

But as she looked back toward the Earth, Mae found, to her dismay, that it was gone.

And, which dot that surrounded her was the Sun? For they all now looked the same.

How far had she drifted?

Her gaze fluttered from dot to dot amongst an endless ocean of stars, frantically searching for the single white dot that was home. Her soul's vantage spun in circles in a frenzied panic that coalesced quickly into utter despair.

Mae flung herself about, blindly searching for the Earth while the stars that surrounded looked on, indifferently.

28

Manifestations

Mae hadn't heard Malaki's voice in nearly a hundred years, and yet it was undeniably his; warm as the day she had met him. She turned her head slowly, and in doing so, sent pink waves rippling all about her.

Indeed, it was Malaki. He stood at the end of a long narrow column of bookshelves running toward the open area where Mae hunched over the Codex. His face was hard to make out, as it was shrouded in shadows.

"It's been a long time, Mae," he said.

She began to move her lips to speak, but hadn't any idea what she intended to say. She'd buried the man in the moist dirt of the forest on that rainy day so long ago. She had felt his final breath dissipate upon her cheek. And yet here he was, walking slowly toward her out of the shadows of the corridor. As he approached, the pink aura again billowed outward from his movement as he disturbed the plane's lingering atmosphere.

A sharp convulsion emoted from Mae's throat, tempting her to fear that she might tumble right out of her trance and back to basic reality if she couldn't keep control of her emotions. It was a tall task, though, and she pursed her lips tightly and furrowed her brow to keep from descending into an outright sob.

Malaki drew near and stood above her. A slight smirk crossed his face and his arms crossed his chest paternally, all while his entire body shimmered as if underwater.

"I've... I've missed you," she stammered finally, tears tumbling unchecked down her cheeks.

Malaki smiled graciously, but only turned his gaze to the Codex which still rested upon the couch cushion nearby. "What's the plan with the book?" he asked.

Mae tried to answer the question, but when she considered her answer, decided it to be too long and superfluous an explanation. At least, for the moment.

"It's... a long story, I guess. I'm using it to fix some... wrongs," she said with a quivering voice.

"That's a lot of murders to undo with one little book," he said directly.

If Mae had been standing, she might have lost her balance and become unended by his words alone. She deepened the furrow of her brow and studied the flatness of his face, noticing a lingering hint of disdain in his eyes.

"My... how did you know that?" she whispered with a growing apprehension of unobserved others listening in from the bookshelves surrounding them.

"How could I not? I'm you, Mae," he said.

The words made no sense at all, despite his confident tone. Mae began to stand, but as she rose, a wave of vertigo overwhelmed her, rapidly dropping her back to her knees. The floor started to spin, and her breathing became labored. It wasn't the impact of his words, but rather the way he said it, as if he were suggesting an axiom that was widely assumed. Something in his tone made her heart race and the oxygen of the room seem suddenly lacking.

She braced herself against the floor and darted her gaze between the blackness's that stood tall and looming between the bookshelves about them. She then came to acknowledge something that she should have understood the moment that Malaki had spoken, or honestly, the moment she saw him standing in the bookshelf's corridor. It wasn't Malaki; not even his ghost. It was a specter of the plane itself. Although unpleasant, it wasn't a thoroughly uncommon experience to cross paths with such a being. They were the reason that she rarely meditated herself into the realm, circumstances of necessity notwithstanding, of course.

She should have known this sooner. Rarely were they anything but malicious tricksters.

"You're not me," she said at last. "You're not Malaki. You're just a visitor. And I'm not afraid of you."

She reached down to grab the Codex. "Get fucked," she proclaimed and turned to walk away, but as she spun about, she found that she was standing at the dark end of a long row of books, gazing towards the clearing where she had been sitting a split second before. Now, however, young Susy sat on the rug with her legs crossed and her eyes closed, as if in meditation, exactly where Mae had been seconds before. Mae knew that it was only another visitor playing off of her memories, but nonetheless the sight rattled her and her lip quivered. She hadn't seen her sister in over a century.

Mae's breath quickened. As she approached the opening, the hue of the air cascaded through a range of different colors. The pink became green, then blue, then orange, then red. An inert lamppost stood beside the couch, strangled in strands of Christmas lights that illuminated the clearing in a shifting and flickering light.

As Mae stepped from the corridor into the reading nook, she found that the bookshelves surrounding the clearing had been fundamentally rearranged. What had been a functional space for casual reading, with aisles and corridors leading to other sections of the bookstore, was now a perfectly circular clearing. Eight perfectly spaced corridors of bookshelves led into dark shadows beyond.

Mae turned her attention to what appeared to be, but what she knew was not, her sister fiddling with wooden blocks upon the rug centered in the clearing. Rather than the endless loop that had once decorated the rug's fabric, its fibers were now midnight black decorated with tiny white dots scattered all about its face.

The sight of it conjured a rogue wave of terror that cascaded across her spine.

"Where'd the Earth go, Mae?" asked Susy in a playful singsong. Her eyes remained closed.

Clomp! Mae spun around and saw a book lying face down on the floor in the corridor from whence she had emerged. Just like the rest, the corridor continued into empty blackness beyond. She approached the book hesitantly, but when she got within a few steps, stopped dead in her tracks. She could recall that leather-bound cover anywhere. It was the *Tome of Instruction*.

She bent to pick up the book, and while holding both it and the Codex in her hands, began eagerly rummaging through its familiar pages. Everything was as she remembered it to be, although a particular page was bent at its corner. She'd never known the tome's pages to accept such a deformity. She turned to the tabbed page and found it to be the opening page of a chapter titled *Manifestations*. Again. That was new. But before she could read it's words or investigate any further, the song being sung by her "sister" still sitting in the clearing behind her drew Mae's attention away from the book.

"Weightless Mae

Floating in the black

Lost in stories

She's never to get back."

When Mae turned to face the clearing, her sister was gone, as was the rug and the couch. All that remained was the lamppost, now without the Christmas lights that had adorned it before. Its lonely light flickered meagerly, and in it, she could see into the bookshelf corridor directly across the clearing. In it, a hooded figure stood on the threshold between the light of the lamppost and the swallowing darkness behind it. It was one of the very same watchers that had descended upon the house on Emerald Acres when Mae had conducted the ritual of mortality.

It stood facing her, without movement. Mae's breath grew ever more shaky as the seconds passed.

Then, abruptly, it began striding briskly towards her.

As it entered the opening, its face was no longer shrouded in darkness and was illuminated by the flickering light of the lamppost. The face was hers.

It smiled a toothy grin.

Clutching the books, she turned and sprinted into the darkness of the corridor. As she ran, she muttered a quick Illuminarious incantation and touched a pendant she wore around her neck. It ignited with radiant light.

The corridor went on and on without change. Mae noticed, though, that the spines of the books in the shelves on each side of her shifted from varied colors and shapes to a monotone grey, but she dared not stop to investigate. She assumed that the face of the cloaked figure was nothing but a trick being played by a malicious entity of the realm, but it disturbed her nonetheless.

At last, she stopped running, and looked back, as well as forward to discover nothing but darkness in both directions of the seemingly endless corridor. Panting, she collected her breath and paused to listen intently. The only sound she heard was the cadence of her heavy breathing.

She looked down at the books that she carried. Both were large and heavy, but she was glad to have them with her. She considered how the *Tome of Instruction* had found her. It was more than a book, after all. It knew who its true master was and had found its way back to her. She cracked its spine to reference a warding spell to protect her from further interruptions, as she still hoped to dig into the Codex while in her state of meditation.

She found the page she had been searching for and began to scan the familiar spell, but before she could finish reading its first sentence, the black letters upon the page began to thicken. The ink bled rapidly outward as if each stroke of the pen had been amplified in thickness a thousand time, and before she knew what was happening, the entire page was encompassed in ink; midnight black.

With a start, she rifled through the pages and found that each page was the same: nothing but infinitely black pages staring back at her.

"No!" she screamed, dropping the Codex. She turned each page of the Tome meticulously but found no variation in the book's empty blackness. A tear fell from her cheek and splattered upon an open page. When it landed, it shattered into a galaxy of white, gold, and silver dots upon the midnight black background of the open Tome.

She froze as she stared into it. The image jostled something loose within her and she abruptly began to sob. She dropped the book, but she didn't heard it hit the floor, as a ringing tinnitus rose to overwhelm all sound.

Her chest tightened and her sight grew thin as the sound of many approaching footsteps echoed and reverberated in the still rising tinnitus of her hearing.

It was time to leave her meditation, she knew, as something was terribly wrong. Never before had the realm's inhabitants been so aggressive and invasive.

There was no exact means of escaping the deep meditation, but it typically wasn't a complicated process. When she's been forced to leave her meditations abruptly in instances prior, all she had to do was induce some minor pain and she would quickly shoot out of her trance. She raised her thumb to her mouth and bit down, hard.

Nothing.

The light of her pendant began to flicker intermittently.

She raised the thumb to her teeth once again, and bit down as hard as she possibly could. *Snap!* "AHHHHHH!!!" she screamed into the corridor.

Nothing.

The sound of encroaching footsteps began echoing louder as the light of the pendant flickered faster and faster. The ringing in her ears became all encompassing, reaching a fever pitch that echoed resoundingly through her skull.

She bit down on her tongue.

"LET ME OUT! LET ME OUT! LET ME OUT!" she screamed in violent despair.

The light flashed rapidly, and in its alternating positive, she saw shadowy figures swiftly approaching from both directions of the corridor.

Blood spilled from her mouth as the shadows imminently encroached upon her with each flicker of the rapidly disappearing light of the pendant.

"LET ME OUT!"

Everything ceased upon a negative alternation of the flickering light. All that remained, in every direction, were clouds of miniscule white dots splattering an endless black canvas.

Puzzlement best described Mae's initial reaction to her change of scenery. What could she possibly be looking at? She went to feel for the Tome, but found nothing where her hands had been. In fact, as she attempted to gaze downward at her body, all she found was a similar view of infinite white dots coating a black backdrop. Where was her body? Was she floating?

Was she... in space?

A long, aching awareness gently returned to her mind while an old, tired, and disabling terror returned to the seat from which it had reigned for longer than she had the capacity to comprehend.

And as she shook off the lingering dust of the dreams that had coated her like the nacre of a pearl, she once again wept and contorted painfully within her tomb of infinity while reality pressed itself tightly to her returning understanding.

But alas, all would be well, she knew. Her timeless hell would be forgotten again as she would find solace once more in the deep stories of her mind. She did her best to close her mind's eye and settle her thoughts. She brought her attention inward, toward an imagined breath, and did all that she could to focus.

She conjured, in her thoughts, the sound of an inhaled breath before a corresponding exhalation. Again, and again. And eventually, after a period of time unmeasurable, Mae began constructing a new pulp fiction, a new imagined existence in which to descend, to pass the lonely eons that refused to cease.

Author's Note

Dear Reader,

Throughout this story, I've explored themes of apathy, self-abandonment, and inner struggle—not as an endorsement of despair, but as an acknowledgment of the battles many of us face. If you or someone you know is struggling with thoughts of self-harm or suicide, please know that you are not alone, and help is available.

Pain and isolation can feel overwhelming, but there are people who care about you, even in moments when it feels impossible to believe. There is hope beyond the darkness, and your story matters.

If you are in crisis, please reach out to someone—a friend, a family member, or a professional. There are resources available 24/7 to listen, support, and help guide you through:

United States – Call or text 988 for the Suicide & Crisis Lifeline (Veterans press 1)

United Kingdom – Call Samaritans at 116 123

Canada – Call Talk Suicide Canada at 1-833-456-4566

Australia – Call Lifeline at 13 11 14

You are valued. You are not alone. **Please stay.**

www.ingramcontent.com/pod-product-compliance
Lightning Source LLC
Chambersburg PA
CBHW071110100726

47908CB00008B/2332

9798998997006